BAYOU BOUND

Jennifer Samson

First Printing, 2018

ISBN: 978-1-988797-12-0

Published by Twin Crowns Press
twincrownspress.wordpress.com

www.arieswriting.com

Cover photo by Zacarias da Mata

This book uses Canadian spellings.

This novel contains mentions of criminal activity, prisons, animal attacks, rape, beatings, injury, illness, illegal imprisonment, foul language and more.

For my cousin Bret

1

The tent door flapped in the breeze. Cold air blew inside and the figure in the blanket curled up into a ball. The roar of a truck on the overpass above startled him out of an uneasy sleep.

Jake Wheeler opened his eyes and stared at the roof of the tent, trying to figure out where he was. It came to him slowly—underneath the I-15 in the wash. Las Vegas, Nevada.

He groaned.

The air was dry and cold, and he shivered. The old Army surplus blanket he'd found was filled with holes and a foot too short for his frame. He braced himself, then tossed it aside.

The cold attacked him, and he shivered, then coughed for a minute. He searched around for a cigarette and lit it.

Jake rubbed his eyes, then sat up, his head swimming.

He'd stepped off the bus at the depot a few days before and looked around Las Vegas for a moment before ditching his plan to get a room somewhere. He didn't want to fall into old habits, and he didn't want to see anyone he knew.

And anyway, he couldn't afford a room.

Instead, he rolled a bum, stole his tent and walked along the railway tracks until he found this spot in the wash, underneath the I-15, in full view of Caesars Palace, the Dunes and the Las Vegas Strip.

If he was lucky it wouldn't rain in the mountains, and he wouldn't have to worry about being swept away in a flash flood.

He was an idiot coming back here.

An idiot, but one with a plan.

Rodeo season had ended months ago, and his small savings had dwindled quickly. Between the time spent in the Dakotas and traipsing all over hell's half acre with Al and the mutt, he was running on fumes.

His debt to the Chicago Outfit was always paid up each month, but it left little for him to live. Not enough for a decent room, not enough for saving.

Never enough to find Darla.

He saw her in a shampoo commercial one day. He was eating at a dive restaurant in the middle of nowhere. There were months to go before the rodeo season started again, and even if he rode well and made enough cash, he was still living on next to nothing. He didn't know how Al could stand it.

He was about to dig into chicken fried steak when, suddenly, in front of his face was Darla Redmond on the small black and white television behind the counter, shampooing her hair and flicking soft blonde locks over her shoulder, giving the camera a come-hither look.

It sat like a brick in his stomach, her eyes boring holes in him through the television. He hadn't been able to finish his dinner, the first decent thing he'd had in awhile, and he stewed the rest of the night over it.

Al hadn't said anything, but the kid knew. Jake brooded a few days, and all kinds of plans raced through his head, but it wasn't until Al suggested maybe they split up and meet back in Las Vegas he realized he'd already decided and hadn't known how to suggest it to Al. The kid was smart.

Jake left him enough money to cover some food for him and the mutt.

He took his duffel bag and hitched his way to Los Angeles before he could stop himself.

He went to Schwabs. Her last letter—her only letter—said she worked there.

But there was no Darla. He'd never answered the letter she'd sent him in the summer, and it was the only place he knew to look.

"Darla? She quit about a month ago. Got some part out in New York or something," another waitress had told him.

Jake slung his duffel over a shoulder and moved on.

Only he couldn't.

She was in his blood, in his skin, stuck to him like glue. Everywhere he looked around Los Angeles he thought he saw her. He wanted to get on a bus and take off somewhere, but he had nowhere to go. It was the dead of winter, he needed money, and he had nothing but thoughts of her that wouldn't leave his head.

He cashed in a dollar bill for dimes and called around to people he knew, looking for work. He avoided all the Las Vegas numbers.

He hit pay dirt when he called his old buddy Monty, a wheeler and dealer from Alabama. Monty was the kind of kid that would trade you all sorts of things, and you'd find out later he'd stolen it all and you could be on the hook for it if the cops caught you.

Jake liked Monty.

He didn't like odd jobs, but Monty's odd jobs were dangerous, illegal, and best of all—profitable.

His call to Monty had come at the right time, to hear Monty tell it. He'd scored a truckload of cigarettes, but the load was hot, and the cops were sniffing around him on a daily basis, making it nearly impossible for him to sell. Couldn't Jake take them off his hands?

If Jake had any money he could.

He had a small pittance saved up to cover his debt for the month, but that was it. No one was going to hire him for anything, not right now, and not the way he was seething. Darla had done it again, and she wasn't even here.

He hung up the phone three days ago, hearing the clink of his change fall into the pay phone. He walked along the boardwalk, staring at the Pacific.

Darla was right about the beach. Sand was appealing when it wasn't the coarse desert grit that buffeted your face when you were out riding. He slept under the Santa Monica pier for one more night, a plan forming.

He resigned himself to making the call and plunked his last few dimes in and called Las Vegas. A few minutes of shooting the breeze and he had the information he needed.

Now he was back in Las Vegas.

No Darla.

He robbed a convenience store in Los Angeles before hitching to the bus station and getting on the Greyhound heading to Las Vegas. The money hadn't been enough, and he couldn't risk getting caught pulling another one without a car. When you were on foot, dogs could find you.

So he stepped off the bus in Las Vegas with nothing but a half-formed plan based on gossip he heard on the phone from Hollis Warner.

He wandered up to Rett's stable and kept hidden. He stayed long enough to see Al was there with the mutt, mucking out stalls. Rett was a bleeding heart sometimes, but Al did good work. Satisfied they were taken care of, he hoofed it back downtown and ended up under a highway overpass.

He turned the plan over in his head, unsure if it would work. If he didn't go for it, Jake was going to have to find a way to double his money in a day or he was done and Darla was lost to him.

Last night he took in the show at the Silver Slipper, something drawing him there when he should stay away. He was surprised he didn't recognize any of the dancers. The girls moved between shows a lot, but he thought he'd see someone he knew.

He ended up at Tower of Pizza, a cowboy hat low on his head, a slice of pizza in front of him, and the grating accents of some Chicago-born pizza

3

slinger shouting in the kitchen. He turned away from the door when Susie and Jackie walked in.

They were the closest things Darla had to best friends.

"I really need to get home," Susie sighed. "I'm drowning in wedding planning. I never thought it could be so awful."

"Don't remind me," Jackie groaned. "As soon as that ring's on your finger, I'm on my own. As nice as Charlie is, I sure wish you weren't getting married. Be a modern woman and keep working!"

"It won't be so bad," Susie said. Jake studied their reflections in the window, confident they didn't recognize his back. "I won't mind staying at home—my ankle's been bothering me more and more every day—and you'll do just fine without me. You're the one always teaching me the choreography."

"I had a letter from Darla." Jackie had lit a cigarette, and it reminded Jake he was down to his last two. "She'll be back in Los Angeles in a week or so. Said she wanted us to come out there."

"You should go," Susie said.

Jackie lifted a shoulder. "I asked her to come here and visit. She hasn't answered yet. She sounded . . . different."

Jake's ears perked up.

"What do you mean?" Susie asked.

Jackie's sigh was bone deep. "I don't know. Just a feeling that maybe she's homesick or something. I sure hope she is. It hasn't been the same without her."

Their talk turned to showgirl gossip, and he power ate his pizza and left out the side door without paying.

He wandered the Strip for an hour, nothing on his mind but Darla.

He returned to the tent under the overpass and fell asleep, his dreams punctuated with her perfume and that lilting laugh, memories of their fights and making up.

Now, in the early light of morning he lay there staring at the olive green tent and decided he was a fool.

But fool or not, he was going to get back out to Los Angeles. He was going to get to Darla, pay off that Outfit debt for good and be free.

He needed a good chunk of money, because what he had was going to make up less than half of what Monty wanted. He didn't have the rest and couldn't steal it in time.

But he knew someone who did have money.

Jake shook his head, clearing away all the memories flooding him and pulled on his cowboy boots. He stood up, his back cracking and his collarbone aching.

Tim Kelly wasn't going to be happy to see him.

The warehouse was worse than cold this early in the morning, and Tim blew on his hands to warm them up. It had dipped so close to freezing last night he was tempted to set a fire in the room he slept in, hazard or not.

He had more pressing issues, though.

The factory next door had shut down, the doors between them were shut for good, denying them access to a bathroom. Now there was no can and no running water. The boys weren't happy taking leaks in the alley like bums, and he looked around the place and wondered if this was all he could offer.

Adam's old man was a plumber, and Adam spent a few weeks bringing supplies and tools around, bit by bit, so his father wouldn't notice and ask questions. They had what they needed, but Tim didn't relish turning into a plumber.

Unfortunately, he and Adam were the only ones who had any talent in the fixing things department.

He stared at the exposed pipes. When their side of this plant was decommissioned they took everything, including the sinks and toilets in the bathroom. Pipes stood out from the cement, taunting him. Adam swore they would work, all they needed was to install everything and turn a few valves. Tim doubted the big man's word, but they couldn't keep hanging around here if they didn't do something.

A porcelain toilet sat on the cement, an old basin next to it, and a busted vanity Adam swore could hold the weight of the sink.

"I say we put in the toilet first," Adam said.

They lifted it in place, and he let Adam worry about the hook ups and placement. He smoked and stared out into the main room, five cigarette machines staring back at him.

Part of the gun sale money went to investing in these machines. Since most of their income was from thefts, robberies and other crimes, they needed a way to hide that when it came to tax time. If Tim had learned one thing watching the Outfit, it was that you had to play ball with the IRS.

Most of the boys had part-time work, and guys like Jimmy could claim tips from working at his old man's bar, while Eddie got paid legit from valet parking full time. Tim and Bill were the only ones without a job to their names, and it would look better if he filed like everyone else and had a way to hide his income.

The machines, being cash only, meant there was no record of what was sold and when. It was the perfect cover for their income.

The downside was having to show they had product. Tim had an idea about that, and it wasn't spending money to buy it.

Getting product was a small hurdle. The bigger hurdle—outside of finding trucks to move the machines—was where to put them.

Rett Gordon was the only one who agreed to place one of the machines. Rett was involved with Sam Wyatt and not the Outfit, and that was probably the only reason he agreed. Rett had the gall to ask for ten percent of the cut of cigarette sales, too. Rett had given him a look, one that had nothing to do with business and everything to do with his sister Ruby.

Tim was an idiot and agreed to the ten percent. He'd take it out of his own end, because there wasn't a soul in this world who was going to know he caved in to Rett Gordon.

The boys were antsy about this, though. Those machines had sat for far too long. Everywhere he'd approached about them wanted nothing to do with them, knowing Tim and his boys weren't a crew the Outfit had okayed.

The Outfit controlled a lot of the vending business, and not just in Las Vegas. Getting someone to take a chance on them meant making the machines look legit, and product inside was the way.

He knew his boys heard everything he did about the things Ray had going with Johnny Moro. Ray was long gone from his gang, if not his life, but he could tell it burned some of the guys to see Ray making money, even if he was doing something as low as running women.

He was probably running drugs too, and if the Outfit ever found out he'd end up in the desert. Johnny Moro wanted too much of the pie, and the minute they found out back in Chicago, Tim wouldn't have to worry about Johnny Moro and Ray Roth again.

But in the meantime, it rankled his boys.

So he needed to come up with some cigarettes for the machines, and fast. Then they needed a way to get the machines around town. He had a line on a truck or two they could steal, repaint and use for themselves. He was the only one that could drive a truck, though, and that was a problem.

The bigger problem was finding cigarettes to fill the machines. They'd have to hit a delivery truck, and that meant bringing in some of the other guys, ones he wasn't so sure about anymore. Guys like Joey the Rat, who always seemed to know what Ray was up to, and Dave and Tom who didn't seem as eager to get involved in some of their operations as they used to be. Tim didn't want to get pinched for an armed robbery, and he was going to have to do it himself if he couldn't trust the others.

If he could hit a truck and get some product that way, they could sell the cigarettes legit as well. A contact of Mendoza's was willing to provide him with paperwork saying he sold Tim the cigarettes. It was payment from

Mendoza, who Tim had encouraged Lupe to push the Castillo brothers toward. From what Mendoza told him, he was sitting pretty now that he had a connection with the Castillos.

Part of his brain told him to forget this idea, knock off a drugstore for a few cartons and strong arm people into putting the machines in their places with stale, old product and letting those machines exist solely to wash their income.

The other part of his brain . . . well, maybe it wanted legitimate income. Maybe some part of him still thought he could save Diana, save his mother, do something about something for once, and there was no way his family would agree to anything if they thought he did something illegal to pay for it.

Diana hadn't stopped seeing Ray, even after she got out of juvie. Coming back from Mexico and finding his sister locked up, he'd gotten into it with Ray in the middle of the Sands. They'd been tossed out by security, and he noticed they worked him over harder than they did Ray.

Then he found out his father had gone to the Outfit to get her out. So now that hung over their heads, another favor to be paid off. Diana was out of juvie and into Ray, and his father wouldn't put a stop to it since Ray was associated now.

He wasn't going to lose Diana to a fucking pimp like Ray. No way.

So he needed the money those cigarette machines would bring in, and if that meant hitting a shipment, that's what he was going to do.

Awhile later Adam had the toilet set up. Adam turned the water on, and the first flush brought a flood of water all over the cement floor and Tim's boots.

"I forgot the sealant," Adam groaned. "I can run home and swipe some outta the garage. I'll be back. See if you can tighten those hose connections, my hand's still hurting from that fight last weekend, I may not have got them tight enough. And those bolts need to be tightened, too."

Adam loped toward the new steel door they'd put in two weekends ago. Tim and Bill had liberated the big, steel door from the factory next door to replace the old corrugated mess. This one was secure, with a real lock. Tim handed out keys only to Bill and Jimmy, with warnings about what would happen if those keys ended up with anyone else.

Tim stared at the toilet and sighed. He picked up a wrench, dried the floor off as best he could with old towels, and laid down beside the toilet, tightening the hose connections. Adam hadn't tightened them very well.

"Tim Kelly lying with a shitter. Sounds about right to me."

That *voice*.

He sat up too fast and knocked his head on the toilet tank, swearing a blue streak as he moved away from the toilet.

Jake Wheeler leaned against the door frame, an amused look on his face.

"What the fuck are you doing here?" Tim hoisted himself off the floor, noting with irritation his shoulder ached from the cold. Ever since Mexico, he knew the temperature thanks to his bum shoulder. "How'd you get in?"

Jake waltzed back out into the main room, lighting a cigarette and looking around.

Jake beat it out of town a few weeks after their dust up in the summer last year. Tim tried to pretend their fight had been all about Jake's attack on Jimmy, but he knew, like Jake knew, it was about Ruby in the end.

Tim hadn't been happy to hear about Jake's cowardly attack on Jimmy Lewis, though—from behind, no less. Jimmy, one of the vainest guys Tim ever knew, now sported a nice scar across his cheek. Jimmy brooded about it more than Tim ever did over his own face, lopsided and filled with scars and metal thanks to the Chicago Outfit.

Jimmy didn't realize his new scar made him more attractive to the bevy of women that always hung around the fringes of their activity. Jimmy whined about it like he'd actually *lost* something.

Tim swiped a hand across his face, thin metal and mesh holding his cheekbone together. Jimmy had no idea what losing something meant.

Tim stared at Jake for a moment, willing the thoughts of Jake and Ruby together to come back into his head with a vengeance and make his vision go red with rage like it used to, but it wouldn't come. The memory was like sawdust, dead at his feet. He wondered what that meant.

Jake took in the warehouse like he aimed to remodel.

"How the hell did you find this place, anyway?" Tim asked. The guys never brought people by—especially people like Jake. He'd never even brought Ruby here.

"Everybody knows about this place," Jake said. "And Barnes left the door propped open. All your guys have shit for brains or just him?"

Jake picked up a pack of cigarettes, and Tim grabbed them out of his hand and tucked them in his back pocket.

"Everybody does not know about this place," he said. He walked over toward the door, raging at the rock propping it open a few inches. Adam needed his bell rung. He kicked the rock out of the way and the door shut.

Jake shrugged. "Everyone who knows anything about you knows about it."

"Ray tell you?"

Jake looked at him with a furrowed brow. "Since when do I talk to assholes like Roth?"

Since when did Jake fuck Tim's girlfriend, or cheat on Darla, or get on the Outfit's bad side and owe them money.

"You'd do just about anything if it came into your head." Tim lit his own cigarette. "You wanna get the hell out of here so I don't have to bust your head open and stain the concrete?"

Jake rolled his eyes. "Thought you might be interested in a business deal."

"What, with you? After all you've done? You're dreaming, Wheeler. Anyway, you haven't shown your face in Vegas since the summer, and I'm supposed to believe you've got shit going on? Whatever, Jake. Take it somewhere else."

Tim turned and walked back toward the bathroom.

"How long have these cigarette machines been sitting?"

Tim turned around and stared at Jake. He had a wolfish smile on his face.

"Awhile, huh? That's what I heard, anyway."

"From who?" Tim asked.

"Does it matter?"

"I need to know whose ass to kick."

"Well, then you better hope Billy boy can take a punch. He moves like an ox, you'll probably land a good one."

"Bill never would've said anything to the likes of you."

"Nah, but he talks to his sister."

And Brenda was seeing Hollis. Hollis Warner had the biggest mouth in Clark County and then some. Hollis and Jake palled around, although it was a stretch to call them friends. It was a stretch to call anyone Jake's friend.

Tim closed his eyes and pinched the bridge of his nose, a headache coming on. He hoped Adam wouldn't show up and see Jake standing here. He wished Jake would turn around and head back out into the ether.

"Alright, you've had your fun. Now get lost," Tim said.

"You don't wanna hear about this deal?"

"I don't want to hear you breathing anywhere near me. It's been a nice few months without you here screwing everything up."

Jake laughed, and it wore on Tim's nerves more than it should.

"I'm willing to be generous with this deal." Jake ashed his cigarette in a cut glass ashtray someone had stolen from Rett's. "I can change your luck with those machines."

"The only luck you've got is bad," Tim said.

Jake flipped him the bird. Tim stared at him, and Jake finally faltered.

"Look, the Outfit's breathing down my neck," Jake said. "I need money to get a load of cigarettes out of Alabama by next week, and I got less than half. You come in on it with me, we split the shipment. I sell enough to get out from my debt and put a little away, you can get these machines out of here."

"Cigarettes?"

He knew Jake had been cagey, the way he looked at those machines. Hollis must know about them.

"Old high school buddy in 'Bama stole a truckload with his crew, but the cops are on him. He's got a warrant, they pick him up and he's toast. He needs to unload them, and he's selling cheap. Guess it was a bad deal all around for him."

"How much are we talking?"

"Only two hundred cases."

Two hundred cases and one hundred and twenty packs of cigarettes in a case . . . Tim almost fell over doing the math.

"That's twenty four thousand packs of cigarettes!"

Jake raised an eyebrow and nodded. "If that's what the math says."

Each pack could go for thirty five cents in the machines, more if he wanted. On half the cases, he'd bring in over four grand.

"How much for the shipment?"

"Two thousand bucks. I can put in a grand," Jake said.

Tim whistled, but did the math. This Alabama guy wanted about seventeen cents a pack, which was way under what they sold for in stores.

"Why so cheap?"

"Like I said, the cops are breathing down his neck." Jake took a drag on his cigarette. "Something about one of his guys getting pinched for the armed robbery. He thinks the guy'll roll, he wants the stuff out of the state so it's not tied to him. He'll go in a long time if they get him on this. He wants to wash his hands of it."

It smelled like a set up.

Tim looked over at the machines. If he put in a grand and got half those cigarettes, he'd have a way into some of the other places he'd approached. He'd have product for a long time, and add the fees he'd charge for the bars to rent them . . . they'd be bringing in guaranteed legit money per month *and* a way to hide their other income.

It'd give him and the boys a legitimate business front, and they could run all kinds of cash through it if they needed to. The Outfit did it on a large scale, all over the country, but he only needed to wash enough from their robberies to make tax time easy. It might not matter now when they were small time, but it'd keep the cops from looking, and in the future, it'd keep the IRS from looking.

He wasn't going to be stupid like Ray. He'd plan ahead and have things set up right.

If only he had enough to buy out Jake's end too. Either way, half the cigarettes would set them up nicely. It was a small price to pay for an operation that could legitimize his gang and hide their criminal work.

To his mother and Diana it would be legitimate work. No more hiding money around the house for his mother to find to cover their rent. He could give it to her up front.

It sounded too good to be true. A cheap deal on exactly what he needed, exactly what Jake said he needed . . .

"So what's the catch?"

"No catch," Jake said. "You think I wanted to set foot back in this town? Hell no. I came here because I knew you had the cash. This deal has to be done soon. I gotta get to 'Bama by the weekend, or it's no deal."

So all Jake had was a deadline and half the money.

"When do we leave?"

Jake was surprised. "*We* don't leave at all. I leave tomorrow if you give me the cash."

Tim's laugh was full of bitter amusement.

"You think I'm gonna hand you a thousand bucks on a promise to deliver me a hundred cases of cigarettes? You gotta be outta your mind."

"I'm good for it."

"You're good for nothing, and that's been the truth since the day you were born. No way. You want that money, it's coming in my wallet, in my back pocket, with me sitting in the driver's seat next to you."

Now it was Jake's turn to laugh.

"I'm not going on a road trip with you, Kelly." Jake stubbed out his cigarette and blew a stream of smoke out of the side of his mouth. "No way. No how. Not happening."

Tim's smile was grim, and Jake didn't like it.

Not one bit.

2

Bill was as dubious as Tim about this deal.

"Are you sure Wheeler's not going to take off with the money?" Bill asked, watching as Tim packed up a duffel bag.

"Why do you think I'm going?" Tim asked. He shoved socks in the bag, followed by underwear. "You really think I want to spend any time with that clown? He'll try and mess with me the first chance he gets, and I'm not letting it happen."

"Yeah," Bill said sourly. "It's just, last time you took off . . . "

Last time he took off Diana ended up in custody and everything went to hell. He came home with a bum shoulder, two deaths at his hands and a busted up car.

At least the gun deal had gone through after that. The Outfit hadn't even taken their cut, a surprise for him, but Sam Wyatt said they liked how he'd drawn the hit men out of Vegas, like Tim had done it for them and not to save his own ass.

He hadn't argued the point, though. That extra money was allowing him to take this trip.

He wasn't going to risk the car this time. He had insisted they rent a cube truck to drive across the country and back. No way was he risking his Charger for one of Jake's schemes. He was lucky to find a deal on a truck that wouldn't eat into his buy-in.

He asked Bill to keep an eye on things last time, and it hadn't gone right. He didn't blame Bill for it—he blamed Ray Roth—but Bill felt responsible all the same. Tim decided to let Bill off the hook this time.

"You don't have to keep watch on Diana," Tim told him, noting Bill's obvious relief. "Diana's on a short leash with the old man, my mother and the law. She'll keep her nose clean, because if she goes in again, they'll keep

1

her 'til she's eighteen. She'll keep out of legal trouble just to stay out and near Ray."

It bothered him, but there was nothing he could do about Diana and Ray. The more he railed against Ray, the more he told her about what Ray was doing and what a scumbag he was, the more Diana dug in her heels.

The last thing he wanted was to chase her straight into marrying the asshole, and he wouldn't put it past Ray to ask. He didn't think the thug gave a damn about his sister, but he was good at playing the part.

His head ached. If he kept thinking about it a full-blow migraine would bloom between his eyes. He didn't need it now.

"Why's Wheeler so eager to pay off his Outfit debt?" Bill asked.

"Don't know and don't care. He said he wants to 'be free,'" Tim said, using air quotes.

He opened a lock box underneath the mattress. They'd propped it up on wooden pallets to keep it off the cold cement, and he'd hollowed out enough space to keep the lock box here instead of the house. His old man still had his service weapon, but Tim hid it in the attic rafters where he knew the old man would never look. He took his lock box with his own gun and bullets just in case the old man knew about it. Or his sister did.

He found the Browning Hi Power, loaded it, and tucked it into the shoulder holster he got from Mendoza.

"Really?" Bill asked, nodding toward the gun.

"Better safe than sorry. How much do you trust Wheeler?"

Bill shrugged. He sat down on the edge of the mattress.

"You think he's in touch with Darla?"

"Why do you care?" Tim grunted and pushed the lock box back under the pallets.

"Well, it's just . . . " Bill seemed loathe to get out the words. "See, she was real good on Dark Shadows, and I thought maybe he'd be able to get me her autograph."

Tim looked over at Bill like he'd grown two heads.

"Never mind," Bill mumbled.

"I'll be back next week if all goes well," Tim said, still staring. "Or maybe a little longer if I end up having to kill Jake. Keep an eye on things, and don't let the boys know what's up. When they see these cigarettes their eyes are gonna fall out of their heads."

"And you don't want Ray finding out."

Tim nodded. "Yeah. So maybe keep your mouth shut when you're talking to your sister."

Bill's face turned red. "I didn't think she was telling Hollis our business."

"She doesn't consider it business, that's why." Tim took a deep breath as he zipped up the bag, not wanting to head out of town again so soon. "Keep things level with the boys. I don't want to come back to everything gone to shit again."

Jake sat in the passenger seat of a 1960 Ford U-Haul cube truck and sulked. He didn't expect to get out of Vegas with Tim's money and nothing else, but he hadn't thought about the alternative. A road trip across the country with Tim Kelly wasn't what he had in mind.

He tried to talk Tim out of coming, claiming the load could be in a big rig and they didn't need to drive out there, but Tim wouldn't budge. He refused to take the Charger, claiming it couldn't haul the load, and he rightfully pointed out affording airfare wasn't in the cards.

So Jake had no choice, since a Greyhound wouldn't get them there fast enough.

He was stuck with Tim Kelly.

It would've been better in Kelly's Charger. It looked cherry enough cruising down the Strip, but Kelly pointed out it wasn't the most inconspicuous car on the road. Jake heard rumours the Clark County Sheriff liked to stop Tim just to check he had papers for the car.

So they were in an old truck together, and Kelly wouldn't let him behind the wheel. It burned him—he drove for a living when he was in the Air Force, and Kelly didn't think he could handle a measly cube truck.

He hated being stuck a passenger. The first hour on the road was an argument over the radio station, the second over not touching anything. He cranked the window down, and they almost got into a fist fight on the highway over the wind.

So Jake sat in the stuffy car looking at dead desert fly by as they drove through Arizona. It was going to take *days* to get to Alabama.

He looked over at Tim's profile and swore.

This better be worth it, or he was going to kick Monty's ass.

Saturday, February 25, 1967

Tim was close to going back on his promise to himself not to let Jake behind the wheel.

He was exhausted from driving for so long. Jake would doze in the passenger seat, and he was well rested and looked it.

They'd been stuck together in the truck, eating greasy roadhouse food and sharing the empty back of the cube truck for a place to sleep for two and a half days. He had more sympathy for Lupe's trip from Mexico and didn't know how she'd done it.

They'd just crossed the state line at the Escatawpa River, and there was only a half hour left before they reached Mobile.

He'd never been to the south before, and so far it was humidity, flat land, trees, rivers and the dull, boring company of Jake Wheeler.

If anyone had told him the day he found out Jake slept with Ruby that he'd one day be road tripping across the country with the bastard, he would have laughed long and hard.

Money. He had to keep thinking about the money those cigarette machines would bring him. It was a business deal, and he could put up with this for a business deal.

Jake got quiet and morose a day into the trip and barely spoke since. It irritated him more than Jake's normal yapping and taunting did. The closer they got to Alabama, the more irascible Jake was.

By the time they reached Mobile, he was ready to pitch him out the truck door.

"Are you going to screw up this deal?" Tim asked. "If you are, I'm turning the truck around right now."

No, *mom*, I'm fine." Jake spat out the window. "Turn here. It's right along the waterfront. Let me do the talking."

Tim spotted a guy loitering near the entrance to a warehouse. He drove the truck inside as the guy opened the double-wide doors. He parked the truck with the front end facing the door—just in case—and cut the engine.

Jake's ol' buddy, ol' pal Monty was a shifty, nervous type that reminded Tim too much of Pete Malcolm. He bit his nails and his eyes darted around the room like he thought someone was watching. Tim thought he was on something. He had a mop of sandy curls in a Beatles haircut and his brown eyes were hooded with frowning brows that made him look instantly suspicious.

Monty ushered them over, looking over his shoulder like the cops were about to show up. Tim was ready to walk out.

He stopped when Monty opened up a huge wooden crate packed with straw. The cases of cigarettes varied from Chesterfields to Marlboro, Winstons to Newports. They were good quality and would sell in the machines. It was too good to pass up, catch or no catch.

Tim ponied up his end of the money, listening to Jake's accent get thicker and thicker the longer he talked to Monty. They sounded like hicks.

Not that Jake sounded like a rocket scientist on a good day, but Tim had no idea what possessed these two to sound more and more like they'd never seen a city a day in their lives.

Monty counted the money, the nodded to his guys. They got in an old Pontiac and took off, leaving them the crate in the middle of the floor. Tim sighed. It'd take forever to move them.

Jake's mood lightened since the exchange, and they sweated their way through unloading the crate and loading up the back of the cube truck. Tim was relieved when they were done.

"Let's get out of here," he said. "I don't like this."

The longer they were there, the more certain he was the cops were going to tear inside the building and arrest them.

"You don't like anything," Jake muttered.

Tim started the truck up and headed out of the pumping station, relief flooding him as he got back on the highway and pointed west. He expected cops at any moment, and the farther they got from Mobile, the better he felt. Jake's friend was an idiot, but not a snitch, so that was something.

"We should go down to New Orleans for the night," Jake said. "You think Vegas is a good time, you oughta see the Big Easy."

He glanced at Jake out of the corner of his eye. "I know all about The Big Easy, it crawled into bed with my girlfriend."

Jake laughed. Tim was glad they were getting the hell out of Alabama. He didn't like the humidity, the vegetation and anything else he'd seen. Slow moving rivers and lazy, dipping cypress and willow didn't do anything for him. Give him the desert any day.

Most of all, he wanted to be back in Vegas and get those machines ready.

With Jake's mood changed, Tim wasn't sure he would enjoy the chatty, annoying version of Jake on the road trip back. Maybe silent Jake was the high water line.

"We need to get back to Vegas," Tim said. "The sooner the better."

Jake looked out at the Alabama landscape. "Yeah."

Tim pressed on the accelerator a little harder, and the rental truck peeled down a desolate stretch of road in central Louisiana. He didn't want to push the truck any harder; the last thing they needed was to get pulled over by a cop for something stupid like a speeding ticket.

The cargo was added weight, and he didn't want to dump the truck over on the side of the road, all their money and hard work littered across two lanes of a back road highway.

He chose the back roads once they got out of Alabama. Cops liked to pull over rental trucks, and he and Jake didn't look like the type that would be driving one without a bad reason.

He glanced at the bald cypress trees in the distance. They loomed over the Louisiana bayou like skeletal sentries. The place had an otherworldly feel to it, strange birds and plants all over the place. Nothing was familiar. He'd be happy to get back into the desert where he belonged.

Tim looked over at the passenger seat. Jake appeared to be asleep—again—the stupid cowboy hat low on his head, blocking the sun that was beginning to dip toward the tree tops directly in front of them.

This part of Louisiana was deep in Cajun bayou territory. Somewhere down there was New Orleans, and Jake wouldn't let him forget it.

"There's still time to turn off and get down there," came Jake's voice from under the hat, as if he'd heard Tim's thoughts.

"Yeah, still time for you to shut up about it, too."

"Hey, you ain't in the mood to celebrate?" he asked. "I been to New Orleans a handful of times, it rivals Vegas for parties. We can celebrate with some beers and broads. Seems to me like things are looking up."

Maybe it was the thought he was going to get out from his Outfit debt, but Jake seemed downright cheerful since they left Alabama. Of course, the only thing he'd done was bitch about Tim not wanting to go to New Orleans.

Tim sighed. Jake was terrible company.

"Next convenience store or gas station you see, pull over. I'm hungry," Jake said.

He'd pull over when he damn well wanted to. Nevertheless, when the gas station appeared on the horizon, Tim pulled in when they reached it. They wouldn't make it even close to Texas on what they had left in the tank thanks to taking back roads.

It looked like there was someone inside, but no one came out to pump. Tim huffed out a breath and got out to pump the gas himself.

Jake stretched outside the car.

"I'm getting five bucks worth," Tim said. "Pay 'em, since he's too lazy to do his job."

"I'm not your butler," Jake said.

Tim shook his head, then fished his wallet out of his back pocket and picked out a five dollar bill and held it out for Jake.

Jake took it and headed into the gas station.

He still didn't completely trust him and this deal. It all seemed too easy, and now they were headed back to Las Vegas and good things were on the horizon. Something had to give. It always did.

He stuck the nozzle into the Ford and started to fill it. He needed to get back to Las Vegas and off the road, stash the goods and lay low until the paranoid feeling subsided.

* * *

Jake walked inside the gas station and wanted to laugh. The place looked like it'd been mummified back in the thirties. The air was stale and warm. It was in the mid-seventies outside, but at least ten degrees hotter in the store, despite it being February. That was one thing he missed about 'Bama. The winters in Vegas could dip into freezing in the desert, and it made his bones ache. The south was more to his liking, but the minute he was back in Alabama, he knew he didn't want to stay.

He was surprised at the need to get out of the state. He thought returning wouldn't bother him, but even though he was nowhere near Birmingham, he didn't want to stick around. 'Bama was bad memories.

An old fan on top of the cash desk blew dull air around the place, its tinny whir working Jake's last nerve.

There was a skinny, pimply kid at the register reading an Archie comic and eating what looked like a peanut butter and jelly sandwich.

Jake looked around at the place, noting the month-old magazines, the slim pickings when it came to candy bars and the whir of the fan. An air conditioning unit sat useless in a back window. This place was as dead as a door nail.

He wished he had some company on this drive that wasn't Tim Kelly. Alo and the dog were better company than Kelly, and Al didn't talk much and the dog not at all. Kelly didn't even want to hit New Orleans, and New Orleans was cheap booze, cheap girls and a damn good time, no matter the time of year, even after Mardi Gras had ended.

Kelly was a damn kill joy and wouldn't take any detours.

Jake pulled a Pepsi out of the icebox at the back of the service station, then looked through the aisles at the other stuff. He would die of boredom on the drive back with Kelly, there was no doubt about that. There were still days to go the way Kelly drove, and he wasn't going to survive it.

He popped the top off the Pepsi, the bottle cap dancing onto the floor.

"Oh, you gotta pay before you can drink it," the pimply kid said.

Jake looked at him, then took a nice long drink from the bottle.

"Yeah?" He belched. "What're you gonna do about it?"

The kid stood up straighter and set the comic book down, like he was considering Jake's question. This kid was more square than any he'd seen back in Las Vegas. Probably sniffed too many gas fumes all day.

Jake felt the weight of the pistol at his back. He knew Kelly had a gun stashed in the truck somewhere, and he hadn't come unarmed himself. As much as he liked Monty, he didn't trust anyone in this world. He wore a .32 at his back and a .22 at his ankle that wouldn't do much, but he liked back up plans when things went south.

Jake took another drink of the Pepsi. The kid looked wide-eyed at him, and he'd probably wet his pants if Jake tried anything.

He wasn't eager to knock over a gas station with Kelly as a get away driver. He shouldn't have used Al that time, but Al was ten times better than Kelly any day. Jake wasn't eager for a bullet to come his way. The kid didn't look like much, but there was probably a gun stashed somewhere. With his luck, the kid would be an expert marksman.

"You really need to pay for that," the kid said, nervously chewing his lower lip. Acne bloomed on both his cheeks, reddening as he waited for Jake to reply.

Jake stepped up to the register and picked out Tim's bill from his pocket.

"The gas too," Jake said, nodding outside. "Five bucks worth."

If it wasn't for the fact there were stolen cigarettes in the truck he'd show this kid how much he was willing to pay for the shitty service he offered. Hell, he hadn't even come outside to pump the gasoline. Probably too scared of them.

Jake looked down at the cooler near the cash register and saw the beer. It would be nice to get some cold beer for the drive. If they weren't heading to New Orleans he'd need all the help in the world to survive the drive back to Vegas with Kelly.

Jake leaned over and pulled out two bottles, feeling his pocket and coming up with some change. Kelly had finished fuelling the Ford and was putting the nozzle back on the pump.

"I'll take these, too," he said, setting the beer on the counter.

He looked over at the magazine rack, and his fingers waltzed to the back row, picking out a girlie magazine.

"And this."

"You got ID? For the beer?"

Jake rolled his eyes, but he pulled out his driver's license and held it out so the kid had to lean in and look at it. He studied it for a minute.

"You gonna stare at it all day or what?" Jake asked.

The kid leaned back wordlessly.

Jake slid the bill over the counter and plunked his change down on top of it. The kid's beady eyes watched him.

"You better start lookin' somewhere else or I'm gonna think you're sweet on me," Jake said. "There nothing better to do out here? Jesus Christ. Just gimme the change."

He grabbed the change the kid put down on the counter, then took his purchases.

Jake walked out, the bells above the door jingling. He headed to the truck and put the beer on the floorboards before he got in.

"You bought beer with my money?" Kelly eyed Jake's purchases.

"No, I bought beer with my money. I was feeling generous enough to share, imagine that. You wanna go take 'em back and tell him we don't need them?" Jake asked, a wolfish smile on his face.

Kelly surprised him by grinning. "Get in."

Tim glanced over at Jake again. He whistled in the passenger seat, an open beer between his legs, and the outdated centrefold open on the dash, Miss December with mistletoe over her head and not much on.

"What're you so happy about?"

Jake looked over at Tim. "I gotta have a reason?"

"Yeah."

Jake laughed, and it set Tim on edge.

"You sure this Monty guy's alright?" Tim asked. "He isn't going to drop a dime and tell the troopers where to find us, is he?"

"Monty's cool, don't worry," Jake said.

Tim glanced in the mirror. He had a prickly feeling between his shoulder blades since they entered the state. Maybe it was the bayou or the fact there was no people around anywhere—not even other cars. Whatever it was, it made him nervous.

He spotted a pull out up ahead and the nose of a car sticking out from a crop of bushes, still leafy despite the time of year. The cops. He slowed the truck as he passed, making sure he was just under the speed limit.

A moment later, a siren pierced the air, and the cop car pulled out from the dirt road and started to follow them. Jake sat up straighter, and Tim glanced at the speedometer.

He wasn't speeding. He was careful not to, and this was a pile of bullshit.

"What's he in a pinch about?" Tim muttered.

Jake shrugged. "Maybe he'll let us off with a ticket."

"Yeah . . . and if he searches the trailer?" Tim asked. "You got a receipt for all those cigarettes? They'll confiscate them, and that's two grand down the toilet. Not to mention if they figure out it was from a stolen shipment they might think we stole it."

Jake shifted in the seat. "Shit."

Tim sped up, hoping the cop car would pass, but the car sped up as he did.

He wasn't in the mood for a run, but it looked like that's exactly what was going to happen.

Jake looked back at the cop and raised an eyebrow at Tim, as if daring him to run.

Tim sighed, then punched the pedal down, and the Ford took off. The cop car stayed with him, and a moment later, another one entered the chase from another dirt road. He would have to lose them somehow—in a cube truck that was asking a lot.

He changed gears, trying to jimmy the truck into giving him just a little more. They shot up the road toward a steel bridge in the distance. He saw the cops back off as they approached the bridge, but Tim didn't back off the gas. Hopefully they were going to stop chasing him if he was crossing a county line or something.

He shot over the bridge and around a bend, then slammed on the brakes so hard Jake's beer bottle flew out of his hand and broke on the dashboard, soaking the truck with beer.

"What the hell?!"

Tim yanked the wheel to the left to avoid the road block—cop cars were parked blocking the road, and he barely missed the nose of one as he fish-tailed across the dusty oncoming lane. The weight of the truck swung the back end around and the front tires clunked down into a ditch at the side of the road.

The hiss of the engine was all he could hear.

He was deciding whether or not to run when the cops drew down on them.

3

Saturday, February 25, 1967

"Hands in the air!"

The gravely voice belonged to a stout man with a sheriff's star pinned above his chest. His double chin would have looked comical on anyone else, but to Tim it just made him look angry and stubborn.

He didn't trust the man for a second.

Not that he was in the habit of trusting the cops, period, but something about this man made Tim want to wipe the smile off his fat face and turn the muzzle of the man's gun around the other way.

"Now open the door, from the outside," the sheriff instructed.

Tim rolled down the window and reached a hand out to pull on the door latch of the truck cab.

"I'm gonna gut you when we get outta this," Tim muttered to Jake.

Jake unlatched his own door. "Me? If you hadn't made like Steve McQueen, we wouldn't be in this mess."

Somehow, Tim doubted that. These guys looked pissed, and it wasn't because they were speeding. Which they hadn't been.

"Outta the truck now, come on, move it along!" the sheriff barked.

A bulldog. That's what he reminded Tim of. A bulldog just a little too used to eating scraps from the table, one that was a little more pudge than muscle.

Tim stepped out, sliding on the bank of the ditch and rolling his left ankle a little. He looked around coolly. There was nowhere to run—the tree line was too far, and these guys looked like they were itching to get a shot off.

"I want y'all to throw out all your weapons, the kid at the gas station said the cowboy had a gun, you toss that out nice and easy on the grass there."

A gun? Kid at the gas station? Jesus Christ.

"You knocked over the fucking gas station?!" Tim exclaimed. "Are you kidding me? I told you to go in and pay for the gas, not hold somebody up! What the hell is wrong with you?"

"I didn't knock over shit!" Jake said, his eyes blazing. "I paid that little weasel for everything."

Tim looked at him, stone-faced. Trust that asshole to try and take him down, too.

"I don't fucking believe you," Tim muttered. "You're a disaster, you know that?"

"Simmer down!" the sheriff said again. "I don't want to hear another word out of either of you. Cowboy, throw out your gun and move on up here, let the deputy cuff you. You back there, hands in the air, high."

Jake tossed a gun onto the grass, then stared down the cop for a minute.

Tim, with hands raised, watched Jake walk toward the side of the road. The deputy approached and put Jake down on the ground, cuffing him. Tim groaned when he saw the deputy toss out a second gun Jake had tucked into a holster at his ankle.

Tim was relieved his gun was hidden inside his duffel bag in the back of the cube truck with the cigarettes. He noticed the cops hadn't moved toward the back yet.

"A smart-aleck, huh?" the sheriff said, looking down at Jake's pistol. Tim willed him to pick it up and bury a bullet in Jake's head. "We don't take too kindly to smart-aleck's here."

"Looks like you take real kindly to bacon and second helpings," Jake said.

Jake was rewarded with a kick to the ribs, and Tim felt a moment's satisfaction. The only way it would've been better was if he was the one kicking Jake.

"You, get on over here with your friend."

"He isn't my friend," Tim said. In fact, the minute these local yokels locked them in a cell together, Jake was going to become Tim's personal punching bag for the foreseeable future.

"I don't care if y'all hate each others guts or not, get your ass over here and down on the ground or I'll put a few holes in you."

Tim sauntered over, taking his time. The sheriff rewarded him by a kick to the back of the knee, and Tim fell over onto the pavement.

"Somebody call Duchenes's to get this truck over to impound. These highway hoods aren't going very far for a long time."

"Well, I didn't do anything, officer," Tim said from his position on the asphalt. The deputy had cuffed him, the metal cuffs cutting into his wrists. Tim watched the deputy haul Jake to his feet and a second later Tim was pulled up. He noted he was at least three inches taller than the sheriff, a fact which the sheriff seemed completely aware of.

"Helpin' a thief escape, one that used a weapon in a daring daylight robbery—" Jake snorted behind Tim's shoulder, and Tim was inclined to agree that 'daring' was the last thing Jake's boneheaded move was. "He threatened to kill the kid, too, so you got uttering threats on that list. You oughta keep better friends."

"He was hitchhiking, I don't even know him."

"Fuck you, Kelly," Jake snarled. "I didn't rob the damn gas station. You see any money here?"

"You two are a real comedy act, oughta go on the road together," the sheriff said. "Get these little pukes out of here and back to lock up. They can see the judge in the morning."

A few of the other officers snickered at that, and Tim was immediately wary again. Something set him on edge about this stretch of highway. He should've gone back the same route they'd come, through Northern Louisiana and away from the bayou, swamp and trigger-happy sheriffs.

He was crammed in the back of a police cruiser with Jake and watched as the tow truck showed up to haul the truck away. He was relieved to see they didn't even try and open the back, until he wondered why. Any cop worth his salt would, and now he wondered if his life was about to turn into even more of a horror show.

The drive into town didn't take long. They turned up a dusty road and ended up in the small town of Strikersville within ten minutes. Trust Jake to rob a gas station that close to the cops.

The sheriff and a deputy marched them into a ramshackle office that looked like it hadn't been updated since the 1930s, then toward cells in the back, down a damp hallway just off all the offices.

Tim kept his mouth shut, wondering why they hadn't printed either one of them or took mugshots. First thing Las Vegas PD or the Clark County Sheriff did was print you, even before they sent you into a cell. This sheriff had taken both of their wallets, though.

The deputy took their jackets, shoes and belts. The cement floor was cold through his worn socks. The sheriff and deputy left them and went back into the office.

"I can't believe you," Tim said. He sat down on a lower bunk, the springs poking through the thin mattress.

"I didn't rob the place, I ain't stupid," Jake said, picking at a nail. "The kid looked like a little wuss, I might've given him a hard time, but I didn't rob the little shit."

"They found guns on you, they'll open up that truck and find all those cigarettes," Tim whispered. "We'll be out two grand with nothing to show for it, and all because you messed with a kid at a gas station."

"I didn't rob that station."

Ordinarily Jake would've bragged about something like that. Tim wasn't sure whether to believe his protestations. Robbing a gas station right after making a deal like this would be the height of stupidity, and if Jake wanted out from his Outfit debt, it wouldn't be smart to get himself tossed into jail where he couldn't pay it. The Outfit wouldn't let it slide until he was out, either—they'd expect him to catch up all payments the minute Jake was released.

Tim sighed. Jake wouldn't risk that, so there was a good chance he was telling the truth, and he hadn't robbed the gas station. That was bad news for them.

Tim looked out into the office area—it was pretty quiet, just the sheriff talking with some of his deputies.

"Hey!" Tim hollered. "When do we get to see a judge?"

"I told you in the morning," the sheriff called back.

It was probably past dinner now. He didn't want to languish in this cell next to Jake clear through until the next day.

"Why can't we see the judge now?" Tim asked. "Get us outta your hair faster."

"Because I said you ain't," the sheriff said, sauntering down the hall and stopping in front of their cell. He crossed his ham hock arms in front of him. "You might not be used to how things run around here, but in Strikersville, prisoners don't get to make a decision about when they go to court. Things might be a little different in . . . where'd you say you were from?"

Tim said nothing, and the sheriff wandered over to his desk and grabbed something from a teletype machine.

"Timothy Patrick Kelly, Las Vegas, Nevada. Rap sheet longer than my arm." The sheriff looked at Tim. "Well, maybe Las Vegas lets you call the shots, but I can assure you things are different here."

Tim didn't like the sound of that.

"And we also got Jacob Wheeler. Born in Alabama, lately of . . . sweet Jesus, where the hell haven't you lived? Rap sheet just about as long. You boys are in for some trouble."

Tim said nothing, not liking the man's attitude at all.

"You boys are looking at a long stint in Strikersville," he said. "I don't envy you but a bit. At least you'll come out of there with your attitudes adjusted."

"I want a lawyer," Tim said.

"You'll get what you get when you get it," the sheriff said, appraising Tim coolly. "Like I said . . . this ain't Las Vegas."

Tim had an uneasy feeling that it wasn't exactly normal Louisiana either.

14

Sheriff Wilson MacGregor sat back in the hard wooden chair behind his desk and looked at the rap sheet that had come in from Nevada over the wire.

The two yahoos in his cell certainly had a lot of trouble up their sleeves—theft, vandalism, robbery, fighting, public intoxication, possession of a weapon, resisting arrest . . . from the looks of it they were hoods and outlaws, destined to end up in a penitentiary at some point during their lives.

His nephew Tommy had called him to say a man with a gun had been in the store. It wasn't so unusual—a lot of Texans came through with guns, but these were younger guys, and that's just what Striker was looking for.

MacGregor took off his hat and laid it on the desk, wiping down his brow. He didn't like the heat, but he noticed with annoyance even when the temperature dipped as low as it had lately, he still felt like he was in a broiler. Even the mosquitoes off the bayou didn't get the message it was winter.

He didn't like waiting after hours for Striker either, but Clayton Striker wasn't someone he wanted to beg off on meeting with.

Striker's great-great something or other had founded the town, and Striker wasn't the type of man to let anyone forget that. He was warden at Strikersville prison, and as far as the town knew, their golden boy, their perfect citizen. He donated to Ladies Aid, the church, the charitable foundation and the hospital over in Lafayette. He personally paid for the Town Picnic each year, and there wasn't a person in town who didn't thank the Lord for Clayton Striker.

Well, maybe just one.

Clayton Striker was the biggest thorn in his side, and he had only himself to blame for it. He'd been indiscreet as hell the year he ran for sheriff, and looked to win until his involvement with Lureen Bell got around town. He assured his wife Marnie it was just gossip started by the opposition, but it wasn't doing his reputation any good around town before the election.

Then one night he wandered out of the Sleep-Rite motel, miles outside of Baton Rouge, and outside of his town and parish, and ran smack into Clayton Striker.

He was leaning against his Cadillac, a cigar between his teeth, like he'd been waiting for him. All these years later, Wilson was now certain he had been.

Striker hadn't said a word, just got in that flashy Caddy of his and drove off, leaving him shaking in the parking lot. For the next three days he waited for Marnie to up and leave him, for the local radio station to announce his indiscretions and the town to force him to pull out of the campaign.

H went to the Whiskey Pig outside of town to drown his hopes in some sour mash, and as he stumbled out the door toward his car in the early morning hours, Clayton Striker had come out of the shadows.

"Looks like you could use a ride."

Wilson had accepted, not thinking until later how Clayton got out there without a car of his own. Thinking about it too much made his head hurt.

Striker had been slick as oil and offered to back his campaign. That sobered him right up.

"Why'd you wanna do that?" he'd asked dumbly.

"Because I think we could work well together."

And that had been the start of a miserable relationship.

Not one week after winning that election in a landslide, Clayton Striker had come down to the sheriff's station and asked for his help.

He'd gone to Strikersville prison to find the body laying there right outside the gates.

"Damn shame," Clayton had said, looking at the man on the ground, shot in the back. "Tried to escape."

And there it was. The sting, the catch, the little prickle on the back of his neck. He always thought Striker threw his weight around because he wanted something from him. He didn't back him because he liked him, he backed him because he needed a patsy.

He found out two months later about the drug operation behind the prison walls. There were stories coming back from a few prisoners that were released. It was ones that went in and never came out again he wondered about.

It wasn't until Striker offered to cut him in that MacGregor decided turning a blind eye wouldn't hurt anyone. But Striker's deals were never fair. With him taking all the risk, it was only fair. Striker had turned down his request for more money, and without something more lining his pockets he decided it was time to get rid of Clayton Striker.

All that was left was figuring out a way to do it. Arresting him meant the town would cry foul, even if they found everything out at the prison. Then the questions would come about how much he knew.

No, Striker had to go permanently.

MacGregor was broken out of his reverie by the sounds of the two Nevada men arguing back in the cells. These were two jackasses he was eager to get rid of. He didn't trust either one of them.

The jangling of the phone startled him, and he shifted his feet off the desk and picked up the line. Striker. Cancelling.

Striker was a headache, these hoods were a headache. The whole damn world needed an aspirin.

He sighed, picked his coat up off the hook and looked over at Paul Round-tree, the deputy that had come to relieve him for the night.

"Leave the lights on in the cells," he said to Roundtree. "We got some real smart mouths back there. Let 'em holler if they're going to. I'll be in tomorrow morning to deal with 'em."

Roundtree nodded, and Sheriff MacGregor left the station, a headache brewing behind his eyes.

The lights were kept on in the cell all night.

It made it hard to sleep, and Tim was sure the sheriff did it on purpose. It also made it even harder to put up with Jake, who couldn't stop complaining about every tiny thing like he'd never been behind bars before.

The bed was lumpy, the springs were poking his back, the lights were too bright, the cell was damp. Tim finally told him to shut the fuck up since it was his fault they were in this situation in the first place.

Jake glared at him, and Tim felt the weight of his gaze.

"You really didn't rob that station?" Tim asked awhile later.

"I swear it. I drank some Pepsi before I paid for it, that was enough for the kid to shit bricks. I bought the drinks, the magazine and paid for the gas," Jake said. "Anyhow, your driving is what got us in here."

"I wasn't speeding." He rubbed his face. "Not until after he blew the siren, anyway."

It was five in the morning according to the clock on the wall. It was hours later before a deputy showed up with some bread, jam and cartons of milk.

"Why not bread and water, the irony too much for you?" Tim asked, watching as he opened the barred doors. The deputy couldn't have been much older than him, with a wispy, wannabe moustache and not enough lines in his face to say he'd lived any years.

"When do we get to see the judge?"

The deputy shrugged, then looked over to the bullpen. "You don't want to anyway."

He shut the door up and walked back down the hall.

"What the hell was that supposed to mean?" Jake asked, snatching up the bigger slice of bread.

"I dunno, but I don't like it," Tim said, staring down the hall. Things didn't add up here.

A few hours later the sheriff was in the office, and the only way Tim could tell was from his booming voice and the creak of the wooden swivel chair he sat in.

"Hey!" he hollered.

The sheriff took his time coming down the hall. The deputy, Roundtree, Tim thought his name was, followed behind, hovering at the door.

"When do we get to see the judge?" Tim asked.

"You're real eager to get in front of a judge. Why is that, boy?"

Tim gritted his teeth. "Just want to get bail set."

The sheriff clucked at him. "I dunno that the judge is gonna let bail be set low enough y'all can afford it. Besides that, y'all are definitely a flight risk being from out of state."

"Why would bail be set high?" he asked. "All I did was drive a hitchhiker in a truck."

"Aiding and abetting is what that was," the sheriff said. He nodded toward Jake. "That one's up on even bigger charges."

So they didn't know about the cigarettes. It didn't make sense, but the sheriff obviously hadn't open the back of the truck. The fact the truck was sitting somewhere untouched was a relief, but the fact they hadn't looked inside was a mystery. As good as that was, there was something very wrong about it. Any lawman worth his salt would've cracked open the trailer first chance.

"What kind of place do you run here?" Tim asked. "Maybe you oughta take us down to the judge and let him decide."

The sheriff looked up at Tim. "You're looking at him."

Tim tried not to let the surprise show, but the sheriff saw his expression and laughed.

"Isn't that a conflict of interest?" Tim asked. He flicked his gaze toward Roundtree, who had slunk back into the bullpen, his desk near the hallway. He could tell the man still listened, and Tim wondered what the hick deputy's game was.

"Elected and elected, and if the town thinks it's okay, so do I," the sheriff said. "Let's make quick work of this. The two of y'all ain't gonna want a jury trial, every citizen in the town's heard how you pulled a gun and threatened to kill my nephew Tommy MacGregor, it's a wonder a mob isn't down here trying to torch the two of you. So that leaves a bench trial in front of the judge."

Tim thought he might want to take his chances with the angry mob.

"We got evidence from Tommy MacGregor identifying the cowboy here as the perpetrator, and we got evidence from a sheriff's deputy who spotted the truck driven by you, with the perpetrator as a passenger, tearing out of the area moments later. You tried to flee the sheriff's vehicles, and were arrested, whereupon the sheriff's department found two unregistered handguns in his possession. Sound about right?"

"But none in mine."

His gun was stashed inside his bag, and if the sheriff said he found it, Tim would know they found the rest of the cargo, too.

"Even so, aiding and abetting, like I said," the sheriff said. "Based on these findings, I find you both guilty as charged."

Jake sat on the bed and glared through the bars at the sheriff. Tim let out a breath, relieved that they hadn't found the cigarettes. Although, if they had, they probably wouldn't say. This whole place was crooked and Tim imagined they'd just up and sell the cigarettes without a word.

"Jake Wheeler is guilty of possession of two unlicensed firearms, uttering threats and armed robbery. Timothy Kelly is guilty of fleeing the scene of a crime and aiding and abetting a fugitive, as well as fleeing the police. Now, based on the criminal code of Strikersville and the surrounding parish, I hereby sentence you to both to five years hard labour to be served at Strikersville prison, effective immediately. We'll be transferring you in a few hours."

"This is bullshit!" Jake rocketed toward the bars, gripping them tightly and pulling, like he wanted to tear them off. The sheriff loosened his night stick.

His puffy bulldog eyes stared at them. "Hoods like you are always in trouble, stealing, hurting people, doing wrong—you need some ironing out. A few years in Strikersville, you boys'll come out of there knowing right from wrong."

"Nevada's gonna know something's up, with you running us like you did," Tim said, gesturing down to the offices. "You think we don't have people expecting us back?"

"Teletype request for a routine traffic stop. Nothing amiss, I sent you on your way." The sheriff looked at Tim with a hard, cool gaze. He was enjoying this. "And with his moving around so much no one'll miss him. You, I suspect, won't be missed for awhile, and even then they won't know where to look."

Jake hocked one up and spat at the sheriff, and it was all Tim could do not to groan aloud.

The sheriff turned a deep crimson, yanked a handkerchief out of his pocket and wiped his cheek. He stuffed the handkerchief back in his pocket and looked at Jake with unabashed hatred.

"It's going to be a different story when the warden gets here," the sheriff said. "Mark my words, boy, you're in for a world of hurt."

The sheriff turned to leave.

"Hey!" Jake hollered. The sheriff sauntered back down the hall toward the bullpen. "Hey, get your fat ass back here! I didn't do nothing!"

Jake rattled the cell bars, then pounded his hands against them. After a few minutes of it, he turned to Tim.

"Why the hell ain't you doing anything?"

"You really think you'll convince him to come open the door?" Tim asked, looking at Jake with a raised eyebrow.

"This is bullshit. He just gave us five years—I didn't do *shit*. We didn't get a phone call—" He grabbed the bars and yanked again, then yelled down the hall. "Hey! I didn't even get a phone call."

"Quit it, Jake," Tim said.

"Fuck you!"

Jake kept beating at the doors until he tired himself out.

"There's something going on here," Tim said.

"Oh, you think so?"

Tim looked at Jake squarely. "There's no use in all that. Like it or not, that sheriff is sending us to prison."

"He never told us we could talk to a lawyer. Never fingerprinted us, nothing," Jake said.

"Yeah. At the least he should've read us that Miranda warning. You and I both know going to his prison has nothing to do with those bullshit charges."

Jake paced. "So you're admitting you know I didn't rob the place? He can't put me away for not doing shit. There's no proof I did anything."

"There's no proof you didn't, either," Tim said. "He didn't make any calls to Vegas. He didn't fingerprint us, he didn't photograph us. He may have run our driver's licenses, but Las Vegas PD and Clark County isn't going to think anything of that if no charges come. This guy doesn't give a damn about us or the law. I bet anything there's not a scrap of paperwork on us. He's got something going on, and I'm aiming to find out what."

"This isn't a Hardy Boys mystery, Kelly," Jake protested. "He's not keeping us in the Las Vegas jail or some reformatory. He's shipping us off to a real prison."

Tim sat down on the lower bunk. This was pretty much a nightmare. He had nightmares about cops throwing him in prison for nothing before—hell, half the cops in Las Vegas trumped up the charges on him whenever they hauled him in. He'd begun to expect it. But this was something different—something sinister—but so far he felt like there was still some kind of way out that could avoid the prison altogether.

"We'd better keep a low profile until we figure out what's going on here. This guy might just be some hard ass cop who wants to rid the world of ne'er do wells, but I don't think so. Something smells rotten here, Jake, and whatever it is got us five years in the clink. I don't want you adding to it."

Tim expected Jake to argue back, but he was quiet for the first time ever.

"Something *is* up with that guy," Jake agreed. "I was expecting him to come in here and beat me down."

"Hell, everyone wants that. What'd you think, I'd lift his keys, we'd lock him in and be outta here like an episode of the Lone Ranger?" Tim laughed in spite of himself. "You got an imagination, I'll give you that."

"It could've worked," Jake shrugged.

"I don't like the feel of this," Tim said.

"We can write when we get to the prison, let people know what happened," Jake suggested.

"You think they'll let us send letters? You're dreaming."

"We could find a way to get word to people."

"And then what? Who's going to shell out money for a lawyer?" Tim looked over at Jake. "My old man'll be relieved I'm not around getting in the Outfit's face. My mom'll cry and go to church more than usual, but we don't have two nickels to rub together. Even if somebody does give a shit, no one's coming, Jake. You have someone waiting on you who's going to make a stink if you don't show up?"

He watched Jake's gaze flick from side to side, knowing Wheeler knew it as much as he did. They were on their own.

"So first chance we get we're out of here?" Jake asked.

Tim nodded. "First chance."

4

Tim was half asleep in his bunk when he heard the voices.

He leaned over so he could get a better view into the bullpen and saw a man walk in. The sheriff, feet up on his desk, practically killed himself trying to get to a standing position.

The man was tall—at least six-three—and wore cowboy boots, jeans, a belt buckle the size of Texas and a button down western shirt with a blazer over top. He bit down on an unlit cigar, and removed his flat topped cowboy hat when he came inside, laying it on hat hook just inside the door.

"Heard you got some new blood for me," he said. "What's their racket?"

"Striker," the sheriff said. "Thought you'd be in last night, the prison said you'd cancelled."

"I was busy," he said. "Who are they?"

"Ne'er do wells from Las Vegas, Nevada. One had weapons on him. History of charges back home."

"Well off?"

The sheriff shook his head. "Not by the looks of their rap sheets or their clothes."

"Good," Striker said. "What did the old town judge give them?"

"Five years hard," he said. "Just like you asked."

"You got someone to bring 'em up to Strikersville?" he asked. "Transport's busy with the chain gang today."

"I can have one of my deputies take them if that does you fine," MacGregor said.

"Something I need to talk over with you," Striker said. "What's say we go over to Rosie's for lunch?"

MacGregor nodded. "I'll call up Roundtree on the radio, tell him to transport these two up to the prison. He knows where to go."

Striker nodded. He picked up his hat and left the station without another word.

MacGregor got on the radio to his deputy, arranged the transport then locked up the station.

Tim let out a breath. Something really bad was going down here.

"Think he's gone?" Jake asked a few minutes later.

"Yeah," Tim said. "I saw him go. No one here but us and the mice."

Tim swung his legs off the bed and put his stocking feet on the cold concrete.

"Did you hear any of what he said?" Tim asked.

Jake nodded. "Prison warden asked him to give us five years or something."

Tim nodded, taking a soft pack of Kools off the floor. A deputy threw the pack in that morning with a pack of matches, apparently not realizing the damage Tim and Jake could do with it if needed. But there wasn't much that could catch fire in the cell, and not with them in it. But you never knew when you might need something. Tim tucked the extra matches in his sock.

"Sounds like they got some kind of racket going on," Tim agreed, lighting a smoke. The menthol made him gag, but it was all the cigarette he was going to get, so he put up with it. The tobacco relaxed him. "I don't like the sound of it."

Jake didn't reply.

"He mentioned a chain gang, Jake."

Jake nodded. "I heard it."

"Thought that was something you only see in the movies," Tim said.

Jake shrugged. "Used to see the occasional chain gang working along the highway on the way to Montgomery when I was a kid. It was mostly Negro men, buncha guards with weapons watching them dig ditches on the side of the road. Haven't seen any chain gangs since then, and I've been around."

The man's last name was Striker, from what he heard. The town and prison were both named Strikersville, and Tim didn't like the thought the man in charge of the prison might be in charge of the whole damn town. Something smelled fishy here, and it wasn't coming off the bayou. A man with that much power couldn't be trusted.

They sat in silence for a few more minutes.

"We gonna try with that deputy?" Tim asked.

Jake shrugged. "Best chance we got. Only I don't know how the hell we're getting out of here. We don't have a clue where they towed the car, and I'm not going back to Las Vegas without that trailer."

"Funny . . . if they'd only looked inside they would've had us here legit," Tim said.

"Yeah," Jake said. Tim could tell from his tone Jake thought it was as weird as he did they hadn't checked.

Jake did present a decent point about escape. Even if they got out of their cell, they had no transportation and no money. He wasn't leaving this place without that truck. He wasn't going to let those cigarettes rot on the side of road or in some junkyard until someone got curious and opened it up.

What he wouldn't give for someone decent to come down here and help them. Bill was the only one he'd trust, but there was no way they could get in touch. The other guys in the gang weren't the type to trust with something like this. Hell, if this got out, he was finished.

"What about Wyatt?" Jake asked.

"Sam Wyatt?" Tim asked. The old Fremont Street gangster had helped him out a few times, but this . . . well, he wasn't sure someone like Sam would want to get involved. "From what I've seen he isn't about to get in a car and come down here. Especially once he hears what we've got in that truck. We'd have to ditch the cigarettes or the Outfit would hear, and I doubt you want to cut them in."

Jake gave him a sour look. "That'd be the end of paying my debt off. They'd probably add to it for keeping it from 'em."

Tim stared at the bars.

Jake crossed his arms and brooded. "We could try Hollis."

"Think he's sober? Warner would probably think it was a big joke and come into town advertising we were getting away," Tim said, thinking about his past encounters with Hollis Warner.

"You don't seem to be suggesting any names, so unless you got a better answer, I think my idea's looking pretty good."

Man, he hated it when Jake Wheeler was right.

"If the cop didn't file any charges for real, then we aren't guilty of anything," Tim said. "That's one thing in our favour. The Outfit won't know if there's no paper trail."

"We need a map," Jake mused. "We gotta figure out where to go. We need a map and a phone."

"We need to find where they took that truck."

"That's the first place they'd look." Jake ran his hand through his hair. "The minute we escape they'll put a cop on the place they towed the truck to, mark my words."

Tim laid down on the bed smoking and thinking. It'd be risky, but they had only the one chance with the deputy. If they could surprise him and bolt out of here, well, it'd just be another place to add to his list of locations to never visit again.

The deputy, Roundtree, showed up a half hour later. He walked into the back and looked at both Jake and Tim. He was young, maybe not much older than they were. He was fresh faced, with his blond hair perfectly combed, his uniform pressed, the creases sharp and fine. He looked by the book, and Tim hated by the book.

Roundtree opened the cell door and tossed two pair of white tennis shoes in.

"We're moving you up to Strikersville."

Strikersville. Last strike and you're out.

Tim and Jake shared a glance. Tim wasn't sure who'd move first, but he was ready. The deputy had cuffs with him as he stepped into the cell. He eyed Tim and Jake.

"Don't." His voice bordered on pleading. "They'll just get a posse together same as they did for the last guys that escaped. They're dead now, and I don't want that on my head."

Maybe Tim had underestimated this kid. At any rate, it had to be done.

Tim rushed the cop first, and Jake was right behind him. They slammed into the bars, and the deputy lost his breath. Roundtree managed to grab his baton and give Tim a hit to the leg, but Jake was on him in a second when Tim stumbled back.

The deputy fought back harder than either of them expected. He had leverage on the door, and used it to crack Jake in the head. Jake stumbled back against the cinderblock wall, and the deputy was out of the cell and locking it up before Tim knew what happened.

"I told you, don't," the deputy pleaded, breathing hard. "I don't want to call for Sheriff MacGregor. He's got a cattle prod, and he's not afraid to use it. You don't wanna go into Strikersville like that. Your best chance is go there, keep your head down and serve the time. From what I've seen, you two could talk your way somewhere decent with Striker, I think. He always looks at guys like you, young guys with criminal backgrounds. He needs you, and you'd find a way out easier if you just went with it."

"What the *fuck* is going on around here?" Tim swore.

The deputy got two sets of shackles from a supply closet down the hall and tossed them in.

"Shackle up your legs, both of you, then each others' wrists. If you don't, I'll have to call the sheriff and that won't go well for any of us. Please."

Tim marvelled at the pleading in the kid's voice.

"You're a piece of work," Jake snarled.

The deputy glanced toward the door. "Hurry. It's better if I take you than if he does. You start out on the wrong foot with Striker, and you could be spending a lot more time in that prison than you're due."

"We're not due *any* time. The whole damn town's crooked," Tim muttered.

"The town doesn't know about any of this," Roundtree said. "And not everyone's crooked. There's just some of us who haven't figured a way out yet."

Tim looked down at the shackles on the floor, and every fibre of his being was telling him not to put them on. They had to run, to escape, to get the hell out of Dodge and not look back.

"There's not a lot of time, come on!" Roundtree said.

Tim bent down and picked up the tennis shoes.

"Kelly, you gotta be kidding me," Jake said.

He put the shoes on, and Jake followed suit. Tim stared at the shackles for a minute.

"Hurry!" Roundtree said.

He shackled his ankles, every bone in his body screaming at him not to do it. He closed the shackle around one hand, but couldn't get the other. Jake refused to help him do the last one up. The deputy opened the door when he saw they were mostly contained and came over to adjust to the shackles.

"What kind of game are those two playing?" Tim asked him. "You have to know."

Roundtree's dark eyes looked into his own. "It's no game."

The deputy led them out of their cell and through the precinct floor. The place was abandoned, no one else working and the phones quiet. Granted, it was a Sunday, and maybe no one came in much on Sundays.

Tim saw their boots, belts and other things bundled together in a paper bag on MacGregor's desk. He was going to get this guy for stealing their things.

Outside was more of the same, with the town looking like it was poised for tumbleweeds to blow through. It creeped Tim out, mostly because he got the feeling it wasn't natural. Everyone was probably at church, but it still felt strange and otherworldly.

Obviously the sheriff and the warden had something going on. It didn't really matter what. What mattered was their plan consisted of Tim and Jake stewing in prison for five years.

The enormity of the situation began to hit him when the deputy sat them both in the back of the car. Five years of prison was something he could do—hell he figured he'd be in for longer than that at some point in his life. But five years in prison with Jake Wheeler? He didn't do anything to deserve that.

26

Knowing the awful luck he had, they'd be sharing a cell. He'd wake up to that smirk every morning, have to see him in the chow line, in the yard, in the work program, whatever they had there. Every living second with Jake Wheeler on his ass like a barnacle.

"Jesus Christ, this is some shit," Tim sighed.

Paul Roundtree wasn't a saint. He got in his share of fights growing up; it was hard not to with a face his mother always called "as pretty as a girl's." He'd smoked, drank his old man's whiskey behind the barn and had made it with Darlene Duchamp after prom. He wasn't a saint, but he wasn't a devil, either.

And he was right up against the fact he was likely working for one.

Crime in the town was extremely low, and everyone seemed happy with MacGregor as sheriff and judge. The Strikersville prison was a model of a well-run prison according to the newspaper, and everything seemed fine in town.

So when he'd taken the test and became a sheriff's deputy, he expected he'd learn more about the man who reminded him of a revivalist minister. Instead, he'd learned that Wilson MacGregor was as dirty as the day was long, and so far, there was nothing anyone could do about it.

He presented a nice package to the town, but Paul saw otherwise. The other two deputies, Hickom and Lee, thought MacGregor rose and set the sun. They were his cronies, ready and willing to take a few extra dollars to look the other way. MacGregor hadn't approached Paul with any kind of deal yet, but it was coming. He could sense it.

Maybe it was because it was evident to everyone that Hickom and Lee weren't exactly rocket scientists. They were no more leaders than a church mouse was. But Paul knew that despite his quiet exterior and baby face, people did look to him as one. They had when he was the star defensive end on the football team in high school, and they had when he had gone on to college and played ball at LSU for a year until he blew out his knee. Everyone looked at him as if he had some kind of authority, and it was ironic as hell that he was beginning to hate it.

He could sense Sheriff MacGregor would come to him. There was something about the way the man watched him. He knew the sheriff was trying to decide if Paul Roundtree could be flipped. Sometimes, Paul himself wasn't sure.

The guys in the back of the car weren't saints either, not by far. They'd been in jail for far worse than he had even considered doing, and there was the fact one of them may have robbed the gas station, and they had guns on them. A few months ago it wouldn't have mattered if these guys had come into town and the sheriff had asked him to look the other way while he pocketed a gun or two. If money was offered to keep quiet about something, Paul probably would've taken it. With Melinda pregnant, he was needing all the money he could get. It looked like being under Sheriff MacGregor's thumb might be a distaste he could stand.

And then he'd come across Josie Landry.

Josie was just out of her teens, but was small and slight and looked half her age. Her family had a name in the town, her mother dead, her old man a drunk who ended up in jail more times than he could count. Last Paul had heard, Remy Landry had up and taken off for greener pastures, leaving his son Jean-René and daughter Josie behind.

He was just coming off a long shift manning the station alone while the deputies and the sheriff had been out with the warden and some guards from the prison, searching for three men who'd broke loose earlier in the day. The evening paper had their three pictures lined up across the front page.

He drove along a back road on his way home, alongside the bayou, when Josie Landry stumbled out of the brush. He swerved to avoid hitting her.

She tried to run when he got out of his truck with his uniform on, and it wasn't until later he understood why.

She was bloody and beaten but wouldn't say a word about who hurt her and what they'd done until he asked her if her brother had done it. She'd said no, then crossed her arms, looking at him defiantly.

"Y'all won't do a thing to one of your own," she said.

He'd looked at her, not understanding.

"Are you soft in the head, cher?" she asked. "They came to the cabin, looking for the men who escaped. They found me."

He told her she could come back and make a statement, press charges.

"They come back, I'm shooting first," she said. "I'll blow their balls off I ever see 'em again, you got that, cher?"

She had tried to limp away, her ankle swollen, her legs bruised. He begged her to go to a hospital, but she wouldn't budge. He finally convinced her to accept a ride back to her cabin, but she refused to ride in the cab, and sat in the bed of the truck. She didn't thank him when they got as close as he could take her, and he didn't expect her to.

Two months later her brother Jean-René beat Hickom up in a bar fight and landed himself in Strikersville for six years, far too long for a bar fight. Paul wondered if Josie felt Striker and the sheriff had won again. It was a wonder Josie Landry wasn't so despondent they'd find her hanging off a tree branch in the bayou.

But she was Cajun stock, a tough girl who walked barefoot through the bayou like it was nothing, had hunted since she was young, and did just fine with no electricity in the middle of nowhere. She wasn't the kind of girl that came to the local high school. He couldn't recall ever seeing her there. She may not have been educated, but she was smart.

Ever since that day, Paul had watched things a little more closely, and he didn't like what he saw. The thought of playing in MacGregor's court held little taste for him now, and all he could think about was what he'd do to stop him.

Only there was nothing—Paul was a small fish in a pond that was probably much bigger and deeper than he had knowledge of.

He glanced in the rearview mirror again. The two hoods back there reminded him of the Landry family—tough, defiant, street savvy and petulant.

The cowboy wasn't someone he'd like to tangle with—the man went straight for his balls when they were fighting—and there was some kind of snap-at-any-moment feeling about him. He had a thick Alabama accent, and he figured he put it on thicker when he wanted people to underestimate him. He was handsome enough to headline the movies, and that probably got him in more trouble than his mouth.

There'd be riots and brawls and all kinds of things with that one at a regular prison. He wondered how he would do in Strikersville, and had a feeling he'd try and con his way out with Striker. Knowing Striker, if this cowboy had something he needed, that was a good way to go.

The other one was quiet, a thinker. He might have looked like he wasn't paying attention, but Paul didn't miss how he flicked his gaze here and there. The dark-haired one worried him.

His face was misshapen on one side, scarred and unsettling, and Paul had no idea what kind of injury could cause that. There was no indication in the teletype how he'd gotten it, but if he was beaten, a person wouldn't come out of it with a sunny disposition.

The two men couldn't be more opposite, in looks and personality, but somehow, they were one and the same. There was some kind of crackling hope there.

"You know he's not doing right."

The dark-haired one had spoken up.

"You two robbed a gas station and fled the scene, had unregistered weapons on you," Roundtree said, testing them.

"Didn't rob shit. The guns, I'll give you that. They were for protection, because Wheeler can't fight worth shit. What's that usually get a first time offender around here? Guns confiscated?"

Paul almost cracked a smile. "First time?"

"Well, in these parts," the man said. Kelly, he remembered his name was.

Paul looked ahead to the road for a second.

29

"Confiscate the weapons, ship him back to Las Vegas with a fine, and rid yourself of him," Wheeler said. "That's my guess. I know those weapons came back clean, all I did was forget to register them, officer."

These guys might be his age, but they were smart when it came to legal things. They'd obviously had a lot of dealings with the police.

"What do you say, Jake?" Kelly asked the cowboy. "If they were gonna throw you in the clink—maybe a year? Probably served in county lock up, out in six months if you're lucky. 'Course, it'd be easier to ship you back to Las Vegas and serve it there. Less drain on the lovely state of Louisiana. Me, on the other hand . . . let me off with a fine for picking up a hitchhiker."

"What's your point?" Paul asked.

"You know this is all bullshit. I can see plain as day you don't want to go along with it. I can also see there isn't anyone else standing on your side of the line."

"Then you see I can't help you. I wish I could."

"I almost believe that."

"Keep your head down in there," Paul said. "Don't go getting noticed by Striker so quick. Trust me when I say he's always watching. I've only got some idea of what's going on in there, but I suspect a lot of the boys on the outside of the cells should be on the inside."

"Nothing unusual about that," Wheeler said.

"You think I'm pissing away five years of my life in that prison, you got another thing coming," Kelly said.

He looked in the rear view mirror again. They were only a few miles from the prison now.

"They have a shoot to kill policy on escapees," Paul said. "They bring out a dog team if anyone escapes. Most escapees go back in body bags. I'd just wait it out if I were you."

"But you're not me," Kelly said. "You're sitting here doing the bidding of that hog on the take back at the sheriff station. You're running his errands, being his lapdog, which is just as bad as if you were railroading us yourself. Don't kid yourself, Roundtree. You're just as guilty as they are."

Kelly's gaze flicked over to the window, and it was clear he was done talking.

Paul drove the rest of the way with great unease settled in his stomach.

The deputy took them as far as the main processing office, then turned around and left without another word.

They were herded into a processing room, and Tim was quick to notice not a single fingerprint or photograph was taken. Both he and Jake were handed orange jumpsuits. The guards made them strip down and change into their prison issue clothes. Tim was sure he'd never see his clothes again.

They were each given a threadbare towel, a face cloth, a small bar of rancid smelling soap and a toothbrush.

They were marched through different secure areas of the prison before nearing the cells. A door was unlocked and they were led down a long corridor. It smelled like wet concrete.

The walls were unpainted cinderblock and Tim could hear the familiar sounds of prisoners whispering down the line. Of course, in Las Vegas it was usually a chorus of hellos from people he knew. The calls this time were a little different.

He couldn't tell if Wheeler was nervous—he didn't know if Wheeler had ever been inside a prison. As it was, he'd only spent six months in the state pen himself, out early for overcrowding a few years back on a robbery charge. It hadn't been fun, but it wasn't horrible. People had heard of him and that helped.

Knowing Jake, he'd probably been holed up somewhere at some point. That would do them both good. Experience was a good teacher.

The guards moved them down the corridors, and the men in the cells came forward to the bars, looking out and clucking at the fresh meat. He studied Jake, walking ahead of him, and wondered what the prisoners made of him.

He was overly handsome with light brown hair and hazel eyes, the kind of guy who should be in movies, although his shit personality would've put a stop to that. He didn't look like your typical hood, that was for sure. If you were a betting man, you might think he'd be easy to flip and make a first rate bitch, and Tim almost laughed to himself. Jake would start a riot first.

It made Tim remember the first time he'd met Jake. Tim was coming out of the Brown Cow, pockets full from winning at craps, and the asshole had tried to mug him. After Tim started laughing, not expecting the hick accented cowboy wannabe to have any game, Jake popped him one. They'd ended up in a fist fight in the alley, broken up only when they got too tired to continue. They'd shared a cigarette afterward, and went their way like nothing had happened. Jake earned a scrap of respect from him then.

Of course, Jake had pissed away that respect over the years, most of all with Ruby.

He wondered if she'd notice he wasn't around town anymore.

The guards stopped at a small cell which already held two men. Tim was surprised the guard unlocked the door.

"Welcome to your new home, boys."

Tim's heart sank as he realized they were sentencing him to five years with Jake. Nope. Not going to happen. If they wanted to guarantee themselves a prison break, they just did.

The guard locked the doors shut behind them, and Tim felt the familiar rise of panic the moment the door clanged shut. He usually felt this way the first few days inside—like the walls were crawling all over him. It would be even worse in here, with two other bunk mates.

The cell was barely big enough for two people, never mind four. A small steel sink and toilet sat against one wall and two bunks were pushed against the other walls. They had thin mattresses and a small pillow and threadbare blanket each.

One of their cell mates was lying on the lower bunk and hadn't taken much notice of him and Jake.

The other man got up from the lower bunk of the other set of bunk beds. He stood there cracking his knuckles like he was waiting for a fight. Tim was in the mood to oblige him.

"What the fuck are you staring at?" Jake asked the man.

"Nothing," the guy said. He was probably in his late 20s, and was pretty well built. His hands weren't scabbed or bruises and that meant he hadn't fought in awhile. Tim sized him up quickly and decided Jake might have a bit of trouble without him.

"My friend here thinks you're a pansy," Tim said. "I don't know about you, but I wouldn't take that coming from him."

"Fuck you, Kelly."

Jake wasn't very original with his retorts.

"You gonna learn I run this cell, I run this block, you got that?" the man said.

Jake stepped up to the guy and looked like he was going to lean in to tell him something. Tim fell for that once. Jake hefted his fist into the guy's midsection, doubling him over.

The cocky guy flew at Jake, and they hit the bars. Jake retaliated with a punch to the man's jaw, while Tim sidestepped out of the way.

The man on the lower bunk, probably in his late 40s, stood up. He had to be close to six foot five, and Tim backed up a step. Jake was going to be in a world of hurt, and too bad for him.

The giant stood and stared at the two fighters for a moment, then waded in and grabbed both of them by the arms. He yanked them apart.

"You two stop acting like children and sit down unless you want the guards in here. Solitary ain't no joke in here, and I want y'all to keep your noses clean, you got that?"

Jake looked cowed by the big man, and the other fighter showed him deference, too.

"How long you been in?" Tim asked him, knowing the answer had to be awhile.

"Fifteen of a twenty year sentence, but you can bet they ain't letting me out. I'm in here legit."

The man leaned against the bars and looked each way down the hall, probably for guards. He came and sat down on the lower bunk again and the metal groaned against his bulk.

"What the hell is going on around here?"

"You haven't figured it all out yet?" the other fighter said.

Tim looked from one man to the other, then at Jake, who was feeling his jaw.

"What's your names?" the big man asked.

"Tim Kelly. That's Jake Wheeler."

"Henri Boudreaux," he said. His voice was a thick Louisiana patois.

"Victor," the other man said. "Molinez."

He didn't look Mexican. The two men had each claimed the bottom of the bunks. Jake had already climbed up to the top of the one above Victor. It reminded Tim of two cats that fought and then curled up by the fire together. The image almost made him bust out laughing. People probably thought the same about him and Jake the way they constantly fought, yet couldn't seem to escape each other.

"You get thrown in by MacGregor?" Victor asked.

Tim nodded.

"Striker has him in his pocket. In case you haven't figured it out, Clayton Striker runs this town."

"Haven't found a way out yet?" Tim asked.

"Haven't tried," Victor said.

Tim frowned. "If it's such a hell hole, why not?"

"I've seen twenty-six men shot trying to escape since Striker took over as warden two years ago. I am sure many more than that died," Henri said. "Men have escaped, I've seen them come back in body bags. Buried in the wastelands."

"The wastelands?" Jake asked.

Henri nodded. "A dirt field here. Too hard to grow anything but weeds. They bury the bodies there. There are far too many. The warden has only a few rules—follow them, and he leaves you alone. Do not follow them, and you'll end up covered in dust."

"Sounds like a real nice guy."

"It is no joke, boy," Henri said. "The guards here are allowed to do what they wish. Victor, show them."

Victor stood and pulled his shirt up, revealing a web of scars across his midsection.

"Burned with hot water," he said.

"So he tortures folks that try to escape? What's he got going on?"

"One of the largest drug operations I have ever seen," Henri said.

"Some prisons punch out license plates. We package grass, pills, all kinds of things," Victor said. "I should say, the lucky ones do. Henri is one. The rest of us it's manual labour."

Henri nodded. "He has those he . . . trusts . . . of the prisoners working inside his drug labs here. The majority of the prisoners are on the chain gangs."

"Chain gang? They weren't lying about that?" Jake asked. "I heard it, but I didn't believe it."

"It is no joke," Henri said. "Groups are taken to work in different locations. There is a quarry and an old train bridge being dismantled outside the prison. You will probably end up there eventually. He will have you work in the prison yard first, chipping rock at the quarry here. If you are good workers, then the chain gang."

"How chained are we talking?" Tim asked.

Henri shook his head. "You cannot escape. Prisoners are shackled at the leg, and you're in wrist shackles for the transport there and back. Guards have high powered weapons and they shoot to kill. I saw a man run like a jack rabbit end up with thirty-six slugs in his back. I know. I buried him."

"Does anyone get out?"

Henri nodded thoughtfully. "Some, we're told, work on the outside for Striker in his drug operation. The ones who are here legitimately, like myself, have no hope of that. Those he brought here secretly, the ones he think he can use, he wants their connections on the outside."

Tim didn't think any of his connections, new or old, would put up with Striker, and he smiled grimly at the thought of Striker trying to pull some shit with Sam Wyatt. He'd end up having a dirt nap next to Bobby Tafani.

He also wasn't aiming to stay in this hole one minute longer than he had to. He wasn't going to be beholden to anyone like Striker. He had enough trouble with the Outfit on his back, the last thing he needed was a Louisiana prison warden running the show.

"I can see in your face I can't convince you to stop any attempt to escape. I say go, try, be successful. If you get away, run. Don't look back."

Tim and Jake looked at each other. Well, the only thing to do was get the lay of the land and see what they were up against. Come hell or high water, they were getting out.

5

Monday, February 27, 1967

Jake couldn't sleep.

It could be all the noise. Or the dampness of the cell. Maybe the spring poking into his lower back, and maybe the way his jaw smarted from the punch Victor got him with. If he was honest, it was because he had no earthly clue how they were going to get out.

Kelly tried to play it cool like he was some kind of Svengali genius who'd bust them out of prison like Steve McQueen in *The Great Escape*. Kelly was no Steve McQueen. And anyway, he didn't like the end of that movie.

He was right about one thing though; they had to figure out how it all worked before they tried. Jake had often fantasized about breaking out of jail, and it'd be kind of fun to do it. He wasn't keen on having to avoid bullets aimed his way, but maybe they'd all aim for the back of Kelly's ugly head instead of his.

He changed positions on the mattress and tried to drown out the part of his brain that said if he hadn't messed with the kid they wouldn't be here. That skinny little bozo lied his ass off and at the least was in on railroading them by telling his bulldog uncle where to find them.

It wasn't his fault the kid was a fink and called the cops, and it wasn't his fault the cops turned out to be on the take and tied up with the second coming of Satan.

He closed his eyes, trying to envision an escape. Something more daring than bolting from a chain gang. No, he'd go out like McQueen, right under everybody's noses.

Jake dozed off with images of prison escape in his mind.

The wake up call in the prison was the guards coming down the hall, smashing their batons against the metal bars.

"Everyone up!"

Tim's head ached and the clanging was enough to make him want to make one of the guards eat his own baton. He got out of the bunk, his feet freezing on the cold floor, and slipped into the sneakers. He'd slept in the jumpsuit, wanting to be ready in case something bad went down.

The prisoners were let out of the cell blocks in sections, and everyone went to line up for chow.

Tim and Jake got into the line for food, near the back, but not at the very end. All the little things about doing time came back to him. There was a hierarchy in prison, way more than there ever was in high school.

Tim looked around the chow line. The prisoners were quiet, no one talking, everyone sitting and eating. Guards wandered around the room with rifles on alert.

Usually the prison cafeteria was a place where you tried to make your rep when you went in.

Choosing where to sit and who to associate with was a big part of things. The first time he went in to prison, he picked one of the meanest looking guys in the cafeteria and dumped his tray. He got into a hell of a fight, but nobody messed with him after that, and cliques opened to him that wouldn't have before he made that move. The guy whose tray he dumped was always a problem, but it was a small price to pay for a place on the ladder.

There was something off about this place, something Tim couldn't put his finger on. There was a decided air of tension in the room, but it had nothing to do with prisoners wanting to make a name for themselves. No one was hassling anyone else.

Usually the prison cafeteria was loud, cons yelling across the room, arguments breaking out and the occasional fight. The jeers and hollering you got used to as background noise. It was a place people came to prove themselves when they were new and socialize when they'd been in for awhile.

Here—there was nothing. It was like a cafeteria in a funeral home.

Maybe the guards and their guns were the reason why.

Tim got his tray of food—something that might be oatmeal—and a glass of water. It wasn't just slim pickings because he was at the end of the line, it was what everyone had.

Tim followed Henri and Victor to a table and sat down.

Jake took the seat across from him and shoved his spoon into the goop in the bowl, letting it slop back into the bowl. "Oatmeal? Are you crazy? This ain't even fit for pigs."

Tim looked at Henri and Victor, ignoring Jake. "Gimme the lay of the land."

Henri looked like he wanted to do anything but. He glanced around the room before looking down at his bowl and talking in a low voice.

"Guards at all the doors, automatic weapons," Henri said. "That's all you need to know. Everyone keeps their heads down because they know what happens if they don't."

"What's that?" Jake asked. "Sent to the principal's office?"

"It's not a joke, boy," Henri said. "You see them over there? They call themselves the Rock. Out of California. They keep their mouths shut. Those Mexicans there? Mexican mafia. Mouths shut too. Because they know that to beef with each other and call attention to themselves is to get themselves into trouble with Striker. The guys in here doing legit time, they either want to be on Striker's crew for the freedoms they might get, or they want to stay the hell away from it so they don't end up dead and can get out someday. New blood like you means nothing but trouble."

"So where does that put us?" Tim asked. "On Striker's radar or not?"

Henri shrugged. "Things changed last fall. He started bringing in young guys on trumped up charges, keeping them to work on the chain gangs. The prison has contracts on the outside, and the state wants them fulfilled. Hard to do when you keep your long term men in here working for your drug operation."

"So everyone stays on the man's good side so they'll get to be part of his crew." Tim spooned some oatmeal into his mouth. It tasted like warm cardboard. "How'd you manage it?"

Henri looked over at him. "Chemistry degree from Louisiana Tech."

"You serious?"

He nodded. "Striker has me working on synthesizing lysergic acid."

"Acid?" Tim asked. "Like those acid tests out in California?"

"Yes, like that," Henri said.

"That's some heavy duty stuff," Jake said.

"He looks for people like me with skills he can use." Henri took a spoonful of his oatmeal. "He's been wanting to branch into opium and cocaine. The men in here on drug charges all work in his labs. You boys don't have anything he'll need but muscle for working the chain gangs."

"We got contacts."

"He doesn't need them," Henri said. "The man has more than enough of his own. He has a farm in Mexico growing the opium poppies and sells half to a drug lord there for grass. He brings that up here for packaging. Aside from that, he has a nice lab for synthesizing the LSD. He has a nice little package to interest buyers. The man is big time. You two are small fish."

Tim ate the rest of his meal thoughtfully. Henri had said things changed late last year. He wondered if it was in September when the FBI picked up Carlos Marcello, the head of the New Orleans family. Joey the Rat had spent an entire night telling them all about the conversation he overheard some heavy hitters in from Chicago having when they were at dinner at the Dunes. A bunch of Family members got pinched in New York, with some New Orleans and Florida mafiosos.

The only question was if Striker was doing this because Marcello was otherwise occupied with legal trouble, or if Striker was hooked up with someone like Trafficante out of Florida. Either way, Chicago wouldn't get involved if it was Family business, and it's not like Tim Kelly was going to count on the Outfit to help him out of here.

Even Sam Wyatt was a long shot. If he could get word to him, it's not likely the former Texan would have any pull this far from Vegas. He was an independent sort, and while he had pull in Vegas and respect from Chicago there, he might not have that kind of legacy here. Sam had stuck his neck out for Tim enough, and it was time he used his own head to get out of this.

"You're still going to try to escape, aren't you?" Henri asked.

Tim shrugged. "Don't know."

But he did know. Just as much as Jake seemed to know, the two of them weren't long for this prison.

Jake and Tim were kept in their cells while everyone else went off to work in various areas of the prison. Jake itched to get out and do something, even if it was chipping rock for hours. Anything so he didn't have to stare at Kelly's face all day.

Kelly got quiet after breakfast and hadn't said a word since. The jerk better be working on an escape plan, because the food in this joint sucked a big one.

Jake had only spent time in prison twice. Once in the Air Force—and you couldn't really call that prison—and once for eight months after he got pinched in possession of stolen property. That had been in Arizona, and it hadn't been a bad way to spend a cold winter.

This place wasn't anything like Arizona. It was on the crazy side, since everyone seemed to behave like model prisoners. He wasn't eager to find out what happened when you broke the precious rules, but it wasn't like he was going to be a model prisoner himself. That was asking for a miracle.

"I think our best chance is to get on a work crew outside of here," Tim said.

Jake looked over at him. Henri had scored them one pack of Camels—a luxury—and they had split the smokes between them. Jake was already half way through his half of the pack.

"I hear you," Jake said. "What about arming ourselves when we do run?"

"Still thinking on it," Tim admitted. "We're going to need a distraction of some kind. A big one. All of it depends on where they put us to work."

"If they put us together."

Kelly shrugged. "If not, you're on your own."

"Asshole."

"You got us into this."

"That's bullshit, and you know it," Jake said, getting angry. He paced the cell. He wasn't taking the blame for this. "Those cops would've arrested us even if we had only bought gas, even if you'd gone in to pay for it, or the kid had done his job and come out to do it, and even if we were upstanding citizens. Hell, I bet they would've run us off the road and claimed we ran from them if you hadn't actually done it."

"Yeah."

Jake raised an eyebrow at Tim's agreement. That was as close to an apology for blaming Jake that he'd get, he supposed.

The day passed slowly. Without a window and just a bare bulb in the cell, Jake was certain he wouldn't be doing five years here. He wasn't even sure about five days.

They realized after noon they weren't going to be called for any kind of lunch break, and they later discovered there were only two meals served in the joint. That was a crock.

"Whatever we do, it's gotta be soon," Jake said. "Otherwise I'll die of starvation."

"You'll die because I'll beat you to death."

Tim had found a little hidey hole behind a piece of loose tile. Jake had no idea what Kelly thought he'd use it for since they had nothing to hide. They had nothing to their names but orange jumpsuits and ill-fitting shoes.

Jake lay in the bunk, his second night in prison, and wondered if anyone had noticed he was gone. He'd told Al he'd be gone a week or so, but Al knew he took off sometimes. He wouldn't think much of it until a lot more time went by.

Maybe Kelly's gang would notice he wasn't around. Jake smiled to himself. Maybe Kelly's boys would assume he skipped town and their whole outfit would fall apart. The thought soothed him, and he fell asleep soon after.

When they were returned to their cell after breakfast the next day, Tim and Jake were fetched by a guard.

"The two of you come with me."

Jake was about to offer up a retort, but Tim shook his head slightly. He could tell the bastard didn't want to take his advice, but he wasn't about to let Jake blow their chance to scope out the prison or get put on a work crew.

They were marched down the halls and joined the tail end of a group waiting at a door that led outside. Tim watched as the guards shackled their legs together.

The door was opened and the prisoners walked outside, in an odd shuffle so they wouldn't trip or fall. Jake kept pushing his back.

"Quit it, will you?"

"No talking!" a guard roared. "You're here to work, you got that?"

Tim wanted to haul off and hit the smug son of a bitch, but instead he looked forward and didn't say a word. He wasn't going to give the guard the satisfaction.

It was only in the low sixties, but he could tell the day would warm up. A dissipating mist of fog was in the distance, probably over the swamp water in the bayou.

They were marched across the prison yard, and Tim wondered where the hell they were going. They left a secure area of the prison and were led out to what Tim assumed were the wastelands at the edge of the prison, tall fences with barbed wire surrounding the top.

The land really was a waste. It was a big patch of yellow, dry dirt, some scrub brush and rocks, and an outcropping at the far end he assumed they were being led to. The ground was cracked and dry in some places, and it looked like the middle of a desert.

The odd thing was that it was surrounded by green vegetation on each side. Tim could even see by the tall chain link fence topped with barbed wire that green grass grew not far beyond it. It was like a bit of the Nevada desert had landed in a tiny patch of Louisiana.

The guards lined them all up, machine guns at the ready.

This was obviously no place for any kind of a prison break. The fences were too tall to scale, and the guards would get a half dozen shots off before they even got to the barbed wire at the top.

"Y'all know the drill," the guard said. "No talking, no breaks until we say, and no trouble. You give us trouble, you get the hole. Got it?"

Another guard cocked his rifle. "Any one of you makes a motion with these pick axes that ain't aimed at the rock and we shoot you down like dogs, no questions asked. Then y'all can have the fun of burying him. You got that?"

Everyone nodded, and Tim nodded along with them. Soon they were each handed a pick axe. The group moved toward the rocky outcropping and men began chipping away. Tim wondered how much of this rock formation had been in the yard—maybe it had covered all this dead area or something. If so, that was a hell of a lot of time chipping rock in this lousy joint.

He swung the axe against the rock, watching as barely a dent was made. His arm jolted from the motion. He snorted with derisive laughter. It was all a goose chase of sorts—they probably would chip away all day for no more than a cup of rock chips.

Most of the prisoners worked with the arms of the jumpsuit tied around their waists. Even though the day was cool, the work was hard. They had no shelter out where they were, and from what Tim saw, no available water. His wish to get on a work crew wasn't looking so hot now.

They worked well for an hour, until Jake started getting restless.

"Move over, would you? Stay out of my way."

"Watch it with that thing, Jake."

The pick axe had come awfully close to his head.

Jake shoved him.

"Hey! You there! Back to work!" A guard levelled his rifle at them and his eyes held barely concealed contempt. Tim turned back to the rocks and swung at them a few times until the guard wandered down the line.

"Stop acting like a damn idiot and listen," Tim said to Jake.

"You're no more planning a break than you are baking cupcakes," Jake whispered. "You're just gonna serve out these five years like a good little boy?"

Before Tim could respond, Jake was felled from a blow from behind and crumpled down onto the rock in front of them. Tim lost his balance since his leg was shackled to Jake's.

"I said no talking," the guard said. "Get up and get back to work."

"Or what?" Jake asked, climbing to his knees. "You'll call my mommy?"

The guard swung the butt end of his rifle at Jake's head, knocking him over again. Blood sprayed onto the rocks.

"You got anymore smart words, tough guy?"

"Yeah," Jake said. "But I don't think you'd understand them."

The guard kicked Jake in the midsection a couple times, then whistled to another guard.

"This one wants a little solitary," he said. "Get up!"

The guard unlocked the shackle at Jake's ankle and they half-dragged him across the hard pan and back toward the prison.

Tim shook his head at Wheeler being led away. He was so stupid.

"He's gonna get himself killed." The man chained on the other side of Tim spoke for the first time. He had a Louisiana accent and looked back at the guards and Jake with a withering expression.

"Better him than any of us," Tim murmured.

Tim glanced over at the man, then picked his axe back up again. His back ached, and he was sweating like a pig. His shoulder, the one he hurt in

Mexico, was on fire, and he hoped he wasn't doing more damage to it. He suspected the chain gang crews outside of the prison didn't have it this hard.

"How do you get on the gangs for work outside the prison? Seniority?" he whispered to the guy next to him.

"No," the man whispered back. "Just luck of the draw. Could be any one of three locations on any given day."

Tim nodded and swung the pick axe again, the metal clanging against the rock. His hands were numb and blistered. Luck of the draw meant their plan would have to be spontaneous to work—a distraction that just happened to happen. He wasn't sure they could create one, and that was going to be a big problem.

He glanced over his shoulder, seeing Jake get hauled in the prison door, his feet dragging behind him.

Of course, he also had a bigger problem, and with his luck, they'd be chained on the same work crew together.

Jake wasn't surprised when he was thrown into solitary, and he wasn't surprised when the guards who tossed him in there came in to hammer home their point about not talking when the prisoners were supposed to be working.

He did his best to not fight back as much as he normally would have, and came out of it smarting more from his pride than anything.

He was sure he had bruised ribs, and he was going to have a mighty big shiner the next day.

His foray into solitary hadn't been without its advantages though. The food was shit, the cell was wet, and there was no mattress on the spring bed, but there was privacy and quiet.

And most of all, no Tim Kelly.

Three days after Jake's episode on the chain gang, Tim was surprised to see him in the cafeteria for what shouldn't be allowed to be called breakfast.

His eye was black and blue eye, and Tim could tell he was hurting the way he favoured his right side.

"I see they made you even uglier than usual," Tim said.

"Yeah, they were tryin' to get me looking like you."

Tim ate in silence for a minute or two.

"What was the wise idea? You call attention to yourself and they're going to be watching like hawks."

Jake shrugged.

"I'm not kidding, Jake." Tim laid his spoon down. "You start doing shit like that all the time and you'll see that we won't be able to move five feet in this place without a guard on us. I'm of a mind to bust outta here on my own and leave you here cracking jokes on a chain gang."

Jake sat back in his chair, looked at Tim for a moment, then leaned forward.

"Solitary is down in the basement, not too far off the laundry area. There's guards on all the in and out points, and it's key and lock like the rest of this place. They use a skeleton key for each section, so all the cells on our block use the same key. Laundry trucks come once a day at noon. Guards are at the door, two of 'em, automatic weapons. Prisoners load the laundry bags. They offloaded some stuff too, and I ain't lyin' when I say one of 'em looked like a dead body." Jake looked around before continuing. "Even if you could get the guard on the door going down to the basement, you still got two to worry about in the laundry area. If you get tossed in solitary, they don't open the doors for nothing. The cells down there have a pass through at the floor for food trays, but they never once cracked the locks open when I was in there. You'd have to convince them to open the door, and to do that, they'd call for back up like they did when one guy tried to hang himself across the hall from me."

Tim looked at Jake with a raised eyebrow. "You got thrown in on purpose."

"You ain't the only one that can do recon and shit."

Sometimes Jake managed to surprise him, even after all these years.

"While you were playing super spy, I got put on each of the outside work crews," Tim said. "They pull guys randomly for it. There's no saying when we'd end up on the same crew or not. Seems to be luck of the draw."

"You escape without me, and I'll follow you back to Las Vegas and make you wish the Outfit killed you."

"The rock quarry is a lot like the prison yard quarry, but it's surrounded on all sides with rock walls," Tim said, ignoring Jake's comments. "There's nothing around, and it's flat enough they could see us no matter where we went. Even if an atomic bomb were to go off, those idiot guards would see us hightailing it out of there easy."

"What about the other one?" Jake asked.

"That one has some promise. They're taking down a steel bridge to replace it. They got construction crews on hand, but they're using dynamite to do some of the work. The explosions from the dynamite would be good cover. There's an embankment that leads down to a creek area. Word is it leads straight to the bayou. You could get lost in there for years."

"Better than this shithole."

"My thinking exactly," Tim agreed. He had no problem spending some time in a swamp if it meant getting the hell out of this prison.

"So we get on the work crew out there. Then what?"

"They chain everyone two by two. That's gonna be a problem," he said.

Jake snorted. "There's gotta be tools around or something."

"Yeah, when the moment comes, you spend precious time searching for something."

"What's gonna serve as a distraction? They're probably all armed to the teeth out there," Jake said.

Tim shrugged. "I haven't figured that part out yet. What we have to do is get on that crew and pay more attention so we can figure something out."

Henri sat down at their table a moment later. He looked at Jake's face and shook his head.

"You must have a death wish."

Jake grinned. "No more than usual."

"Striker asked me about you two."

Tim glanced over at Henri. This could be bad. "What'd he ask?"

"If I knew much about you. He does this with all the new fish, asks the cellmates."

"You've had other cellmates?" Jake asked. "What happened to the others?"

Henri looked at Jake. "One made a shiv out of his toothbrush handle and slit his throat in the night. Two others tried to escape out the laundry area and were shot and killed."

"Is this bad news that he wants to talk to us?"

"I told him you may have connections," Henri said. "It might be worthwhile to see if he'll put you on his crew. Might make your time go faster."

"What kind of crew?"

Henri shrugged. "He has men working in the labs, men processing the marijuana, packaging and so forth. He also lets some out to act as runners. Ones he trusts."

"He lets them out?" Jake asks. "What's to say they won't take off like jack rabbits?"

"He has reach," Henri said. "I've seen runners return in body bags."

Jake's gaze flicked up to meet his. It was possible that Jake really had seen a body being unloaded, but then, sometimes Jake was full of shit.

He didn't think Henri was, though.

"He'll have the guards come for you some time," Henri said. "Don't commit. Don't be memorable. Just tell him what he wants to hear."

A better idea would be keeping their damn mouths shut entirely, just like around a cop or a judge.

45

They were put on the work crew on the prison grounds again that day, and Tim had a lot of time to think about how his conversation with Striker would go.

6

Jake was the first to be hauled into Striker's office. He liked to think it was because he'd made a name for himself, but Striker didn't seem to know who he was.

"You're the one MacGregor picked up robbing the gas station?"

"So he says," Jake said. He leaned back in the chair in Striker's office. It was in an administrative section of the prison and had soft furniture—plush chairs, leather couches and a big mahogany desk. They'd only been on the inside for just over a week, but already he'd forgotten what soft things felt like.

"There may be opportunity around here for you."

"Yeah? For what?"

Striker lit a cigar, then paused, opened a desk drawer and pulled out a package of cigarettes. He tossed them to Jake. Jake lit one up warily, fully expecting some guard to come out of nowhere and pull the thing out of his mouth. He stuffed the pack inside his jumpsuit so Striker wouldn't ask for them back.

"I'm not sure where," Striker said. "Takes awhile to see where some people would be most useful."

Like ten feet under maybe, Jake thought.

"Your rap sheet is . . . impressive . . . for someone so young."

"Let's not fuck around, you put me in here against the law, what is it you want?" Jake asked, knowing he was playing with fire. Sometimes he couldn't help himself.

Striker's smile didn't reach his eyes. "You'd do best to remember who's in charge here. I don't much like that kind of language."

Jake tried not to snort with laughter.

"We put you in here because you need the kind of discipline this place can dish out. Given some time . . . I think I may be able to use you."

"Doing what?"

47

Striker shrugged. "I'm sure you've heard there's lots of opportunities around here."

Jake nodded. The asshole sure played things close to the vest.

"Think about it, Jake," he said. "I may be able to use you on the outside."

"What, chipping rocks?"

"No, something a little more enterprising and up your alley."

Jake sat up a little straighter. If Striker offered him a way out this soon, then maybe he didn't need to go along with Kelly's stupid schemes. Kelly would spend a year coming up with a decent plan, then fuck it up when it was time to do it.

It might be a better gamble to work with Striker. If he could get on the outside, then he could take off back to Nevada and see how eager Striker would be to chase him into Outfit territory.

He wouldn't have the cigarettes or the money to pay his debt back, though, and that could be a problem.

Of course, if Striker had him moving grass or something, skimming a little into his own pocket could make back what he'd lost and then some. He could make it back to Darla if that happened.

He felt a moment's compunction, thinking about him on the outside while Kelly toiled away behind bars, but shoved it out of his head. Kelly wouldn't think twice about leaving him behind, not after what he'd done with Ruby.

He knew the minute Tim beat him in their fight after he jumped Jimmy that every strike was for Ruby. Kelly wouldn't forgive and forget, even if he did say yes to working with Jake. Kelly was all business, and Jake's game with Ruby ensured Kelly would leave him if he had to.

Jake looked across the desk at Striker.

"I'll think about it," he said. "You make a lot of good points."

Striker smiled, then the door opened and a guard was there to take him back to his cell.

Hoods were so stupid.

It was one reason he liked it when MacGregor arrested them. They usually had a record, no one to care what happened to them and they were eager to get back out into the world and would do just about anything to get there. It was never very hard to turn them.

This one was extra stupid if he didn't see how Striker could see through him. The glint in the kid's eye when he mentioned the outside, and Striker could almost see the wheels in the kid's mind turn.

He always needed a few guys to act as runners, and he couldn't let lifers out without the state knowing about it. That's where all the delinquents came in. Arrest them, throw them in here without charges, and they were ghosts. Striker could use them for any purpose, inside or outside of the prison.

Most of them seemed to think getting to run outside the prison meant they were off the hook. The first kid that tried ran to Tampa, which was funny since Trafficante helped to bankroll everything in here. Trafficante's men returned the kid in three pieces and Striker made sure some of the others saw his return.

It hadn't stopped the jailbreak attempts; in fact it had increased them, which baffled him. The last three that took off were gone for longer than any of them, but in the end, they were found.

Striker had enough reach to get these guys back into his prison, but it wasn't a good use of his money or his men. It was just easier to cut his losses, get rid of them entirely when they fucked up and tried to run. There was always someone to replace them.

These young cons were so dumb they never realized there was nowhere to run. Prison breaks sent the town into a panic, and every time he caught them the townspeople breathed a sigh of relief and he was the hero. Not a person in town would help escaped prisoners, and there was nowhere to go that the dogs couldn't find them.

He sat back and looked at the rap sheet for the other one—Tim Kelly. Both men had been in a lot of trouble, but there was a lack of big prison time. They were small fish who ended up in his pond.

Striker relaxed in his office chair, smoking his cigar down. Sometimes this job was too easy.

Tim was pulled off the prison yard gang to go talk to Striker about an hour after Jake got back.

Tim was drenched in sweat and smelled pretty ripe, but that was Striker's own fault. He was led down the hall with his hands cuffed together, doing that shuffling walk in the leg shackles that reminded you every step where you were.

He wasn't surprised Striker's office was dry and well-appointed. A jackass like him probably held meetings with new prisoners in there on purpose so they could see who ruled the roost.

Tim's shoulder blades itched. He'd like nothing more than to watch the warden's face as someone shoved him into a tiny cell and the doors clanked shut behind him.

Instead the guard showed him into the office and sat him down in a chair.

Striker came in a minute later, a lit cigar in his mouth and a big Stetson on his head. He looked like a used car salesman.

"Kelly. Timothy Kelly."

He sat down at his desk and picked up a file, which probably held Tim's rap sheet. Tim wished he was on his feet; sitting while shackled made him feel like the prisoner he was.

"Public intoxication, public brawling, disturbing the peace, theft, robbery, aggravated assault, receipt of stolen goods, witness intimidation . . . my my."

Tim rolled his shoulders, cracked his neck and looked out the window of the office. There wasn't a cloud in the sky. In the distance he could see the tree line. Beyond it, he was told the gully led straight to the bayou.

"You like being on the work crews?" Striker asked.

Tim dragged his gaze away from the window.

He shrugged. "Nothing else to do, it seems."

"Now, that's not exactly true, and I suspect you know that," Striker said. "We've got all kinds of opportunities here. Lots of different areas of work. What would you be interested in?"

"I'm not." He looked Striker in the eye. "Just gonna serve my time, that's all."

"Your time really depends on a lot of things, Timothy," Striker said. "How you do in the prison, for example. We don't like troublemakers, like your cellmate, Jake Wheeler. He was hauled off to solitary once already."

"I don't control his fat mouth."

Striker chuckled. "I don't suppose you do. But sometimes, when one person gets out of hand, it takes a punishment to the lot of them to control that mouth. I'm sure you understand."

Striker's speech was interrupted by a ringing phone. He answered it.

"I can't come down. What are we talking about? When?" Striker sighed. "Hold on. I'll be right down."

He hung the phone up and looked over at Tim.

"I'll be just a minute."

He shoved Tim's file in a drawer in his desk, then called the guard in. Instead of letting Tim sit down in one of the plush chairs, they pulled a wooden rail back chair over and the guard shackled Tim's legs to the chair. The chain was run through the back, so if Tim wanted to run, he'd do it with a chair on his ass.

"Just a precaution," Striker said.

Tim nodded blandly.

Striker and the guard left the office together, and their footsteps faded. He stood up, holding the chair up off the floor and moved it with him toward the window. A horn sounded, and a truck backed up right below the window. Tim could see the back end.

It was a laundry truck, and he surmised the laundry area was probably a few floors underneath him. He watched the back open and a man in a laundry uniform got out, clutching a towel to his head. It was drenched in blood.

Striker was yelling—a big contrast from Mr. Nice and Calm he presented in the office. Another man held a gun on the back of the truck, and a prisoner in an orange jumpsuit got out.

Before Tim could see who it was so he could find the guy later and ask him how the fuck he got out, a shot rang out.

The laundry worker fell to the ground, the prisoner in the jumpsuit shocked beside him. Striker stepped forward. He gestured to some men around him, and guards came and picked up the dead man, hauling him out of Tim's view.

Prisoners started to unload the back of the truck, and Tim saw a bunch of bloody towels and laundry bags. He spotted Victor with the crew, and his cell mate looked up as he was handing towels and bedding to another prisoner.

Victor spotted him in the window and shook his head. Bad scene down there.

Victor walked out of view. A moment later a spray of water washed the blood off the pavement.

Tim shuffled around the room with the chair, trying not to make any noise. It was bad news if Striker shot people and worse if he shot unarmed laundry workers. Maybe it was punishment for letting the prisoner escape.

Tim made it to Striker's desk, hoping to God there wasn't some kind of surveillance system in his office. He made sure to use a tissue before touching anything, in case the man was paranoid enough to dust for fingerprints.

He found a folder in the lower desk drawer with MacGregor's name on it and took it out. Tim smiled as he recognized the bank statements at the top. He tucked a few inside his jumpsuit, then flipped to another folder and found the print out of both his and Jake's rap sheets. He grinned as he picked those out and shoved them inside his jumpsuit.

A sheet of paper fell from between the file folders.

A map.

He unfolded the map quietly. It was a map of the prison and grounds, but not done to enough detail to be helpful. It showed the land surrounding them, including the two work sites. Tim noted where the bayou was and where it lead.

There was one area—out near the wastelands he thought—that was marked with tiny x's, all in different colours, but there was no key as to what it was marking. Tim tucked the map inside his jumpsuit, hoping it could help him figure out where to go after the escaped, then he replaced the files and eased the drawer shut.

He scooted back to where the chair had been, trying to line up the dents in the carpet with the chair legs. Keys jangled outside the room, and he adjusted his jumpsuit, smoothing it down to hide the map and papers. He had just enough time to take a deep breath and let it out.

Striker strode back into the room and behind his desk. Tim lifted a bored gaze up to his face.

"As I was saying before we were interrupted," Striker said. "There are lots of places to work in here. I may need someone like you in other areas."

Tim kept quiet.

"You don't seem too interested." Striker studied Tim.

Tim shrugged. "Just waiting for the catch, is all. So far there's been one at every turn."

Striker smiled, but not in a friendly way. "There's a catch with everything in life, isn't there, Timothy? From getting a good deal on a car to finding a dollar on the street, everything comes with a catch. Sometimes the catch is worth it though, wouldn't you think? I mean, wouldn't it be worth it to be out of here a little early?

"Depends on the cost." Tim looked at him. "Like you said."

"You're going to be a hard nut to crack," Striker said, his façade dropping for a moment.

"That's what Johnny Moro said." Tim dropped the name, happy to see the look in Striker's eyes when he heard it. "Got a pretty hard head on me. Chicago tried to take it off, didn't work out for 'em."

Striker's gaze flicked from Tim's eyes to his ruined face.

"Maybe hard labour should mean hard labour for a man like you, Timothy. Everyone has to learn where they belong in the food chain. I could have given you a chance to work your way up."

Yeah, he thought, work my way up to your fall guy.

"If you're content working on a road crew in all kinds of weather, well then, I guess I ought to respect that."

Striker opened his office door and hollered for the guard. He unchained Tim from the chair.

"I have a feeling you'll come to change your mind on this, Timothy," Striker said. "I may or may not be willing to entertain your plea when that happens. But you can always try."

Tim nodded noncommittally.

"I thought you were the smart one," Striker said, as if he was unable to stop talking and had the need to make Tim react. Tim learned a long time ago that silence rattled people more than any words could. "I guess your friend Jake has a bit more in the brains department than you give him credit for. I think he'll be a welcome addition to my crew."

Tim tried not to let the surprise show in his face, thinking Striker was probably trying to lie his way to a reaction. As he walked back with the guard toward the entrance to the prison yard and back to the chain gang, Tim wasn't so sure. Jake Wheeler was a piece of work, and maybe it was time to cut his losses if the idiot had decided to work with Striker.

They didn't get a chance to talk on the work crew, and Tim was glad Jake kept his mouth shut while he worked. They had dinner in the cafeteria, a silent affair since everyone was dead tired.

When they returned to their cell, Tim saw Victor was already there, staring up at the bottom of Jake's bunk.

"Who was the guy they shot?"

Victor glanced over at him.

"Which guy?" Jake asked. "Who'd you see get shot?"

"When I was up in the boss man's office a laundry truck came by, a worker all bashed up, a guy in a jumpsuit in the back. Striker shot a laundry worker who wasn't even involved."

"He wasn't a laundry worker, he was the prisoner," Victor said. "A guy named Michael Mandolo. Been here about three months. He managed to get out, had a scuffle with the driver and held him with a shiv, made them switch clothes. The driver got the jump on him and came back with the truck."

Tim sighed. It made a lot more sense than Striker killing random workers. But now he knew Striker didn't give a shit about shooting prisoners.

"So this guy doesn't mess around," Jake said.

"Maybe that'll give you pause to think about joining up with his little crew," Tim said.

Jake shrugged. "Doesn't hurt to keep your options open."

Tim climbed up on his bunk. He should've asked some questions of Striker to try figure out how others had escaped, but the man would've spotted his reasons a mile away. He was irritated with Jake. Hooking up with Striker might mess with his plans to escape. He didn't much like the idea of leaving Jake to deal with Striker on his own. The man was cagey and had a hair trigger temper, and Jake would set him off in no time.

Why he was trying to save Jake's ass was a mystery to him. He should leave him to rot, because he knew Jake would do the same to him.

"You get involved with Striker's crew, you're on your own," Tim said.

"Why not get on it yourself? It'd make it easier to escape."

"No such thing," Henri said. "You'd be under his thumb."

"I ain't under no one's thumb," Jake said.

"That guy is the king of shifty, underhanded deals. No . . . he knows I'm not interested," Tim said. "I'll be working a road crew the rest of my time in here."

"You mean forever?" Jake asked. "Because I don't think he has any intention of letting us out."

Henri nodded. "It seems you are finally understanding. There is no way out."

Tim wasn't so sure about that.

Monday, March 13, 1967

They were kept within the prison walls the rest of the week, working at the small quarry on the grounds, and rested on Sunday. Tim figured folks on the outside would be suspicious if they worked on Sunday.

On Monday they were both put on the chain gang and loaded onto a bus. Tim never knew where the bus was going until it left in the morning, and no one saw fit to tell him. It would rumble out of the prison gates, and only when it reached a dusty paved road did he know. Left was to the big quarry, right was to the bridge.

From his time on the chain gang while Jake was in solitary, he was learning that the big quarry was the worst option for escape. There was literally no way out. The rock quarry had one way in and one way out, high bluffs of rock and guards at every turn.

Tim could see no means of escape at the quarry, and there wasn't much chance of a distraction that could help them.

The bridge site was a better option. It was an open site with a big construction area, and there were construction crew members working alongside the prisoners. There were more guards at the site, but it also provided more chances for escape.

It was Jake's first time out of the prison on a chain gang, and Tim hoped he paid attention.

The bus rumbled to the main road and turned right, and Tim breathed a sigh of relief. He hoped to return to the bridge site as much as possible. The more he knew the site and understood how it worked, the easier an escape plan would form.

The shackle and chains presented a problem. He tried to find something to break the chains, but so far nothing presented itself. He and Jake wouldn't get far if they were chained together.

As they were unloaded off the bus at the bridge site, the guards chained prisoners two-by-two at the ankle, then assigned them to an area.

Their wrists were uncuffed and they were handed tools, something Tim thought might come in handy. It was usually hammers or pick axes.

He had been chained to a quiet guy a few years older than him when Jake was in the hole, but they chained Tim to Jake this time. He was relieved, only so he could update Jake about this place.

The guards handed them each a mallet and directed them over to some railroad ties. Tim looked up at the completed track and realized the prisoners were actually building the train tracks and probably the bridge once the old one was down. Guards ordered some of the men to bring the metal tracks over, lying them on top of the wood ties, where others, like him, would drive stakes to anchor them to the ties. It was a slow procedure, and they were silent until they got the hang of it.

One benefit to the bridge site was the prisoners were more spread out and so were the guards. It allowed the prisoners to talk more, and that was just what Tim needed.

"I'm working on something," he said to Jake.

"What's that?"

"A way to get out of the shackles," Tim said. "Gotta be able to move when things go down."

"What things? Look around you, Kelly. Ain't nowhere to go."

Tim did look around. There was a creek bed to follow, the tree line, and beyond it, the bayou. There were plenty of places to go.

"You need to start paying attention to everything, this place is our best hope."

"I ain't so sure about that," Jake said.

Tim paused what he was doing, but Jake moved toward the next tie, and Tim was forced to move with him.

"What are you talking about?" Tim asked. "Striker?"

"I'm just saying, we got other options."

"You heard what Henri and Victor said, working for Striker isn't a way to get out of here."

"I think it could be."

"Then why isn't Victor doing it? You ever think of that?"

"Maybe Striker never asked him," Jake said. "Maybe he only asks ones he knows he can use."

"Are you thick in the skull? Right, forgot who I was talking to," Tim said. "Jake, he chooses people he knows he can get rid of with no mess. Come on. You don't have any family, no one's coming looking for us. Striker knows we're on our own. He wants people like that because we're easy to get rid of."

Jake rolled his eyes.

"It's the truth," Tim said. He leaned in closer. "Look, I found some shit in his office, and none of it looks good. I think he lets some guys out as runners for him, but as soon as they get any wise ideas about leaving or he thinks they know too much, he gets rid of them. Permanently."

"He's not the damn Outfit, not by a long shot. You think he's Al Capone, you're crazy."

"I don't think he's in this alone." Tim swung at the railroad tie. "I think he might be hooked up with the New Orleans family or some people out of Florida. And anyway, Capone was a shit leader who barely last three years. You know where he ended up? Alcatraz, full of syphilis."

"But he got out. He died years later in Florida, dipshit."

Tim looked over at Jake and cracked a smile. Sometimes the idiot surprised him.

They worked silently as one of the guards walked by, his rifle at the ready. Tim watched him pass as he hammered a railway tie.

"We gotta make a run for it," Tim said.

"What, now?"

"No, not now," Tim said. "Like I said, I'm working on something to handle these shackles. We need a way out of them or we'll never make it when we do run."

He looked around at where the guards were, then bent over and shoved a few long nails into his jumpsuit. They only did a cursory pat down getting them on the bus, and Tim was confident they wouldn't find them. He could work on popping the locks on the bus ride and carry some with him all the time, just in case.

Jake watched him stow the nails, then went back to swinging the axe.

"What about all them guards?" Jake asked.

"We need a distraction. That's the part I'm thinking on."

He hoped Jake would catch a bit of the fever about taking off. Tim figured the more he talked about going like it was a sure thing, the more likely Jake was to go along with it. Jake always wanted what everyone else had, but didn't want to do any work to get it.

"Asking for a distraction is like waiting for rain, Kelly," Jake said. "You got no idea when it's gonna come."

"So we have to be ready," Tim said.

He swung the mallet a few times and anchored in more ties as the guard approached again.

"What kind of ready?" Jake asked after the guard passed.

"Well, we gotta figure out the best way to go."

"Down that creek, I figure," Jake said. "Follow it down and it oughta send us into the bayou. That could be dicey, but it's better than sticking around here. They'll have a hard time getting a shot off with all the cover the shrubs and trees will give us."

Tim tried not to smile. Jake was more into taking off than he said.

"You two are crazy if you think you're gonna get away," someone said.

Tim looked over—it was the guy he'd talked to briefly in the prison quarry, the one with the Louisiana accent.

"Better than sitting on our asses," Tim said.

"I'm not kidding, they'll shoot you down like dogs."

Tim glanced over at the guy. He was probably around their age, maybe closer to thirty than he was. His face was thin, and he had deep circles under his eyes, like he hadn't been sleeping.

"Tim Kelly," he offered. He nodded at Jake. "Jake Wheeler."

"Johnny Ray," he said. "How long you in for?"

"Five years, but he railroaded us." Tim looked around at the railroad ties. "No pun intended."

"Shut up before the guard hears you," Johnny Ray's shackle partner said. "You're talking too much."

"Mine was seven, but it was earned, although the time was longer than it should've been. I've been here awhile already. Seen too many killed to make a breakaway out of here."

Tim was tired of hearing this from everyone. "Yeah, well, I'd rather die trying than not at all."

"It's a fool's errand. There's nothing around here but bayou, and they know every inch of it," Johnny Ray said.

"Let them try, we haven't had a good round up in awhile," the partner said.

"Shut up, Ernie."

"The bayou could be a good place to hide," Tim said.

"You'll die in there if the guards don't shoot you down. Lots of stuff there to trap you. Gators, quicksand, hunting traps. Not to mention the warden would have a dog team out there pretty fast."

"Sounds like you've seen it before."

His face darkened. "Once or twice. Last time was the worst. Things get bad out in the bayou, friend. No one wants that kind of trouble, least of all me."

"He may look green, but I know my way around places like this," Jake said, his accent heavier than usual.

Johnny Ray shrugged.

Tim didn't know what it mattered to the guy if they escaped or not, but all the people stuck inside this place were fucking weird. He didn't know if it was the monotonous days of work, living with threats or the reality they'd probably never get out, but they were all weird.

They had a break for "lunch" which consisted of water and a fifteen minute break, taken in shifts.

"Stop fucking moving," Tim said. "I want more water."

"I need to take a leak."

"Hold it, for Christ's sake!"

Tim felt for the nail in his pocket. He hoped he'd have enough willpower to hold onto it rather than stab Jake in the neck with it. No matter which way he moved, Jake seemed to go the opposite way. They were constantly under the other's feet, tripping, shoving and jostling each other. The guards had told them time and again to quit it, but they just weren't coordinated together.

Tim watched the other shackled prisoners move and none of them were having as much trouble and him and Jake.

Jake asked a guard for permission to take a leak and the guard escorted them both to the side of the tracks. Tim turned around while Jake took a piss, tempted to pull his feet out from under him.

The rest of the day went slowly, and by the time they were herded back on the bus, everyone was exhausted and no one talked.

They all ate in the cafeteria, then returned to their cells. Tim was asleep before his head hit the thin pillow.

7

The next morning at breakfast, Tim spotted Johnny Ray across the cafeteria. He sat with a group from a cell block that was at the end of their row and avoided Tim's looks. Johnny Ray seemed to have a lot of knowledge about the bayou, and Tim needed his information if they were going to make it out of here.

He was concerned about a few things—Johnny Ray had mentioned alligators, and a key part of Tim's plan was traveling through the water so they couldn't use dogs to find them. Alligators in the water would make that a ridiculous and dangerous idea. He needed to know how likely the chance was they'd run into one.

If Johnny Ray was local he might know of a place they could hide out until the heat blew over and they could find their way out.

The only hiccup would be Jake. He'd probably want to get back to Las Vegas five minutes after they left, and convincing him to wait things out in a hiding spot was not going to be easy.

After breakfast they were put on the bus again and taken back to the bridge site. Before they got off the bus, one of the guards stood up.

"Y'all will be coming back here from now on. The construction crew wants people who know what they're doing and the best way for that is the same people working. They're telling us they need consistency, and that's what you bunch of shits are gonna be. Any of you have a problem working out here, you shut the hell up and do it anyway."

Relief flooded Tim's body. Knowing he would be coming back here every day—even if it was with Jake—was a load off his shoulders. Now the planning could begin in earnest.

Tim manoeuvred himself so he was standing closer to Johnny Ray, and he got shackled in with him that day.

"You're going to ask me, I can tell," Johnny Ray sighed when they were assigned to move railroad ties. Johnny Ray moved with ease, even with the shackles on, and it was a relief not to be tripping over someone else every five seconds.

"I need to know about this place." Tim looked around. The guards were pacing up and down the line. "You're a local?"

Johnny Ray nodded. "All my life. What's left of it, anyway."

"Bayou's down that way, right?"

He nodded. "The crick takes you right down there. But I'd stay away. Nothing but danger if you don't know what you're doing, and you look like you're more comfortable in the streets instead of the swamp."

"You're not wrong about that," Tim said. He lifted his section of the railroad tie and they moved together to set it down in the row that was laid out. There was a few hundred yards left to build before it reached the bridge which had yet to be constructed. The old one was still half up and half down.

"The bayou isn't easy to move through," Johnny Ray said. "And anyway, where would you go?"

"Haven't figured that part out yet," Tim admitted. "I was hoping you'd have some ideas."

"My idea is to shut up and do your time."

They walked back to the pile of ties slowly, their footsteps in sync so they wouldn't trip or fall.

"The sheriff railroaded us in here. No fingerprints, no paperwork, no nothing. And we didn't do shit, so I'm gonna get out of here with or without your help," Tim said. "It'd go a lot easier with it."

Johnny Ray looked over. "I don't think you understand. You see this?"

He held his arm out and Tim saw deep ridges cut into Johnny Ray's wrists. They reminded him of the marks on Lupe's wrists.

"I got letters out," Johnny Ray said, his voice low. "A few to my sister. They learned I smuggled them out."

"How?"

"I worked in the laundry," Johnny Ray said. "Convinced one of the laundry drivers to take it to my sister. I told you I was local. So are they. Everyone knows me, and the driver felt bad for my sister. So they took the letters. Only Striker found out somehow."

Tim picked up another tie and moved it with Johnny Ray, keeping silent every time a guard passed.

"He cuffed me and hung me from a light for three days. I would've begged him to cut my hands off if I thought he'd do it. But that would have been too compassionate for him. Striker likes it when people lash out or escape. It gives him a reason to do things like this."

"I get it," Tim said. "Shit's bad here. All the more reason to leave."

"All the more reason to disappear into the walls, be quiet and serve your time," Johnny Ray said.

"Not my style," Tim said. "Anyway, they didn't get us on any real charges, they made up every damn thing. I'm not sticking around for that, would you? Come on. Help me out."

Johnny Ray sighed, and it sounded like it came from his very soul.

"Alright." He looked resigned. "What do you want to know?"

"Anything you can tell me. How big is the bayou?"

"Huge," he said. "Part of it is a state park, protected land. You can make your way along the creeks to the river, to another river, and all the way to the Gulf, if you stay with it."

"Anywhere to hide out there? Cabins, hunting blinds, anything like that?"

Johnny Ray hesitated. "There's cabins, quite a few dotted around. Some are hunter's cabins, some are people who live there year round, but they'll be the first place Striker looks. He caught prisoners there before. Everything I tell you, you gotta know they already know it. They're locals too, don't forget that."

"Anything they wouldn't know?"

He shrugged. "Like I say, it's always seemed like an impossible escape, so I don't see the purpose in trying. Y'all could find a boat, maybe travel the length of the bayou. Strikersville is inland enough that the town folk and the bayou folk don't mix much. Just a small grocery store and a bar on the old highway, really. Y'all follow the bayou, it bends away from Strikersville and passes out of the parish. Y'all won't see any towns. No one builds that close to the bayou, although people live there. Towns are all inland."

"Any chance of boosting a car?"

"Yeah, but then you have to get past roadblocks."

"What if we waited it out, hid in the bayou."

Johnny Ray smiled for the first time, an easy grin. "I don't think y'all'd last long enough to hide out."

Tim shook his head. "I might surprise you."

Johnny Ray stifled a laugh, and Tim frowned. A little bayou wasn't going to stop him.

Johnny Ray looked over at Jake, busy hammering the railroad ties, alternating hammers with his shackle-mate. "You taking him?"

Tim looked over at Jake and saw him like Johnny Ray might have. Jake had the jumpsuit tied around his waist, and his build was all muscle, probably from all the rodeo riding. He hauled a railroad tie, sweat on his face, but looked like he was used to a life of hard living.

He looked cool, tough, and completely at ease outside. Tim realized for the first time Jake was comfortable here. Maybe not in the prison, but in Louisiana.

"You're going to die. Both of y'all," Johnny Ray said, a hint of a smile on his face.

"If I stay here, I know I will."

They moved a few more ties, making sure the guards didn't pay much attention to them.

"What's there to eat out there?" Tim asked.

Johnny Ray shrugged. "Plenty. Gator, fish, all kinds of stuff to hunt. But you won't be able to do that without starting a fire, and that'll give you away."

Tim started to wonder if there was any way to hoard their food. He was starved by the time they got back to the prison, and he had no way to save any food.

"These cabins," Tim said. "Would you be able to draw a map to them?"

"With what?" Johnny Ray said.

Tim knew as well as anyone that prison was all about commodities. Victor and Henri had already shared cigarettes, so Tim knew the prisoners had contraband. The guards didn't seem to care the prisoners smoked, and he didn't know where the cigarettes came from, but after meeting with Striker, he wondered how much Striker did to gain favour with the prisoners.

He could hand a pack off to someone like Henri to use to do just about anything. Paper and pencils and other things like that might be something Johnny Ray could come by if he tried.

Tim still had the maps tucked into his jumpsuit. He had studied the prison one, and the little symbols beyond the gates . . . well, he had an idea those were graves. He would've thought unmarked ones, but here were the markings. Striker was an idiot.

The map wasn't much use to him though—it didn't go far enough. He wished he'd thought to take a map of the larger area.

Tim was about to tell Johnny Ray to find some paper at any cost when he thought of something.

"Okay, think of the bayou like the prison. Where the cafeteria is, that's the prison. So where would other stuff be?"

He saw Johnny Ray working it over in his mind.

"Then the bayou is everything down the hallway that goes past the showers and out to the prison yard, then beyond the prison."

"Okay, so where are we?"

"On Foret creek, it's what this bridge crosses. It's dry part of the year. Leads down to the west arm of the Guidry. You cross that, you're on some land that's an island part of the year. Other times, you gotta cross the east arm of the Guidry. The two arms merge pretty far downstream and then travel on until they reach the Atchafalaya."

Johnny Ray was good at description, and using the prison as a model managed to get Tim oriented.

"You said some prisoners were found at a cabin last time," Tim said. "Where are these cabins?"

"All over. On the west side of the west arm there's a few hunting cabins and blinds. Between the east and west arm are more, but it's too dangerous. I wouldn't go between the arms if you take off from here. Likely to get caught stuck if it rains and it turns to island."

"If you escape from the prison, where do you end up?" Tim asked.

Johnny Ray huffed out a breath. "Down between the arms. But then you're stuck. You'd need a boat to get out, especially this time of year." He hoisted another tie.

"Sounds like heading for a cabin is the way to go. They probably wouldn't expect us to go between the arms if we escaped from here."

"If you escape from here you'd be foolhardy to try and cross the arm to get to the middle. Too much chance of running into something you don't want to. And like I said, you'd need a boat."

"When did the prisoners get caught?"

"Which time?" he asked. "People have tried to escape a lot. None of them came back. Alive, anyway."

"The ones that escaped awhile back, three of them who got pretty far."

"Before my time," Johnny Ray said. "They were stupid. Escaped from the prison and were between the arms. Stole a boat and still got themselves caught. You need to stay away from those cabins between the arms. The whole area is filled with gators and snakes. That part's bad news."

Tim figured Johnny Ray was right that the warden and his cronies would probably search cabins first. But if they could escape from this side, crossing the river at all might not be what they'd expect. They'd search all the closest cabins on the west side first.

"You haven't mentioned the most important part," Johnny Ray said.

"What's that?"

"How you're going to get away from here at all."

Tim looked around. There was a light breeze and clear blue skies.

"Yeah," he sighed. "I'm still working on that part."

* * *

On the ride back to the prison, Tim had Jake block everyone's view of his hands, and Tim used the nail he'd snagged to try and work the cuffs shackled onto his wrists. He worked it until his fingers were red and sore, but never managed to pop the lock.

"This plan of yours sucks already," Jake said.

"I didn't say the plan was going to go right off," Tim said. "We may have to wait a few weeks or even months for a good chance. You need to be ready."

"I'm always ready."

As the bus rumbled near the prison, Tim tucked the nail away in his sock. He was pretty sure it wasn't going to work. He had some experience with picking locks, and he picked cuffs once when O'Lafferty had cuffed him in front and sat him in the car. He'd found a paperclip in the backseat and had them open in seconds. The big Irish cop wasn't too impressed, but Tim got the distinct feeling his boss, Sikone, found it amusing.

The nail was a bit too big to get it in far enough to pop the lock. He didn't want to risk leaving scratches all over the cuffs either. The last thing he needed was a guard noticing and giving Striker a heads up.

The bus rumbled to a stop and everyone was unloaded and taken in to the cafeteria.

Tim's mind wouldn't stop working. He looked at Jake as they ate.

"I mean it when I say be ready," Tim said. "Johnny Ray gave me all kinds of info about where cabins were on the work site side of the river, down in the bayou. There's cabins on the east side too, this prison side, but I can't get much out of him about those. Prisoners got caught there."

"That's all fine and well, but you don't even got a distraction planned so we can get out."

"I know," Tim said. "It's the unplanned one I'm waiting for."

Monday, March 20, 1967

A week later, Tim's entire plan—what little there was of it—was ruined.

They were taken out to the site six days a week, given only Sunday to rest. On Monday, about two and a half weeks after they'd been sentenced, Tim was cuffed to Jake, working on the last few feet of railway ties, when one of the prisoners, the one who'd been cuffed to Johnny Ray most of the time, took off.

He was unshackled at the time to help the construction workers. With all the work going on around them, they needed some of the prisoners unshackled, without another person attached to them.

The guards were wary at first, but after a week and a half with no problems, they seemed to relax as everyone worked, probably assuming that no one would try and make a break for it out here.

Tim wasn't paying attention at first and only heard the shouts of the guards. He and Jake stopped the work they were doing—moving old parts of the partially dismantled trestle bridge—and looked around to see what the commotion was.

A man in an orange jumpsuit was headed to the tree line, struggling to run for cover. It looked as if he might make it, too. Tim figured he must have been inching his way toward the fringes of the site before he took off running.

"We should go now!" Jake pulled on Tim's sleeve. Tim glanced around, seeing the guards watched the action and not them.

The only problem was their route to the edge of the creek was blocked by the guard's Jeep and two of them standing there with high-powered rifles.

"Come on!" Jake said, urging Tim the opposite direction of where he wanted to go. The tree line was much further away—there was no way they wouldn't be shot or caught up to with that much open space. Hell, if they ran, the only good it would do was giving this other guy a chance to make it himself.

"Hold still, Jake, not now."

"Fuck you and your not now! You talk about getting outta here and now you won't go?!"

"It's not the right time."

Jake kicked at some stones by his feet, and Tim looked at the escaping prisoner again.

The orange jumpsuit served its purpose—he was easy to spot. Tim saw some of the guards aim and take fire and he cringed, watching the man duck and continue to run. Two guards jumped into a nearby Jeep and pulled out, while the other guards pulled their guns up on the working prisoners, ordering them all to stop what they were doing and move closer together. Guards came by and shackled everyone together in a line.

The Jeep gained on the man quickly. A guard in the Jeep took aim, and the crack of the shot echoed. Tim looked down as the man fell to the ground. The Jeep was at him a moment later. The man struggled to his feet, shot in the back. Instead of cuffing him and shoving him into the Jeep, one of the guards raised his gun and fired. Tim saw the man fall over into the foot high grass. He'd almost made it to the trees, and beyond that, the road and the bayou.

"Son of a bitch," Tim whispered.

"Now you all see how pointless it is to run," a guard said. "We can always find you, we can always catch you, and we will shoot to kill."

The prisoners were instructed to sit down, and soon the guards came back.

"Search them!" a guard roared. "I don't want Striker thinking we're not taking this seriously."

"Get rid of it, man," Jake said, under his breath.

Tim picked the nail out of his pocket and palmed it, then as everyone stood up, he dropped it on the ground, lost in the noise of boots and chains on gravel.

He had left the map and papers back in his cell, crammed into the space behind the loose tile. He had forgotten to tuck them in his jumpsuit like he did every day, just in case an escape opportunity presented itself. He was thankful he'd forgotten.

The guards came to pat down each prisoner, and Tim noted nothing contraband was found. It seemed like no one on the chain gang was looking to get away.

He wondered why the guy had up and done it. He didn't seem so into it before. He hadn't even waited for a distraction.

The prisoners returned to work shortly after, and it was late in the afternoon when Johnny Ray made his way near them.

"He thought your idea to escape here could work," Johnny Ray said. "Tell me now you won't try it. Y'all can see for yourself it doesn't work."

Tim shared a look with Jake, and he could tell Jake knew he wasn't backing out.

"You still in?" Tim asked.

Jake nodded. "I am now."

Maybe seeing that guy killed had knocked some sense into Jake.

"Good," Tim said.

"You're both crazy," Johnny Ray said. "If they catch you, they'll kill you, you saw it."

"They ain't gonna catch us," Jake said. "I'll get us out of here."

Tim bit down on a retort. At least Jake wanted to leave.

Johnny Ray shook his head. "You're stubborn, like mules."

Tim picked up the crow bar he'd been given to work with that day and continued to pull metal spikes out of the old railroad ties.

The Jeep was going to be a problem.

Their best chance was to try and get down the steep bank to the creek and follow it to the bayou. Running to the trees would give them a clear shot in the Jeep. The Jeep wouldn't be able to make it down the steep embankment. The only problem is it left the guards with high ground to take shots at them.

The other option was heading for the south tree line like the prisoners just had. It was further away, but disappeared into the creek and would lead them to the bayou. Of course, the Jeep would be on them in seconds. There would have to be a major distraction in place for it to give them any sort of cover. Tim had been trying to think of something—maybe setting fire to the gas tank of the Jeep and exploding it or something.

That might not be too difficult. He could smuggle matches to the site with him and use the towels laying around to stuff into the tank. It would disable the Jeep, start a fire and give them some cover.

He sighed, looking at the sun dipping low in the sky. The day was almost over, and he was starting to feel discouraged about their chances. He pulled up an old railroad tie and moved it out of the way, tangling in the chain and almost tripping against Jake.

Something had to give.

Later that night, in the cafeteria, Jake was quiet and morose.

"We could've gone."

"Yeah, and get shot in the back for our trouble. You saw it," Tim sighed.

"What I saw was them guards so distracted they wouldn't have noticed us leaving."

"Sure," Tim said sarcastically. "Us two hobbling off wouldn't give them any sort of reason to shoot."

"You figure out a way to get those shackles off?"

Tim looked up. "Not yet. I need a bobby pin or paperclip or something. Something metal, thin and bendable."

Jake nodded. "We may have to figure that out later."

"Yeah," Tim said, not relishing the idea of tripping through the swamp with Jake. He looked over at Jake again. "I guess that calls for some practice."

For the next week, Jake and Tim made every effort to get shackled together, and when they were, they worked at walking and moving like a well-oiled machine. It was hard going at first, but soon they both seemed to get the hang of it, and Tim was more confident in their ability to run and move together in the shackles.

Tim couldn't get hold of another nail, but he did have the papers with him. Victor and Henri said nothing when they saw him pull the papers out of his hiding spot. Henri had shook his head like he expected this kind of stupid behaviour from him.

He had thought and rethought his plan. There were some days where he felt it was just the right time to do it, but something always held him back.

He was glad it did the day he overheard some of the construction workers talking.

"That dynamite is really sweating," one of them told the guards. "We need these guys to move faster, we gotta get to the blasting. This is the sawdust kind and this stuff is so unstable, I don't even wanna touch it."

"Just get them to touch it."

"You don't understand, you need a license to have and use dynamite on a work site, we'd been in deep trouble if it got out we used prisoners to do it, and I don't wanna lose my license. It's getting unstable. We need all of the track removed so we can blow the supports, at the latest by midweek. I can't just hand this stuff over to inmates."

The guard chewed on a piece of grass. "We'll get it done."

The construction foreman wandered off, wiping sweat off his forehead and looking just as worried as he had when he'd approached the guard.

Tim had forgotten about the dynamite.

"You hear that?" Tim asked.

Jake nodded.

"Is he for real?"

"It's a bad deal," Jake said. "Shit like that can go off anytime. My grandfather had some dynamite once, to blow a giant boulder in a field he was clearing. I snuck out there with Monty once, and that kid . . . man, he started flicking off the nitroglycerine with his finger, and every time that shit hit the ground it'd pop like a gunshot."

"What's it sweat for?"

"The nitro leaches out. If it's doing that, they got some old stuff they didn't store too well," Jake said. "Won't take much to set it off."

Tim looked over at him and grinned.

"I smell a distraction," he said.

8

Tim planned to try and set the dynamite off a week later, but the guards were paranoid after the last escape attempt. Aside from the guards, the nights were cold, and he wasn't sure how they'd fare in the bayou with it dipping close to freezing each night. They'd be better off waiting until it warmed up, but time was a luxury he didn't have.

He didn't know what was going on back home. Diana could be in juvie again, Ray could have up and married her, his father could've lost his latest job and taken it out on his mother's face. He tried to keep his mind from thinking about the possibilities, but at night, when the lights went off and he lay in that top bunk staring at a water-stained ceiling, there was nothing to do but think.

Jake was anxious to go now, his eagerness to leave turning into worried pacing and a hair trigger temper. He hadn't antagonized the guards thankfully, but Victor was a breath away from beating Jake to death, and Tim couldn't blame him.

He didn't know what got Jake thinking about leaving, but whatever it was, at least Jake was on board one hundred percent now.

Striker had left them both alone, and Tim was grateful for it. Jake agreed it was probably best, although he seemed to say it through a veil of regret. Tim suspected Henri may have waived Striker off them somehow. Maybe he fed him bogus info about their usefulness, because the man hadn't asked to see them again. He also hadn't noticed the papers were missing, and Tim was relieved. The more time that went by, the less likely Striker would think it was him.

Tim's plan for the dynamite was to pick up what he could from the ground, be it a rock or a spike, toss it toward the box, and see what happened.

That morning, a week after the break, he felt the guards had finally relaxed enough. They were unchaining them to work more, and the hawk-eyed glances he'd gotten used to were not as quick in coming. He thought Friday would be the best time to try. The guards would be eager for the day to be over and the weekend to come, and maybe they wouldn't be at their best with thoughts of a day off before them.

Monday afternoon, fate stepped in.

He and Jake were unboxing a bunch of railway spikes brought in by Jeep that morning. Tim wondered if Striker was egotistical enough to build his own railway to ship all his drug shit out and decided he probably was. As they set a box down along the south border of the work site, a huge explosion rocked the area.

Tim and Jake both were knocked off their feet and flew into the air before hitting the ground unceremoniously. He looked up, his ears ringing and saw others closer to the blast bloodied and on the ground. His ears were tuning in and out like a broken radio, the sounds coming from far away, then suddenly loud before getting drowned out by silence. He remembered Cubs games on the radio, his old man cursing at them, and the sound fading in and out. The station never came in clear.

Another fireball of an explosion erupted, and then a ripple effect began, explosion after explosion. Tim realized the dynamite was going off in a chain reaction. People ran for cover, guards and prisoners alike. As the guards nearest the explosion ran away from the commotion, a stick blew and started a fire right near the Jeep.

Another stick caught, and a moment later the Jeep exploded into a fireball. The rest of the dynamite sitting in the back of the Jeep went off, sending a portion of the edge of the work site, Jeep included, down into the gully, part of the old steel bridge with it.

"Come on!"

Tim yanked on Jake's arm, and they got up from where they crouched. Tim pulled him toward the south, toward the trees, with Jake trying to yank Tim toward the gully, right where the burning Jeep was.

"It's not safe down there, they got the high ground, come on!"

Jake finally got into step with him, and they took off for the tree line, getting further than the man shot in the back had. Tim glanced back and saw other orange jump suits running. Shots rang out, and he and Jake ducked into the sparse trees.

Another explosion echoed through the air, and Tim didn't bother to look back this time, even with the ground rumbling under his feet. They stumbled through the thin forest, the ankle chain catching on roots and small plants. It slowed them down.

"Come on!" Jake yanked his foot and almost pulled Tim's out from under him.

Tim hustled along, seeing the tree line come to an end as they reached the road.

"Slow down, slow down, the road!" Tim said. "I don't want anyone spotting us."

"Fuck that, we need to move!"

Tim tried to slow, but Jake yanked on the chain and pulled him forward. They rocketed across the road and Tim stumbled, taking Jake down.

"Come on," he said. "Get up, you son of a bitch."

"Fuck you!" Jake snarled.

"Come ON!" Tim got up and moved away from the road. The tension on the chain lessened as Jake got up, and they dashed into the trees again.

"Creek," Tim said, with barely any breath left in him. "We need to get to the creek."

Jake bolted to the right, and Tim smacked into a small tree when Jake bumped him. The guards would catch up in no time with them like this.

"Stay on my left! On my left!" Tim growled. Jake was chained to Tim's left leg, but Jake kept pushing over to the right, like he was running on a diagonal.

They headed toward where the creek should be, running at breakneck speed, and suddenly Jake slid to a stop. Tim was unable to stop his forward motion and went hurtling over the side of an embankment. He tucked, then felt a sharp pain in his leg as the chain caught. Jake swore, and they both tumbled down the embankment, hitting every rock on the way down.

Jake bounced over Tim at one point, crashing into him. Tim hit a tree, then was yanked around it as Jake continued his tumble. Tim saw the ground rushing up to meet him and held his arms out to brace himself. A moment later they were both lying in a heap at the bottom of the creek bed.

"You fucking moron!" Tim said, trying to catch his breath, the dust clouded around him. "We've got to work together."

"Me? You're the one who went headlong off the cliff like a maniac."

Tim struggled to stand and winced as he tried to push himself up. His right wrist was sore and swelling. Great.

He stood up, limping slightly, and lifted the pant leg of the jumpsuit. He could see the deep marks the shackle had left on his ankle when the chain caught.

He looked over at Jake, who was already on his feet and looking impatient to go. Jake started unbuttoning the snaps on his jumpsuit and tied it at his waist.

"Good idea," Tim said, following suit. They had issued all the men white undershirts, and with all the dirt they were falling into, it'd be much more inconspicuous than the orange jumpsuit.

"We gotta move," Jake said. He looked around at the creek and the greenery and shook his head.

Tim nodded, cradling his wrist as he tried to tie the sleeves of the jumpsuit around his waist.

"Hold up," he said to Jake. "Inside legs first, alright?"

Jake nodded and they began to move, stumbling on the rocks. The creek was no more than a trickle, and it wasn't going to do much to hide their tracks or their scent. Tim glanced behind him and saw the swath they'd flattened falling down the hill. The guards would find them in no time.

They picked up the pace, running along the almost-dry creek bed for what seemed like an hour. Tim noticed the vegetation was starting to change. The trees got thicker, and soon the creek bed started to get wetter and the creek grew. It emptied into a large pond, and brambles blocked their progress.

They climbed up an embankment and found themselves in what had to be the beginning of the bayou.

The land didn't look swampy yet, but it did look like it was headed that way. From what Tim remembered from the maps, they just had to keep going the direction they were. Soon enough they'd end up coming to the west arm of the Guidry, at least that's what Johnny Ray had told him. The closest cabins were on this side, not too far once they reached the arm, but he aimed to find a place to cross the river once they found it, despite Johnny Ray's warnings to stay away from the middle of the two arms.

Tim and Jake jogged along, doing alright until the trees got thicker and the environment more treacherous. Jake stepped out in front, trying to move between all the of the branches and not disturb them like Tim was. Tim tried to move in front of Jake again, and went around a tree, tangling the chain.

"What the hell are you doing?" Jake asked. "We're gonna get so tangled up in here they'll find us both tied to a tree. Watch where you're going."

Tim turned back to look at Jake. "Yeah, well I didn't see you work out the lock on those shackles, at least I tried. Don't come complaining to me about it."

"You should've had them off before we ran two steps."

"Fuck you, why don't you do it? So far I've done just about everything!"

"You set the dynamite to explode, huh?" Jake said. "I must've missed the part where you turned into James Bond."

Jake took another step backward, and Tim tried to stop the momentum as Jake slipped down a small embankment. Jake's weight was too much on his sore ankle, and he let go, tumbled down with him and crashing again onto the ground.

"That fall better have snapped that chain, because running with you is like having a boulder on my ass," Tim moaned.

Jake rolled over, wincing as he got up. "Fuck."

Tim glanced down. The shackles had never looked stronger.

He saw the cypress trees and live oak covered with hanging moss right over top the still waters of the small creek. If they followed it, it would probably take them to the river arm.

"We should go through the water," Jake said. "Throw the dogs off. You know they'll bring them in, that cop said as much. Watch where you step. I hate the damn bayou."

Tim nodded. He didn't see any signs of gators—not that he knew what to look for—but he'd rather deal with them than Warden Striker.

Striker got out of the Jeep and looked around at the remains of the construction site. The trestle bridge was blown completely to hell, part of the new railroad line was mangled and there was thick black smoke coming from the creek below—what he was told was the remains of one of his Jeeps.

Two guards were being tended to near the prisoner bus, both bleeding from head wounds, and three members of the construction crew also held bloody towels, while another was on the ground, a splint on his leg.

Two prisoners lay on the ground not far away, blood from gunshot wounds dried around their chests. If his guards kept shooting people like this, they'd have no one to work.

A tarp laid over another—well, part of another. He wondered if his men had shot him to shreds or something else got him.

There'd been so many attempts in the last few weeks he was ready to fire the entire security team.

The remaining prisoners sat on the ground, shackled together in leg irons.

"Sir, we haven't located the two other prisoners."

Striker looked over at his head guard. He'd always trusted the man to lead the work crews, but he wasn't so sure he could lead anything right about now.

"What the hell happened here?"

"Dynamite exploded."

"Who caused it?"

"No one, sir," he sighed. "Apparently the dynamite was sweating, made it really unstable. One of the prisoners was moving it and dropped a stick. It set off just about all of it, caught the Jeep. There were a lot of explosions, a lot of chaos. The guy who dropped it was . . . everywhere."

"And in the chaos, two of my prisoners got away."

"Five, actually, but we recovered three. One's in cuffs, two are dead."

"The other two?"

"We don't know. We think they went south, toward the bayou. Do you want us to call Sheriff MacGregor and get the dog team in here?"

"You should've done it already. Who are the escapees?"

The guard flipped through his papers. "Timothy Kelly and Jake Wheeler, both of Las Vegas, Nevada."

Striker closed his eyes. Those fucking kids.

Henri Boudreaux had told him he didn't think the kids were worth it. He told Striker they talked a big game, but couldn't find their peckers in the dark. Henri was smart, and Striker had backed off, waiting to see if the two kids showed any kind of promise. He knew Kelly wasn't buying anything he was selling, but he had a lot of confidence that Wheeler saw it would be better to work with him. He saw the greed in Wheeler's eyes. That other fucking kid probably talked him into escaping.

"They went into the bayou?"

"Seems that way," the guard said. "We've got guys trying to follow their trail, but we didn't get moving on it until at least a half hour after they ran. Things up here were nuts, we thought we were gonna lose some of our men because of the accident. One guy got blown onto the steel truss, was hanging by his shirt and it took us fifteen minutes to rescue him. Everyone else was trying to corral the prisoners."

"We'll get the dogs in there," he said. "They can't go far. They don't know the area, and they don't know the bayou. We'll have them back in no time."

Tim was out of breath, and every step he took was making his ankle hurt and his wrist ache. He looked behind them, and it seemed like their trail blazed up behind them like a beacon.

Jake turned to look as well and sighed.

"Okay," Jake said. "Let's get into the water, waist deep only. We'll wade through the water awhile to try and throw off any dogs they bring in."

"You think they will?" Tim asked.

"Oh yeah," Jake said. "Once that sheriff finds out we took off I wouldn't be surprised if he calls in the damn Army to hunt us down. You think you can find these cabins?"

He nodded. "Johnny Ray explained where a bunch were. He kept directing me off to the ones on this side. He said the last guys to get caught got caught on the other side of the west arm of the river, and he thought it'd be the first place they'd look. I don't know if I believe him. Something wasn't right with him. Maybe he wanted to use it as a hide out himself."

"Maybe it's his cabin."

Tim had thought about that—it was possible.

"Come on." Jake headed toward the water.

Tim moved into the still water, tripping on the mushy bottom. He was glad he had the prison sneakers.

It was much slower going in the water, which drove him crazy. He wanted to get out ahead of the search teams they'd call in as much as possible, and while the creek might offer protection from the dogs finding their scent, it came at the cost of speed.

They had to use each other for balance, and Tim got sick of having to lean on Jake whenever he lost his footing. His ankle wasn't too pleased and Jake grunted every time Tim tripped.

"Quit it!" Jake said. "And try not to fall over again, I don't wanna get dunked in this stuff."

The water was murky and impossible to see through, and he tripped with every step. Things floated on top of it and water bugs jumped out of the way as they moved. It was slow going, since they didn't want to churn up the water in case the guards were closer than they thought.

"Ah!"

Tim stumbled and braced himself against Jake, who slipped and ended up under the water for a second. He came up sputtering water and coughing.

"I swear to God, if I get some kind of disease from this water, I'll drown you in it and leave you for the gators," Jake said. He spat more water out, looking at Tim with barely concealed hatred.

Tim tried to steady himself on the bottom, but his feet kept slipping in the muck. It took him a second to balance.

Jake stared at him, then turned and started to move again.

"You think there's really alligators in here?" Tim asked. "For real?"

Jake tried to move, but Tim stood still waiting for him to answer.

"They're more scared of you than you are of them," Jake said. "I'm more worried about water moccasins. Let's go."

"Water moccasins? Like snakes? Venomous snakes?"

Jake glanced over his shoulder. "You've lived in the desert your whole life, you've never seen a rattler?"

"I've seen plenty," Tim said. "Never had a bath with 'em though."

Jake chuckled. "Yeah, and we gotta watch out for other shit too—snapping turtles aren't very friendly and they can bite your finger clean off, then scratch you to hell afterward with their claws. The perch will nibble on you just for fun. And gators. Can't forget them."

"Wasn't going to," Tim said.

"They're nothing to be scared of. Mostly keep to themselves."

"I didn't say I was scared," Tim said. "I just know that alligators can drown a grown man."

"Where'd you hear that?" Jake asked. "*National Geographic*? I know it's not personal experience."

"From that Cajun guy, Johnny Ray," Tim said. "I asked him about this stuff in case we ran off in here, and he said the gators can lunge faster than you can blink. He told me this story about how a gator down in the brackish water—"

"'Brackish water?'" Jake asked with a laugh. "Do you even know what that is?"

"Fuck off. He told me about this gator, the biggest thing going in the bayou down south of here somewhere. And he lunged at this guy fishing in a boat, toppled the boat over, grabbed the guy in his jaws and started to roll him—you know it's bad when they roll you. They drag you down and drown you, then eat you whole."

"You are so full of shit."

"That's what he told me," Tim said with a shrug. "I don't know about you, but I'm not real eager to go and prove Johnny Ray wrong, you know what I'm saying?"

"I grew up in 'Bama, never once had a gator drown and roll me."

"You grew up in Birmingham, that's the city."

Jake shrugged. "I was stationed at Keesler in Biloxi for awhile, and trust me, they got gators and shit down there. I know what I'm doing. You just have to listen to me."

Tim seethed as they moved through the water. Listening to Jake Wheeler. His life was a drag.

Jake looked back at him and grinned at Tim's expression.

"You either try your luck with me and the gators or Striker," Jake said. "Seeing as we escaped his chain gang, I'm liable to think the gators will be friendlier."

MacGregor got the call around three in the afternoon.

Warden Striker had called a few times when prison breaks were made. Usually the calls came in the dead of night. Once, he got a call from him cancelling the hunt, saying his guards had put down the escapees. If Striker kept on doing that there wouldn't be enough cons in the country to run his precious prison operation.

He hung the phone up quickly and looked over at Roundtree.

"Get on the horn and call everybody in," he said.

"What's going on?" Roundtree asked.

"Prison break at Strikersville," MacGregor said. "Those two mouthy delinquents we had in here a month back."

"Where are they headed?" Roundtree asked.

"South of the prison, in the bayou. Just get on the phone, roust whoever you can, get them to meet us at the Strikersville bridge construction site."

"I heard there was an explosion out that way," Roundtree said. "Some construction crew was hurt."

MacGregor nodded. "Something to do with this break, I'll reckon. Get on the phone."

Roundtree got to work, and MacGregor turned around in his chair to look at the map posted behind him. Sliding by and south of the site was the creek, which led right into the bayou. Both arms of the Guidry river went south, finally meeting up before merging into the Atchafalaya. It was the biggest bayou in the state, miles of water, ground, trees, gators, animals, hunting blinds, cabins, roads only known to locals and more. It would be a hell of a hunt in there.

"Call the dog team too," he said, not bothering to look and see if Roundtree was listening.

He studied the map. He hated going into the bayou. Despite living out here, he really was a townie at heart. He hated the woods, the forest, the trees, all the plants mucking everything up. He always got snagged in something, cut and scraped up. He hated that damn place, and he hated those two mouthy hoods for dragging him in there.

His forehead creased. Last time he'd been called in it had been pretty bad. Three men had escaped from the prison during the night. The dog teams and chased them right to the Landry place. Jean-René was out, probably rabble rousing it up with friends at a local watering hole, and MacGregor needed to get his hands on those escapees and keep his record impeccable. Capturing them sooner rather than later would inspire confidence.

They found them miles down the waterway in the Landry skiff, but that proved nothing. They could've stolen it, the Landry kid could've given it to them, under duress or not. They headed to the Landry place and questioned Josie Landry. She was a mouthy one herself, looking like a mirror image of her dead mother, complete with contemptuous eyes and a penchant for getting more Cajun the longer she spoke to them, like she didn't want them to understand a word she was saying. She lapsed into French more than once, calling them names.

The kid had pushed him off the porch, and he'd landed in a mud puddle that soaked him clear to the bone and ruined one of his good uniforms. He hadn't argued when Hickom had slapped her, or when he and Lee had started poking at her, touching her hair, saying off-colour things. When Striker told MacGregor to take a walk with him, he knew what it meant for the kid. He was so angry about his good outfit and brand new hat he stalked off in a rage, railing at Striker that he'd throw the mouthy brat in jail.

He'd rethought his walk when he heard her screams in the bayou. Striker had lit up a cigar, cicadas and frogs having a duet in the dark.

"She won't be harbouring fugitives next time they escape," he said, blowing smoke out of the corner of his mouth.

MacGregor's mouth was a dry as sawdust, and it stayed that way a long time.

Jean-René had beat up Hickom in a bar fight not too long after—he'd never seen a man look the way Hickom had and survived. It made him sick to see Hickom's face. The townsfolk had no idea what Hickom had done and they wanted Jean-René to pay dearly. He'd gone in for six or seven years for that, too long for the charge, but everyone had been satisfied. Jean-René had never talked, and he suspected Striker was holding his mail.

He looked at the map again.

The best route for the escapees to take would keep them on the west side of the west arm of the Guidry river. They'd be foolish to try and cross it—even though it was March and the weather was warm during the day, the gators were out. It was nearing breeding season, and they could get mighty aggressive if they detected a threat, and two prisoners were just that.

If he was lucky, nature would take its course and they'd find the two loudmouths half-eaten by a gator.

If they somehow got away . . . he started to sweat at the idea. Those two could go to a neighbouring parish and God only knew what they'd seen in that prison to blab about. If anyone other than him got hold of his nephew Tommy, the story about the gas station robbery would be blown to hell—Tommy would shit out the truth like he had the runs.

He wiped the sweat from his brow with a handkerchief.

They had to find those two escapees. Anyone else he could handle, but those two would be his undoing.

9

Roundtree put the calls out with trepidation. He didn't like manhunts—everyone was too desperate to find the escapees that the outcome was never good. He was on the periphery of the last big hunt and only found out how bad it was in the centre of things after it was all over. This one had the potential to get even worse.

He was afraid the escapees would head to the Landry place, but once he saw the map he realized they wouldn't risk it. Coming in to the area, you'd cross the Atchafalaya, then the east arm of the Guidry before reaching the prison. The train bridge the prisoners worked on was miles down the road and crossed Foret Creek. If you followed Foret Creek, it'd take you right into the west arm of the Guidry. They'd have to cross the west arm to get close to the Landry place, which was between the arms. The previous escapees had escaped from the prison, which put the prisoners closer to the Landry place. These city boys wouldn't risk crossing a river, not with the chance of running into a gator. They'd stay on the west side of the west arm.

That left a handful of cabins he'd do his best to direct everyone to on the west side. He'd keep the searchers away from the Landry place, more for their protection than Josie's. He'd seen her eyes when she said she'd shoot next time she saw them, and the girl wasn't kidding. The last thing he wanted was her dead after what the deputies did. She'd be shot—in the back, in the head—and they'd spin a story. That wasn't going to happen.

Hell, these escapees didn't deserve this either. He knew the robbery story was bull. Tommy MacGregor admitted as much when he gave his statement, a rambling, incoherent one the teenager contradicted over and over. Sheriff MacGregor had railroaded those Las Vegas hoods, and dozens before them, and as much as he hated it, there wasn't anything he could do. He didn't like the idea of helping these guys get caught, but he had more loyalty to Josie Landry than some Las Vegas criminals. He sighed.

They'd end up dead and he'd have murders on his conscience. He knew MacGregor and Striker had no intention of letting them survive. No matter what he tried to do it seemed like someone was going to end up with the short end of the stick.

He glanced over toward the map above MacGregor's desk.

There wasn't a lot he could do aside from keep the search party on the west side of the west arm. Well, maybe that wasn't strictly true.

Depending on how they found the escapees, he could help them, maybe. And if he did, they'd need to get away from here as quickly as possible.

He thought for a moment then searched MacGregor's desk and came up with the envelope with the car keys for the rental truck. He knew MacGregor hadn't searched it—the man had what he wanted and didn't need to go looking for real charges. The truck was over at Duchenes, and he was close to where the two arms merged as the Guidry before it made its way to the Atchaflaya. Roundtree took the keys and tucked them into a pocket.

Their things were in the filing cabinet that passed for evidence lockup. He picked out the paper bags with their boots, belts and ID and put them in his truck.

If the escapees could get down the bayou enough, get to one of the smaller towns, they could make it out. Out of their parish it wouldn't be their problem—hell, he didn't see MacGregor putting the word out on the wire or anything.

Roundtree smiled to himself at that thought. No, MacGregor wouldn't put the word out. MacGregor didn't want anyone to know.

And that was his ace in the hole.

MacGregor pulled up to the construction site around three-thirty. They had about three hours of sunlight left, and they needed to get that dog team here as soon as possible.

Roundtree pulled up in his own truck, as the sheriff department only had three vehicles, and Hickom and Lee each had a car today, and the sheriff with his own.

"We'll catch these sons of bitches," MacGregor said to Roundtree as he exited his car.

Roundtree nodded. "Where do you think they've gone?"

MacGregor looked around. "Looks like they went into the trees, crossed the road and into the bush and down into the creek. They'll head south down to the bayou and the west arm most likely. They'll stay on the west side of the arm. They may be dumb, but I don't think they're dumb enough to cross the river."

"What do you want me to do?" he asked.

"Wait for the dog team."

MacGregor got out of the car. He was already sweating and short of breath in the late afternoon heat. Flies buzzed around his head.

He put his hat on and walked over toward Striker.

"What the hell happened here?"

MacGregor took a look around for the first time, seeing scorched earth, blood dried in the dirt and a row of prisoners sitting on the hard ground.

"Explosion was set off, dynamite too, the Jeep went over."

"What happened when they ran off?"

"They weren't the only ones," a guard said. "We fired on everyone that ran, but didn't hit those two. They had a head start, I guess."

MacGregor was relieved when he saw Hickom and Lee show up. They weren't the sharpest tools in the shed, but they'd outshine every one of Striker's guards.

They were each in a marked car and got out, surveying the damage with their mouths hanging open.

"How many escaped?" Hickom asked.

"Two they still haven't found," MacGregor said. "You have any idea if the dog team's on the way?"

Roundtree approached the group. "I got Pender on the radio, he's on his way now, but he's coming from Opelousas."

"I want those two caught, any means necessary," MacGregor said, his voice low. "They can't get out of this parish, that clear? They do, and it's your badges."

Hickom and Lee exchanged glances.

"Any means?"

"Anything," MacGregor said. "Striker wants 'em back alive, I think, but I don't give a damn. I'd prefer you bring them back in body bags."

"Sir, they're kids," Roundtree said.

"Mid-twenties ain't a kid, that's the same age as you. They got records longer than my arm, attitudes to match. They robbed my nephew at gun point and now they caused all this mayhem. We got people dead here. I want them brought down. If they end up in the bayou in a gator's jaw, then all the better for us. You got that?"

All of his deputies nodded. MacGregor stepped into the shade, waiting for Gil Pender and his bloodhounds.

An hour later, before the search officially started, MacGregor ordered the deputies to talk to the prisoners. Roundtree spotted Jean-René Landry cuffed along the line. He had a guard uncuff him and took him near the bus, but he didn't have to ask him a single question.

"You know they've gone in the bayou," Jean-René said. "You know what the sheriff will do if he thinks they went across the river. Josie said you aren't like the others."

Roundtree looked over at Hickom and Lee. He looked back at Jean-René, but didn't say anything.

"I know not everyone can agree with what he does. He put me in here, that's fair for what I did, but you know Hickom and Lee should be in here for what they did to Josie."

Roundtree nodded.

"The Kelly kid, he's smart, but he's out of his element. I told him about the cabins on the west side of the arm, but he knew I was holding out. I think the stupid son of a bitch will cross the river. He's in over his head, grew up in the desert." Jean-René looked over at the deputies. "The other one, he might give Kelly a chance. Grew up in Alabama. I think he knows places like this."

"Lucky for them." Roundtree looked toward the tree line then at the line of prisoners shackled together. He turned to Landry. "Are they still shackled together?"

Jean-René nodded. "They were stupid to go, but there was no talking to them."

"Damn," Roundtree muttered. Shackled together they'd head for a cabin as soon as they could—if they could make it there without being caught, and in shackles . . .

He sighed. These guys weren't giving him a lot to work with.

"Where would they cross?"

"If they cross where I think they will they won't be too far from the cabin. I'm not worried about them running into her, but you know as well as I do Hickom and Lee will follow."

Roundtree looked at Jean-René. "I know they already want to search the east side. And not because they think those boys are running there, either."

Jean-René looked him in the eye. "Then you keep them on the west side of the west arm as long as you can, and you get to Josie first. I don't think she'll hurt those boys, but if they find her, so will the badges. You find her first. Else you'll have two dead deputies to worry about."

The sun dipped low in the sky, and it cooled off quickly. The skeletal bald cypress trees were just greening up, but the weeping willows provided some cover and everything was a strange shade of green-brown.

"I don't like this," Tim said.

"I heard you the last time," Jake answered.

They moved slowly through the swampy water, waist deep and colder than either of them expected. They hadn't seen anything in the water yet, and Tim would never admit it, but it was creeping him out.

It was slow going in the water thanks to the chain, which kept getting caught up on branches, rocks and other things at the bottom. Tim kept envisioning it tangling around an angry alligator.

Jake stumbled against him, almost knocking him off his feet. This whole escape would go a lot more smoothly if they weren't chained together. Jake tripped again.

"Watch where the hell you're going!"

"It wasn't me, it was the damn chain," Jake said. "We gotta get this off. You ever think about what's going to happen if they catch up to us? We start to run and they'll be on us in a heartbeat."

Tim had thought about it. The chains and shackles needed to come off if they had any chance. Even if they made it out of here to some kind of civilization, they would stand out like crazy in prison clothes shackled together. They wouldn't be able to be seen anywhere without someone raising the alarm. Hell, they'd probably get shot on sight by just about anyone.

The arms of his jumpsuit unravelled at his waist and trailed behind, and Tim took a second to tie them back up. He hoped the papers pinned in the pocket would survive the water. Jake stopped in his tracks a minute later.

"What are you doing?" Tim asked. Jake had lowered himself in the water up to his neck.

"Dirtying up the shirt a bit. It's too white, we should try and make it blend in more."

"I think we stick out just fine ourselves."

Tim hesitated a second, then took the shirt off and tossed it in the water to dirty it up. He tied it onto the sleeve of the jumpsuit after and moved ahead shirtless.

"You're gonna get eaten alive by mosquitoes that way."

"Shut up."

They moved through the water again, moving slowly and pausing every so often to listen for the sounds of dogs or men. They approached a bend in the water and Jake froze as they moved around a log.

"What?" Tim asked, his voice a harsh whisper.

Jake nodded ahead of them, and Tim craned to look beyond Jake and his blood ran cold. About twenty feet away was a large alligator, sailing through the water. It seemed they were now in alligator territory: the deep of the bayou.

"Holy shit," Tim whispered. "What do we do? That thing is fucking huge."

"Don't move," Jake said. "And keep your damn voice down. I don't think it cares about us."

"Yet," Tim said morosely. "It hasn't had a good look at us. We probably look like grade A chuck to that thing."

The alligator approached the bank and slid out of the water, it's large tail flicking it easily out of the water. It's head was pointed right in their direction and Tim could see its beady eyes.

"It's staring at me," Tim said.

"Don't look at it!"

"I'm not walking past that thing in this water," Tim said. "We're in that guy's backyard, he's got an advantage."

Jake looked over at the bank closest to them, and nodded toward it.

"Come on."

He moved slowly, but the water rippled with every motion. Tim grabbed for a low-hanging branch, and tried to pull himself up the slippery slope. The alligator began to make an odd huffing sound.

Tim shoved Jake forward. Jake was almost out of the water, and Tim slipped on the bank, losing his balance. It caused Jake to lose his and slip back into the water. The chain tugged at his ankle as Jake launched himself back up on the shore.

"Move!" Jake said, yanking his leg so it pulled the chain. Tim slipped again on the bank, and Jake finally rolled his eyes and moved forward to grab Tim's hand and haul him to shore.

It was the only benefit to the chains—neither one was going to be able to leave the other behind, and as much as Tim hated to admit it, he wouldn't want to be alone out here. Jake was better than nothing.

Jake let him go, and Tim flopped down on the ground beside him. They both lay on their backs, looking up at the trees stretching to the sky, their arms stretching up like skeletons. Tim breathed hard. It was exhausting traveling like this.

He sat up a minute later and watched the alligator, motionless on the opposite bank. It's mouth was open, all of its teeth visible.

"What the hell is it doing?" Tim asked, watching it with suspicious eyes.

"I don't know," Jake admitted. "Daydreaming about convict soup, how the fuck should I know?"

Jake stood up and must've forgotten about the chain, because he yanked on it, hurting Tim's already sore ankle.

"We need to get rid of these things," Tim said. "We're sitting ducks with this shit attaching us. I'll cut my own fucking leg off if I have to."

"Here," Jake said. "Gimme that rock."

Tim scooted over and picked up the triangular rock sitting nearby, forcing Jake to move over as well. Jake grabbed the rock from Tim and tried to smash the shackles.

"Not there," Tim said. "You gotta hit it near the cuff."

"Stop it," Jake said, shoving Tim's hands away. "Let me do this."

"You're fucking it up, give me the damn rock."

"Get your own fucking rock."

"Just give it over!"

Tim yanked it out of Jake's hand and aimed it for the shackle on his ankle. He missed and ended up slamming it against Jake's leg.

Jake pounded the ground with his fist, making every effort not to scream and alert anyone they were there.

"If them guards don't kill you, I will," Jake said between gritted teeth. He pounded a fist into the spongy ground again. The alligator huffed in the distance.

"You moved," Tim said, feeling a deep satisfaction at the fact Jake's leg might be hurting as much as his did.

"I didn't fucking move, you have lousy aim."

"I do not."

"I've seen you take a piss, you can't even hit the bowl."

"Fuck you!"

"What, you want to do everything your girlfriends do?"

Tim lunged at Jake and caught him with a right hook to the jaw. Jake pushed him back and tried to knee him in the crotch, but Tim blocked him. He hit Jake in the midsection, then pulled back and ducked Jake's punch and got him in the eye.

He stopped his fist in mid-air at the noise and froze. Jake hadn't heard it and kicked him away. Tim landed in the dirt, breathing hard. The alligator bellowed, and they both froze.

Tim got control of his breathing and dragged his gaze away from the alligator and toward Jake.

"That was low, even for you."

Tim sunk down onto the spongy ground and flexed his hand. Jake had a hard face. His wrist throbbed again, the pain in concert with his ankle.

Jake was silent, his gaze on the alligator.

"It's what you deserved," Jake said. "You got to Darla first, it was payback."

Tim looked over at Jake. "You're out of your mind. I told you—more than once—that I never slept with Darla. Not even once. Never even got close. That night she got me upside the head with her purse was the closest we ever got."

Jake stared into his face for a minute, then looked away quickly. He believed him. The jerk would never say it, but he finally believed him.

"She wasn't in her right mind," Jake said, his voice low. "She only did it because she wasn't in her right mind."

He meant Ruby, and Tim knew it. He'd known she wasn't in her right mind, but it hadn't mattered then. He shut his eyes and tried not to think of Ruby. Her face, the way she frowned all the time and the way she couldn't keep how she felt off her face. The terror the minute a storm hit. He'd known her dalliance with Jake was nothing more than terror looking for refuge.

Maybe one day he could forgive her that.

"Let's get the hell out of here," Tim said, looking around the bayou. He wanted dry hard pan, alkaline air and dust storms, none of this wet, messy place.

"Yeah, let's beat it," Jake said.

All Tim heard were birds and that strange breathing sound coming from the alligator.

"This place is giving me the creeps."

Jake moved through the brush as best he could, finding areas which almost looked like trails sometimes. The dry creek bed turned into a flowing creek which turned into a narrow, deep flow like the bayou and then met up with a wide, swampy river a mile back. Jake hoped it was the west arm of the Guidry, the river Tim kept yapping about.

"Are you sure we're going to find a cabin?"

"Yeah," Tim said. "Johnny Ray said they were on both sides of the river. He said there were plenty on the west side. He said they caught the prisoners from the last break between the arms and we should avoid it because they'd search there first."

"I doubt it," Jake said. "Maybe if we'd escaped from the prison they would."

"Just what I was thinking. He was trying to keep us on this side. Dunno why. I figure we cross the river at some point, then find a cabin on the east side. It could buy us some time."

"You better know where the hell you're going," Jake said. "I'm not going back inside because you have a lousy sense of direction."

"Yeah, well I don't see you leading the way, Mr. Alabama."

The sun was beginning to set, low in the sky and casting long shadows. He wanted to be across the river before it was dark—all his years in Alabama he'd only seen gators a few times, but according to Tim that made him the expert. He wasn't sure if alligators were nocturnal or not, and he wasn't itching to find out.

The sun was almost down as they moved down the river bank, keeping close to the water's edge in the hopes it would erase their footprints. Jake wished they'd crossed it further back when it was lower water. The river had widened and looked dark and foreboding, even with the last of the day's sun still in the sky.

He paused, not sure he'd heard the sound, then the panic rose.

"Did you hear that?"

"Hear what?" Kelly asked.

"Shh," he said. "Listen."

In the distance a plaintiff yowl was heard, then a deep bark.

"Shit," Kelly said. "Dogs."

"Yeah, dogs. Come on, we gotta move. Even with us moving through the water edge like this, they'll still find us."

They started moving again, but it was slow going with the sun going down and it being harder to see in the dark bayou. Jake yanked on the chain as he moved, Kelly swearing behind him.

The dogs got louder.

They sounded like bloodhounds.

"We need to get outta here," Jake said. "Those sound like bloodhounds."

"What of it?"

"Their sense of smell is the best there is. They'll find us in no time. Our only chance is getting across the river, it'll at least give us some time. We can make it look like we headed off this way, maybe throw our shirts into the bush or something. They won't stay confused for long, but it'll give us a few minutes at least."

They tracked into the wilderness away from the river for awhile, throwing their shirts into the dense brush, then tracked back to the water's edge.

"We really gotta swim it, huh?" Tim asked. Jake noted with satisfaction Kelly's back was covered in mosquito bites.

"Yeah, we gotta swim it," Jake answered.

They approached the shore and got into the water, surprised by how much colder it was.

"We're gonna freeze to death tonight," Tim said, his teeth already chattering.

"Come on."

They walked into the river as far as they could before the ground vanished from under them. Swimming was hard, since the shackles and chain weighed them down, along with the weight of their jumpsuits.

Jake was making it okay, but Tim struggled to keep his head above water.

"You are not going to drown," Jake said. "You'd be like a lead weight dragging me to hell with you. Come on, swim you lousy son of a bitch!"

"Fuck . . . you," Tim managed.

Jake looked back, seeing Tim's head barely above the water. He could still hear the dogs in the distance.

"Can you even swim?"

"'Course I can . . . swim." Kelly's head disappeared and reappeared for a second and that was not the act of someone who could swim.

"Shit," Jake breathed.

He grabbed Tim's arm and yanked him forward, but he barely moved. The shackle was weighing him down. "Come on, I'm not dragging you all the way over."

"I'm . . . fine."

"You're swallowing half the river. You end up with some kind of disease, I don't want you puking on me."

Tim was trying to move and not getting far. Jake was tired after their run, and the chain wasn't making life easier. The weight was getting hard to swim with.

"Didn't you ever learn to swim?" Jake asked.

"Where?" Tim asked. "We live in the damn desert."

"Oh, I dunno, the fucking swimming pool at the Sands," Jake answered, out of the breath. "And I suppose you forgot we got lakes in Las Vegas, dumb ass."

"I spend my time making . . . out with chicks . . . next to the lakes," Tim said. "Not swimming in . . . them."

Jake had to chuckle at that.

Jake looked around and spotted a log floating, then stopped to think. It might not be a log and it was hard to tell now that the sun was just about gone.

Tim made a choking sound, and Jake decided to risk it. Jesus Christ, it better not be a sleeping alligator floating down the river.

He reached out for the log and was relieved to feel that it was wood. He pulled the small log toward him, then back toward Tim.

"Here, I got you a life preserver," Jake said. "Don't fucking drown."

"We need to get these chains off," Tim said, sounding more alive now that he could keep his head above water by holding onto something other than Jake.

"If we can find a cabin, maybe there'll be tools or something."

"Hold up," Tim said, floating in the water. "You hear that?"

Jake didn't want to stop swimming—they seemed to be moving downstream, although slowly, and he didn't want to get lost or disoriented. He could hear the croaking of frogs, the hooting of owls and other birds, and crickets or cicadas somewhere in the bush. The howls of the dogs were in the distance still.

For a moment he remembered sitting on his grandparents back porch in the late summer, hearing the world come to life as the sun went down. You could hear every creature in the world then.

What he couldn't hear was anything Tim had.

"I don't hear anything."

"It's an engine of some kind, I think," Tim said. "Listen."

Jake stayed quiet for a second and heard a medium pitched whine in the distance. He hoped it wasn't a cop. Whoever it was, they were going to spot the two of them bobbing in the middle of the river, the fat moon lighting them up like a searchlight.

Jake looked toward the shore. He could've made it, but Tim probably wouldn't, not that fast.

"We're going to have to duck under the water," Jake said.

"Are you nuts?" Tim said. "I'll have to let go of this thing, it'll float away."

"Oh, okay, let's risk getting spotted by the cops and hold on to your precious log, Kelly."

He could almost see the angry look Tim must be giving him in the dark. The sky was a deep blue, the sun gone and the moon was above the trees.

"Wait 'til it's a bit closer, then take a deep breath and go under," Jake said. "Hold your breath until I tell you, and when you come up, don't be sputtering all over the place and coughing and choking like a moron. Be as quiet as you can."

The engine noise got louder, and a moment later Jake saw the bow of a small skiff come around the river bend upstream.

"Now," he whispered.

They both took a big breath and slowly sunk under the water. Jake prayed there wouldn't be any hungry alligators deciding to take a bite out of them at that instant.

He heard the whine of the motor and stayed under the water as long as he could. The shackle pulled him under farther than he wanted to go, and he knew he couldn't last much longer.

He heard the noise as the boat passed very close to them, and hoped it wasn't so close it'd take one of their heads off with the propeller. He wished there was a way he could get the propeller to cut the damn chains off. He was starting to think having Tim along was going to increase their chances of being caught.

He stayed under longer, feeling Tim struggle to get to the surface. He tried to hold him down, but Tim scratched at him, then kicked him in the midsection. Jake lost his air and sailed up to the surface, his lungs burning.

He took a large gulp of air as quietly as he could, but then the surface was broken by Tim, who was gasping for air like a little girl, and trying to stifle his coughs.

"Great," Jake said.

He looked downriver—the boat wasn't visible anymore, but he could still hear the engine, and as far as he could tell, it was still heading away from them. As long as it didn't stop or turn around, they were okay.

Tim struggled to stay afloat again. The log Jake had got for him was too far down the river to catch up to, and the shore was much closer.

"Come on," Jake said, trying to yank Tim through the water, his head slipping below the water as the shackle weighed him down. "How someone who says he's so tough can't even kick through the water, I'll never know. Just wait 'til everyone hears about this."

"Fuck you," Tim said. "I've done more work than you on those chain gangs, I'm more tired."

"That's bullshit, we're chained together, we do the same amount of work," Jake said. "Come on!"

Tim half-heartedly kicked, and Jake wondered if he was playing feint just so Jake would do all the work. Tim's head slipped under the water again for a minute, then re-appeared. He was going to get nabbed for sure with this clown chained to him. They needed to be unshackled and free, to either run together or go their separate ways, but this chained bullshit had to end.

"You weigh about two hundred pounds, help me out, man," Jake said, tired. The chain dragged him down again, and he struggled to pull the shackle through the water. He hit Tim's leg with his own.

"One-sixty, if that," Tim choked out. "You asshole."

A moment later Jake's shoe hit the soft river bottom, and he just about threw a damn party. He hauled Tim toward the shore, and Tim finally found his legs. The two of them crawled out of the river and collapsed on the shoreline in the mud, exhausted and cold. Steam rose off their bodies, but Jake was cold and shivering. It was warmer in the water.

Tim breathed heavily, and Jake stared at the sky. Without the sun to dry them, it was going to be a really cold night. They couldn't risk starting a fire—the smell and the light would give away their position in no time.

That'd sure be insulting—to get all this way and be caught because they were cold. What they had to do was find a cabin, find a way to get the shackles off and then get dry.

"We gotta move," Jake said, hearing a baying hound in the distance. He was exhausted, hungry, cold and dying for some water, but they had to move.

"We're gonna trip over our own feet and kill ourselves if we keep traveling at night."

"It's not night, it's seven thirty at the latest," Jake said. "And maybe you'll trip over your own feet, but I'm fine."

Tim gave a harsh laugh. "What a damn joke this is, huh?"

"Yeah," Jake said. He stared at a star shining through the canopy of trees overhead. "Some joke, right?"

"The joke'll be on Striker if we get outta here. I stole some stuff from his office. He'll piss himself when he realizes."

"Those papers? Anything good on them?" Jake asked. He'd seen Kelly hide them, and he'd seen the one with the little x's, but figured Tim's plan involved blackmail. Kelly always thought too much.

"I took the paperwork he had on us," Tim said. "So now there's no record we were ever there."

"Good, I always wanted my record," Jake said. "At least I'll get something out of this shit experience. Come on, we should move."

Jake got up and looked around, concerned to note that he couldn't see very far in front of him. The whole bayou was loud and alive, but surprisingly dark. There should be an almost full moon out there, but Jake didn't see hide nor hair of it from where he was—the tree canopy, even without leaves, blocked out most of the light.

"Where are we headed anyway?" Jake asked. "You have any idea where these cabins are?"

"Johnny Ray didn't say," Tim admitted. "He only told me about the cabins on the other side, but that's the side they're going to check first. You know it as well as I do. I know there were some cabins over here. He was hedging when he was telling things, I think he was trying to keep me away from here."

"Maybe there's a reason for it." Jake took a few steps forward, stopping when the chain pulled. "Maybe he's keeping you away for a reason."

"Like what?"

"I don't know. Like he's got his own hideout here he don't want us to find."

"If he had his own hideout he would've taken off himself ages ago," Tim said. "He wasn't too eager to do anything but serve out his sentence, and he was in for over five years. He wasn't like us, I think he was in there for real."

"Then maybe it's a trap," Jake said. "Maybe he told you where not to go because he knew you'd go, then he'll tell the warden and the sheriff to nab us and he'll get all the credit. I bet those old boys would knock a few years off his sentence."

"Somehow I doubt that."

Jake took the lead for awhile. He was cold to the bone, trying not to shiver and sound like a wuss.

He glanced back at Kelly. He cradled his right wrist and limped, but the limp wasn't from the shackle. It'd be a problem if they couldn't get the shackles off and Kelly was hurt. Kelly was going to slow him down if he got any more crippled, and then it was back to the big house for the both of them.

They needed to find some tools as soon as possible.

Branches scratched his arms as he walked by. His shoes were cold and squished with water. What he wouldn't give for a hot shower and some food.

Kelly crashed through the underbrush behind him like a rampaging elephant.

"Watch where you're going," Jake said. "Don't light up a trail for 'em or anything."

Tim stopped and looked at him. "You didn't seem too worried before."

"Because we needed to get distance. Now we need to make sure they can't find us. The dogs will make it easy. If they cross the river, they'll find us."

The chain jangled.

"Yeah, we're pretty quiet and unnoticeable," Tim said sarcastically.

"I swear to God, we get these things off and I'm taking off my own," Jake said, sick of Tim's complaints and comments. "You can fend for yourself. You'll probably crash through all the underbrush and lead the dogs right to you."

"And you'll navigate your way back to the prison," Tim said. "Shut up and keep moving."

Against his better judgement, Jake turned and marched forward again, the chain pulling and dragging. Making more noise than he wanted, Kelly crashed on behind him.

10

Monday, March 27, 1967

Roundtree glanced around at the trees as they headed into the bayou. It was spring, everything was blooming and budding, but there wasn't as much cover as there would be at the height of summer.

There was an easy trail to follow at first as they found their way to a flattened section of bush that led into the dry creek bed. Down there it was harder to follow, the rocks hiding many of their footsteps. But the dogs got a scent quickly, and the two bloodhounds pulled at their leads, and everyone went crashing after them.

The creek got wetter as it got closer to the bayou, and soon it seemed to bubble up from out of thin air and turn into a deep, slow moving mess as it crept toward the west arm of the Guidry. The arm wasn't much at first, but the further south they went, the larger the arm became.

Roundtree had grown up in the area, but the bayou wasn't his favourite place. There was something creepy and otherworldly about the Spanish moss hanging off everything, the bald cypress growing from the water, and the prehistoric-looking alligators staring at you.

He stepped across the spongy ground, sighing at the damage. These two certainly didn't think much about covering their tracks. He saw broken branches, marks from their shoes and disturbed rocks and soil.

He didn't want these two guys getting killed, especially when he knew all they were guilty of was having guns without a permits, and around these parts that was par for the course. MacGregor seemed to be taking this one personally, and he knew it was because these guys getting away could blow his whole cover as the beloved sheriff of Strikersville.

He would give anything to have the town realize that Striker and Mac-Gregor were just as dirty as the water in the swamp.

They hiked for awhile until he heard the huffing breath of an alligator nearby. Gators didn't have vocal cords, but they managed to vocalize a little by pushing air out of their lungs. The roars and bellows could be pretty loud.

93

"Hold up here," Hickom said. He stopped near a tree to take a leak. "What say we put a little wager on this, huh, Lee?"

"I spot 'em first, then you gotta lend me that new skiff two weekends in a row."

"And if I nail 'em first, you gotta lend me your pickup for four weekends."

"Sure, sure," Lee said.

Hickom gave Lee a look. "The '66 pickup, not that piece of junk '48 you got."

Lee huffed out an agreement. "Well, then it's two weekends, just like the skiff. What if we each shoot one? What then?"

The two men argued about the possibilities.

Roundtree rolled his eyes. Hickom and Lee looked at this like some kind of a game preserve. He didn't like hearing these men, who had vowed to uphold the law just like he did, talking about killing these guys.

No one had coming looking for Kelly or Wheeler, just like the sheriff thought, so these guys probably didn't have families that gave a rat's ass about them. He doubted they'd ever hear from a lawyer if they ended up dead. They were the type of hoods who died and people said "Well, we always knew it'd happen some day." Only this wasn't what anyone would have assumed was going on, not some place like Strikersville.

The dogs circled around, howling and confused, uncomfortable being so near the gator. The sun was almost set, and it was getting dark—they hadn't come prepared with lights, so Lee went back to the cars to get outfitted for a night search. Hickom, Gil Pender and Roundtree waited for him to return.

"Dogs lost the scent," Pender said. "They probably went in the water. We'll move downstream and pick it up again, they won't have stayed in the water for long around here."

"Pretty damn stupid," Hickom said. "It's getting into breeding season, and them gators ain't too kind if you get in their way. These yahoos could've been eaten alive. Dammit, I hope not, I'm gonna win that bet with Lee."

Roundtree looked at Hickom, tired of the man's blood thirst. "Yeah, maybe we'll hit pay dirt, and they'll get killed that way."

Hickom was either ignoring or not understanding his sarcasm, because he gave a deep laugh.

"Nah, I still want to have at 'em. Me and Lee came up with a game about it. Fastest to empty our six shooters plus most hits wins."

Roundtree bit his tongue to keep from speaking out. Hickom was the type of man who'd shoot him during the search and call it an accident with his gun. A memory fluttered across his mind of some town gossip about something like that surrounding Charlie Hickom and a shooting, but he couldn't remember the details.

"They probably stayed at the water's edge," Pender said. "Dunno for how long. We can follow along the shore, see if they came out anywhere."

"As soon as we get some lights," Roundtree said. "I'm not going in there blind."

He meant it, but the longer the search took, the better. He wondered if there would be any way he could find the escapees on his own, but figured everyone would probably notice if he took off. Hickom and Lee were competitive and stupid enough to think he would take off on his own to find them to get all the glory, since that's exactly why they'd do it.

No, the best he could do is keep them slowed down and held up, away from the middle of the arms. He feared Hickom and Lee would try to make their way to the Landry cabin, just to see if Josie was there.

On one hand, he didn't think they'd all come out of this alive. He saw the look in Josie Landry's eyes when she said she'd shoot them, and she wasn't kidding. Hickom and Lee would step onto her property and be dead a few seconds later. It would solve a lot of his problems, but bring new ones to her, and she didn't deserve that.

Jean-René didn't trust cops, but he told him where he thought these guys would go. They wouldn't stay on this side of the river—even Roundtree could see that now. These guys took risks and played against the house— they were from Las Vegas, after all, home of gambling and the mafia. Taking chances was probably bred into them.

They'd cross the river to the middle of the arms, and soon Hickom and Lee would figure that out. Or at least want to take a side trip. He couldn't let that happen. Maybe, if he could play it right, he could protect Josie and get those Las Vegas idiots out of the bayou alive too.

It was about time the Landry's learned they could trust someone in uniform.

They had been moving through the bayou between the arms for at least an hour. There was still water nearby, and Tim wondered if they were on an island or something. He didn't relish the idea of getting back in the water again.

It was hard traveling, not only because of the chain getting held up on all the roots and bushes, but because it was so dark through the trees and brush they couldn't see more than a few feet in front of them. They were moving slower than they were a few hours earlier.

The light was better toward the watery areas, where the moonlight could shine down, but Tim didn't want to risk being spotted moving along the shore by anyone.

That was another risk. These cabins could be full of people, and he didn't know how they'd react to two prison escapees. From what he could see in town, no one seemed to have a problem with the sheriff. There was a good chance no one had a clue what was going on in the prison. They'd probably be shot on sight. So even if they came upon a cabin, there was a chance they'd have to move past it to the next one and find one unoccupied.

Jake cursed a few feet ahead of him, then stumbled again. Both of them were getting more unsure on their feet as they moved.

"Watch it, Jake," Tim said. He was sick and tired of the trees, roots, stones, mud, and all other manner of stuff out here in the bayou. Give him desert any day.

"I tripped over something."

Before he could get out another word, Tim's own feet tangled in something and he almost fell over himself.

"What the hell is it?" He felt around and realized what he was touching. "It's chicken wire. I think it's all strung up around here."

"Like a property line or something?"

"I dunno," Tim said. "If it is, we better keep quiet and try and see if there's a cabin around here. If there's people in it, we gotta move on."

"Yeah," Jake said. "No sense in getting our asses shot off for nothing, right?"

Tim hauled himself up, and he and Jake stepped as carefully as they could through the bayou. He heard that weird huffing sound again.

"Sounds like a gator," Jake said.

"Yeah," Tim said. "Nearby, too."

At least it didn't make that awful bellowing noise. They moved forward, and Tim noticed with some trepidation the noise was getting louder.

"Let's move," he said. "Over to the water."

"Yeah," Jake echoed. "Better for him to eat us. You're out of your mind. We should stay inland."

Tim moved closer to the water, which was away from the sound, and Jake followed, despite his protests. As they moved to where they thought the water was, Tim heard rustling nearby.

"What was that?"

"How the fuck should I know?" Jake asked. "I think it came from over there."

It was dark. Tim closed his eyes, then opened them, hoping he could see better. He spotted something light, like a log from a birch tree, about five feet in front of them. A second later a groaning noise broke the relative silence.

"I think it's here," he whispered.

"You got a match?" Jake asked.

"Soaked, remember?" Tim said.

They both inched forward. A dark log was right in front of them, and the pale log five or six feet beyond it. Tim thought the alligator might be on the other side of the pale log.

"Go around it," Jake said.

"You go around it!" Tim insisted, his voice a sparse whisper.

Jake stepped forward over the dark log then toward the pale log, Tim right behind him, the chain jangling between them. He couldn't see the outline of an alligator anywhere, but he could hear the weird breathing. The creature was definitely nearby. He kept his eye on the pale log, expecting the alligator to jump out and lunge at them from behind it. He was glad Jake was in front and would become the gator's meal first.

Jake froze, and Tim almost ran into his back. He blinked—he could've sworn the log just moved.

"Kelly," Jake said, only two feet away from the moving log.

"What?"

"Don't move."

Jake was silent for a second. Tim saw the pale log move again, and Jake must have too.

"What the fuck?!" his voice was a strained whisper.

Suddenly the log moved around to the side, and Tim saw that it wasn't a pale birch log, but a white alligator, his tail whipping behind him. Jake stumbled backward and fell into Tim, who pushed Jake off of him and tried to crawl away. The chain pulled at Tim's leg and he and Jake both scrambled backwards as the gator log moved toward them.

"What the hell is it?!" Tim asked.

Tim got to his feet and moved back, pulling Jake with him. He paused when the thing stopped moving. It didn't seem all that interested in him as far as eating them went.

"I think it's an alligator," Jake said.

"Gators are green. That thing is not green," Tim said.

"I think it's an albino." Jake's voice was full of wonder. "Christ."

Tim shoved Jake in the back.

"I'm serious man, you see it?"

As the alligator moved around slowly, Tim could better see the outline. It was definitely not a dark green or even a light green colour.

"I've heard about albinos, but never seen one. Christ, how'd it get so big, wouldn't it get eaten?"

"You'd figure." Tim watched as the gator paid no attention to them, skulking around the bushes and then moving toward the water. It walked right past them like it didn't even notice, then slunk into the water.

"Come on, let's get the hell out of here before it works up an appetite," Jake said.

They shivered in the cold and moved past the area where they'd first seen the gator.

A minute later Tim made out another shadow in the distance and stopped Jake.

"Don't tell me there's another one."

"No . . . I think . . . I think it's an outhouse."

"What, here?"

Tim moved forward and felt around for a door knob or latch, and found one. He yanked the door open and found a flashlight hanging on a hook inside.

"Jackpot," he said.

"Only you'd say that about a shitter."

He flicked the flashlight on and then directed the bream right into Jake's eyes. He swore and rubbed his face.

"I get the picture, turn that thing off."

Tim shined it around the area, then moved down the path and shined the light toward the water's edge. He saw the alligator.

"I'll be damned," Tim said. "It really is white."

"An albino alligator," Jake echoed.

He shined the flashlight around some more and saw the makings of a fence.

"Jake," he said.

"What?"

"I think we walked into its pen."

Tim looked around the perimeter, noticing they'd trampled over part of the fence on their way into the area. Just beyond the outhouse was more of the chicken wire fence.

"If that's a fence, then someone built it," Jake said. "Come on."

He yanked on the chain with his foot and Tim followed along, shining the light along the ground. They stepped over the fence and realized they were following a pretty well-worn path. A second later Tim almost whooped in excitement as the light shined up on a cabin, built up on stilts.

There were no lights on, but Tim turned the flashlight off anyway.

A few stairs lead up to a warped porch, and to the left of the cabin was a makeshift dock, but no boat. Tim cursed. A boat would've been the perfect thing to get them out of here.

He and Jake moved up the stairs as quietly as they could.

The place looked abandoned. There were old fishing nets hung from the rafters on the porch, and he saw curtains with holes in them on the windows. He pressed the edges of his hands to the window and looked inside.

There were very few pieces of furniture—an old worn couch, a table and what looked like a desk with no chair. He could see beyond to a small kitchen with maybe a chair and table, then another room to the right. There was no sign of anyone.

"We need to look in the other windows," Tim said.

"How?" Jake asked. "They're up on stilts, and we ain't seven feet tall."

It's not like they could boost each other up with the chains on either.

"You wanna risk it?"

"Try knocking." Jake reached forward and knocked loudly.

Tim looked at him like he was crazy.

"You do realize if people are in there, they're gonna come out and see two people chained together wearing prison jumpsuits, right?" Tim asked. "Tell me how eager you'd be to help?"

"We ain't the cops," Jake said. "That should be enough."

No one came to the door.

Tim reached forward and turned the knob, and the door swung open with a creak.

He crept inside the door and looked for a light switch before realizing they were in the middle of nowhere and the house didn't even have indoor plumbing. Jake came in behind him and shut the door.

"Search the place," Tim said. They each tried to go a separate direction before being yanked back together thanks to the chain.

"Find something to get this fucking thing off!" Jake said. They went to the desk first, but nothing was inside but a few papers and a deck of playing cards.

The kitchen had a few knives in a drawer, but nothing thin enough to fit into the key lock to pop it open. There was a small closet in the living room, and all he found were a few towels and wash cloths.

"I need something thin, like a bobby pin or paperclip," Tim said. There was nothing there. The house smelled a bit musty and old, and he wondered when someone had been here last.

He opened the door to the single room. There were two twin beds against a wall, made up with feminine quilts that didn't match anything else in the cabin. There was a homespun rag rug on the floor, and a three drawer dresser against another wall, but that was it. The drawers held nothing but clothes, and female ones from the looks of it.

They moved over to a small closet and opened it. Inside a cardboard box Tim found a collection of men's clothes, including some jeans and flannel shirts. If they could ever get their cuffs off, they had some street clothes to wear.

Tim found an electric lantern and switched it on. The battery probably wouldn't last long, but it was something. There were some other lanterns through the house, oil ones, and those he couldn't light without matches.

"Let's get back to the kitchen, there were matches there," Tim said. He found the pack in the drawer and lit one of the lanterns. Jake directed him back toward the cupboard and Jake took a towel out, shook it and proceeded to dry himself off.

"No shower?" Tim asked.

"Don't look like it," Jake said. "Anyhow, I ain't in the mood to shower with you."

"I'm so tired of you," Tim muttered. "I meant after we get the cuffs off. We don't want to be too obvious climbing out of the bayou looking like we've been running for days."

Tim searched every nook and cranny, but there was nothing he could use to pop the cuffs off. Maybe there was something outside, but in the dark they'd never find it.

Jake pulled him toward the kitchen and picked out a knife, then began to cut off the jumpsuit at his ankle.

"What the hell are you doing?" Tim asked. "You cut that thing up, now you got nothing to wear."

"I don't fucking give a shit. I'm not wearing that damn jumpsuit anymore."

Jake took the knife and slit up the side of the jumpsuit, opening it up and cutting into the front where the buttons were. It fell off and he kicked it off the other leg. He stood there, chained to Tim in his underwear.

"Yeah," Tim said. "You're not gonna stand out in public at all."

"Fuck public," Jake said. "I'm sick and tired of being wet. I can figure out a way to get some of those clothes on later. Right now I just wanna be dry."

"You're unbelievable."

"We're gonna get these shackles off, okay?" Jake said. He started picking at the lock with the knife. He looked around. "No clocks in here."

"It's probably close to nine at night."

"You think anyone lives here?"

"Clothes say so, but the ice in the icebox is melted and there's not much food in the cupboards," Tim said. "Maybe it's a hunting cabin or something."

Tim sat down in one of the chairs and took off his shoes. He squeezed the water out of his socks and onto the floor boards. His feet were wrinkled and blistered.

Tim rolled up the cuff of the jumpsuit and saw his ankle was raw and bleeding, swollen from the shackle. If this got infected he was a goner.

He wrung out the sleeves of the jumpsuit, which was now a muddy and dingy orange, then dried off with a towel. He didn't relish spending the night wet, but he wasn't cutting the jumpsuit free.

"We can move those twin beds closer and each of us has a bed," Jake said. "You can take off that jumpsuit, let it rest on the chain so you ain't soaked all night if you don't wanna cut it off."

"Yeah."

The weariness overtook him completely. Tim was so bone tired he didn't think he could move. All the adrenaline was fading from his system and exhausting him. He could sleep for a year if he closed his eyes now.

He forced himself to get up and move into the bedroom with Jake, shoving the beds closer together. Tim did slip out of the jumpsuit, then tried to dry off his underwear as much as possible before lying down on the bed.

It felt better than anything he'd rested his head on in months.

He closed his eyes and heard the noises from outside—frogs were croaking, crickets chirped, an owl hooted. He even thought he heard the sound of the alligator moving around on the bank of the river.

He took a deep breath and fell into a deep sleep.

There was yelling, pain at his ankle and someone screaming at someone not to shoot.

Tim's eyes flew open, and for a moment, he had no idea where he was.

It came flooding back a moment later, and he thought Striker and the police had caught up to him, they'd found them and now they were going back to that prison hell hole.

"Don't shoot!" Jake bellowed. "Put the fucking gun down!"

Tim blinked. A flashlight shined right at him and he got up from the bed, an arm across his eyes.

"Do not move, cher, or I'll shoot," a female voice said. She had a thick Cajun accent. "It's a twelve gauge shotgun, I can hit you both where you stand."

"You're not the cops," Tim said.

"I'm no such thing," she said. "Get up! Get out of here!"

"Hold on, now." Tim lowered his voice. "Hold on. I think we can talk about this."

She pumped the shotgun.

"I don't think she wants to talk, man," Jake said, his own voice low.

"Y'all got that right," the girl said.

"We don't want trouble," Tim said. He moved forward, and the chain, his clothes still hanging on it, scraped across the floor.

She shone the light down.

"You were at Strikersville," she said, her voice flat. "You escaped."

"Yeah," Tim said. "Yeah, we did. We were working on the chain gang they got at the bridge, you know it?"

She nodded.

"There was an explosion. We took advantage."

"You crossed the river, then? In the dark?"

Tim nodded.

"Stupid, the both of you."

Her breathing was less shallow, and the light seemed to waver a little.

"You know what's going on up there, don't you?"

"I suspect a lot." The light moved from him to Jake and back again. "Where's your clothes?"

"He's a moron and cut the jumpsuit off before we could get the shackle off. I'm just trying to dry mine out is all."

"Fuck you, Kelly," Jake retorted.

Tim moved forward a little more, holding his hands up in the air.

"We don't want any trouble. Just a place to lay over for a few hours. Just a way to get the shackle off."

"Yeah, then I'm out of here and off of you," Jake said to him.

"Same here," Tim told him. He turned his attention back to the girl. "What's your name?"

"You don't get to ask the questions. What's yours?"

"Tim. This is Jake."

"What are you doing in my house? You always break in to peoples' houses?"

"Not on the regular," Tim lied. "The door was unlocked. We had a run in with a gator outside, thought it best to stay out of the bayou in the dark."

The gun lowered a little. He couldn't see much of her face.

"That's Gummy," she said. "He's mine."

"The gator?" Tim asked, surprise in his voice.

"He has to be hers," Jake said. "Albino."

"Yeah," she said. "Albo gators usually die in the wild—no camouflage. I took him from the nest when he was small. Mother didn't want anything to do with him. He has a pen here."

"Chicken wire?" Tim asked sharply.

"Yeah?"

"It's broken down in one place. Dunno if by us or not."

"It wasn't us," Jake said, a bit defensively. "The chicken wire was down, it's what I tripped on."

"Where?" She lowered the gun.

Tim considered leaping toward her and grabbing the shotgun, but she looked quick, and he figured she'd be able to aim and shoot before he reached her. He didn't think he needed to try and get the weapon from her anymore. She seemed to be in the midst of deciding they weren't dangerous.

"You have to tell me where," she said. "He stays in the water pen at night, sometimes on shore, he won't wander far until the sun is up."

"We can do that," Tim said. "'Course, it'd be easier if I could move around without this giant barnacle attached to me. It'd also be nice if we could put some clothes on him so you wouldn't have to look at him."

Tim tried to ignore the fact he stood there in a pair of Jockeys himself.

"Eat it, Kelly." Jake crossed his arms in front of him.

The girl's weapon pointed to the floor. A pop and hiss sounded and a lantern was lit on the dresser. She lit another with the same match, and soon there was light.

She was about five foot four, with frizzy reddish blonde hair. He couldn't tell what colour her eyes were, but he could see the smattering of freckles across her face. She wore a western shirt tied up at her waist and a pair of denim shorts, frayed around the edges. He assumed they'd once been long jeans. He noticed she was barefoot. Maybe that's why he hadn't heard her.

"You never told us your name," Tim said.

"Josie." She hesitated a moment. "Josie Landry."

"Tim Kelly. That there's Jake Wheeler."

"You're not from around here," she said.

Tim gave a harsh laugh. "No, not from around here. Las Vegas, Nevada."

"So how did you end up in Strikersville, then?"

"Bullshit charges created by your lovely sheriff," Jake said.

Josie's expression clouded over.

"He's lower than a snake's belly in the mud. I was half hoping it was him and his cronies in here so I could do what I promised and blow their heads off."

Tim raised an eyebrow. This girl had some fire . . . and a hatred for a common enemy. What was that quote he'd read once? The enemy of my enemy is my friend.

"Well, whatever beef you got with them is alright with me," Tim said.

She glanced at both of them, still wary, but not itching to shoot them, and that was an improvement. The gun was pointed at the ground and that's where he hoped it would stay.

"We can show you where that break in the fence was."

"I can find it," she said. "Just tell me where."

Jake tried to describe the area.

"Where exactly are we anyway?" Tim asked.

"You crossed the west arm of the Guidry," she said. "East arm is about a fifteen minute hike east. You go south and the arms meet up, and about fifteen minutes by boat after that the Guidry meets the Atchafalaya."

"You have a boat?"

She nodded. "I went in to the road to meet someone who delivers supplies to me earlier tonight. The engine died out on the way back, and I had to paddle. Happens all the time. Lots of things choke the engine up."

He wondered if her boat was the one that passed them in the river.

"Stay here," she said. She glanced at Jake, probably figuring he wouldn't want to go anywhere without clothes anyway. "I'll fix the fence and come back."

She turned and left, and Tim sat down on the bed, grabbing the prison jumpsuit. It was still soggy, but he pulled it on anyway.

"What do you think?" Jake asked.

"I think she might be our best shot," Tim said.

11

Monday, March 27, 1967

Lee returned to the search party with lights, and Gil Pender led his dogs around, calling out when they caught the scent again. Roundtree, Hickom and Lee went down creek further and caught up with the dogs. Roundtree assumed the escapees had ducked into the water for awhile and came out again.

That act alone worried him, as it was obvious the prisoners had gone across the river. Soon Hickom, Lee, the sheriff and the warden would figure it out. They followed the west arm for awhile, the dogs not losing the scent.

"How much farther is the first cabin?" he asked.

"We'll reach the trailhead soon, then it's a ten minute hike or so to the west," Hickom said. He was an avid hunter, and Roundtree remembered again about the gossip years ago about an accident of some kind, but he couldn't grab it in his mind.

Hickom spat a stream of tobacco onto the ground. "There's about six cabins down this branch."

"We need to search them all," Roundtree said. "These boys aren't from around here. They aren't going to want to mess with gators and snakes. They're city boys."

Hickom nodded slowly. "Yeah. Yeah, they ain't like us."

Lucky for them, Roundtree thought.

"They'll find a cabin first thing," Lee agreed.

They trained their flashlights on a barely noticeable trail that led to the first cabin. The dogs still hit on the trail, pulling their leads into the brush. A few minutes later they came across a dirty shirt.

"Here!" Lee called. "We got sign they went this way."

Hickom whooped and Roundtree let out his breath.

Roundtree was pretty sure they weren't there, but he was no tracking expert. He could tell Lee spotted things he didn't—maybe broken branches or something. Lee was a good tracker and Hickom was a hunter—he had to hope he could distract them with enough possibilities to keep them from trusting their own instincts.

Roundtree's radio crackled.

"What's going on?" Sheriff MacGregor asked. "Any sign?"

"We're about to go search the first of the cabins here," Roundtree said into his radio. "Found one of their shirts."

"Keep me apprised," MacGregor told him. "Find them. Or I'll have your badges."

Roundtree turned down his radio and looked up at the heavens. He saw the tops of old bald cypress trees reaching for the sky, and hundreds of stars. He could use some help on this one.

Tim spotted Josie making her way back to the cabin, her light bobbing around outside. He wondered how she didn't get eaten alive by the giant gator. Or the mosquitoes for that matter. His back itched like crazy.

"I could really go for some clothes about now," Jake shivered.

"I told you so." Tim couldn't resist.

The bedroom door creaked open.

"Just a small break. I think he ripped it down himself," she said. "He swings his tail a lot, hits a lot of things."

"He won't attack you?" Tim asked.

She shook her head. "He's lazy. I raised him since he was a baby, he relies on me for food. Still, I don't turn my back on him. Gators aren't going to attack like people think. For the most part, they slink off into the water, they don't want to be bothered by you. Gummy's the same way. I stay out of his way, he stays out of mine."

"Why do you call him Gummy?" Jake asked. "My guess is he's got plenty of teeth."

"Eighty," she said. "They use them for attack, but gators swallow their food whole. I call him that because he looked like a little piece of chewing gum when he was a youngin'."

"What do you feed him?" Tim asked.

"Oh, all kinds of stuff. Fish, chickens, mice, possum, rats," she said. "I figured you two would be more interested in this than my gator."

She held out a pair of bolt cutters.

"Hallelujah," Jake said, grabbing for them. He cut the chain between them and finally Jake and Tim were free. The shackle was still on his leg, but Jake wasn't. Jake cut the chain link closest to his shackle so there was nothing dragging on the ground, then passed the bolt cutters to Tim who did the same.

"You got no idea how you just saved his life," Tim said.

"Why's that, cher?"

"Because I would've killed him had we been chained together any longer."

"That goes double for me," Jake said.

Josie went into the closet and came out with the box of clothes they'd found earlier. She handed each of them a pair of jeans and work shirts. Jake held a pair up to him and passed another pair to Tim.

He stripped off the cold jumpsuit and dried off with the towel. His skin was pale and wrinkled from all the time in the water.

"I'll start a fire," she said, staring at them with no shame. "To dry your other things."

She left the room, and Tim stripped his underwear off, pulling the jeans on.

"Thank God for fire," Jake muttered, buttoning the fly on the pair of jeans he'd pulled on. "These things are gonna chafe like a bitch until this stuff dries."

Jake sat on the bed and went to work with the bolt cutters, trying to work them between his skin and the shackle.

Tim pulled the work shirt on and buttoned it. It felt good to be in real clothes again.

Tim left the bedroom and went to the kitchen, where Josie stoked a fire in a round woodstove in the centre of the room. She took his underwear wordlessly and laid it out on a rack nearby.

Tim limped to the living room couch and sat down, happy to leave Jake in another room for the first time in ages. He hoped the swelling would go down and then he could try at getting the shackle off his own ankle. Jake was probably having more success than he would—his ankle was swollen enough that the shackle was a lot tighter than it should be.

"Whose clothes are these?" Tim asked.

She looked over. "My brother's."

"Where is he?"

"Strikersville."

"What's his name?"

"Jean-René," she said. "MacGregor threw him in there because he beat up a police officer."

"Good on Jean-René, then," Tim said.

"The deputy deserved it," she said bitterly. "They all deserve it."

"I'm not going to argue," Tim said. "Don't much care why you hate them so much either, just as long as you're not gonna pick up the phone and turn us in."

"I couldn't even if I wanted to," she said. "No electricity, no phone, no plumbing."

"No shower?" Jake asked, coming out of the bedroom. His ankle was free of the shackle.

"There's one rigged outside," she said. "Collects rainwater. 'Course there hasn't been none for awhile, so I use the river water."

Jake stood closer to the woodstove, warming his hands.

Tim rolled the cuff of the jeans up on his leg and looked at his ankle, swollen around the shackle.

"It's been cut like that this whole time?" she asked.

He shrugged. "Shackle cut into my skin when the genius over there fell down a hill."

"If I remember right, I ain't the one that fell."

"You're favouring your wrist too, cher," she said. "Escape hasn't been so easy, I see. It wasn't easy for the last that tried."

"There were others?" Jake asked.

"Three men," she said. "They came by here, but I told them to move on, I knew the sheriff would come looking. They escaped from the main prison. This is one of the first cabins you reach if you escape from there, so I knew they'd come looking and I sent them on."

"Did they come looking?" Tim asked.

Josie looked at him, something hard and angry in her eyes. "Oh yes, they came looking."

He wondered what they'd found. A girl alone in a cabin . . . he wouldn't put it past any of them. Except for one.

"There was one cop. Blond, kinda square. Seemed pretty resigned this was happening, like he knew it was all wrong."

"Paul Roundtree," she said. "He's as bad as they are, because he won't do anything about it. He's a lapdog like the rest of them."

"The town's gotta know something's up," Tim said.

"Really?" Josie asked. "They're blind, and they don't want to see. They live in their nice houses on their nice streets and they go to town picnics and they don't care. They think the sheriff does a wonderful job arresting all these awful people, and the warden is there making sure they don't get out and ruin everything for all those nice people. They think all of us that live in the bayou are criminals, when they elected the criminals in the first place."

"Doesn't sound much different from anywhere," Jake said with contempt. "Some of the cops are in the Outfit's pockets back home, you got the cops in cahoots with some of the biggest criminals in the country. Never fair for folks like us."

Jake wasn't wrong. Joey the Rat told him about a couple of LVPD cops who were on the Outfit payroll. They had the money, and everyone wanted some.

"We need a way out of here," Tim said. "You got any ideas?"

Josie looked around. "They'll come looking here. Probably by morning if not before. Longer if Roundtree is with them."

"Why longer with him?"

She shrugged. "I think he'll try and keep them on the other side of the river. Was my brother on your chain gang?"

"I don't remember any Jean-René," Tim said.

"Jean-René?" Jake asked. "Johnny Ray."

Tim looked over at Josie for confirmation.

"It could be what they call him in there, I don't know," she said. "Here."

She got up and searched the bottom drawer of the desk, coming up with a faded picture.

"It's a little old."

She handed it to Tim.

"I'll be damned," he murmured.

"It's him? You know him?" she asked eagerly.

"Yeah," Tim said. "He was the one that told me where all the cabins were on the other side. He didn't say anything about this place. In fact, he wanted us to stay pretty far away from here. He told us not to go between the arms."

Tim looked at Josie, remembering what Johnny Ray—Jean-René—had said.

"He told me he wasn't going to tell me about the cabin the cops searched first and found the guys last time. He meant this side of the arm, wouldn't tell me about them. I thought maybe he was keeping a hiding place to himself."

"He was," Jake said.

Tim looked over at Josie. "He was trying to protect you."

"What brother wouldn't keep prison escapees away from his sister, right, cher?" she asked.

"No," Tim said. "I don't think it was us he was protecting you from."

Josie turned away and went to the porch. She opened the door and came in with a large block of ice which she deposited into the ice box.

"How long does it last?"

"A day at most. Few weeks from now it'll be too much trouble to bother. I cure everything in the spring and summer, or just make enough for a single meal," she said.

She went back out and brought in two paper bags of groceries. She put them away in the ice box.

He felt his leg, wincing as his fingers touched the wound. It looked angry and red.

"Well, if you can't walk on it, I'm out of here," Jake said with a grin. He gestured to his own leg, free of the shackle.

"Shut up," Tim said. "It's fine, just a bit sore. It's all your fault anyway."

"How's that?"

"You were the one who kept yanking the damn chain so hard it broke the skin."

"Did you go in the river with it like that?" Josie asked.

"And the creek. And the mud," Tim answered.

She approached him and sat down on the coffee table and eyed the wound.

"It looks infected," she said matter-of-factly.

"Tough shit, Kelly," Jake said.

"Hush," Josie said. "I'll need to clean it out. I have some remedies. You stay there."

Jake was bored.

He supposed it was from coming off all the adrenaline of running, but he was tired, bored and keyed up, all at the same time. It reminded him how he felt every time he got off a bucking horse, every time he sat on a bull in the chute waiting for it to go.

In those days, he'd end up under the covers with Darla until he was spent and sated, the adrenaline gone and replaced with something far different. He'd tried since he left Vegas to replace her with others, but it hadn't been the same.

He wanted to run some more now, but he wasn't so eager to get outside in the dark with everything. He might be a Southern boy, but he wasn't a swamp kid, that was for sure. Give him horses over gators any day.

The girl went into the kitchen, rummaging around in cupboards, and Jake had no idea what she was up to.

"You got any smokes?" Jake asked.

"I don't smoke," she said. "Jean-René does, or maybe he did, I don't know now. He may have some lying around. Try the desk."

Jake managed to find a broken Pall Mall and a pristine Lucky Strike. He gave Tim the broken one.

"So you're brother's in the joint for a legit reason, huh?"

"Depends on who you ask," she said. Jake watched her bang and mash things together, and she filled up a kettle and put it on the wood stove sitting in the kitchen. He wondered if she was putting something together for Tim.

It kind of burned him that she wasn't paying a lick of attention to him. Tim had talked to her like an injured kitten when she had the gun on him, and since he'd talked her out of shooting them, she directed all her questions at Tim, like he was in charge or something.

110

"What's that mean, 'depends on who you ask?'" Jake said. "You said he beat up a cop, did he or didn't he?"

"Drop it, Jake," Tim said, his voice low.

Jake looked over at him, irritated, and went into the kitchen. Kelly had his foot up on the table and instructions to stay put, and for some reason, Jake knew he'd do it. Maybe it was the way Kelly cradled his arm. Jake had noticed it was in pretty bad shape too. Kelly always was a pain in the ass, but if he was going to slow things down, both of them would be back in that prison in no time.

"Come on, did he do it or not?" Jake asked, moving into the kitchen. She was mashing up some kind of herb.

"Yeah, he did. Beat up Charlie Hickom so bad he didn't wake up for two days," she said.

"What'd he do that for?" Jake asked. He leaned against the wall, watching her. She had more lanterns lit in the kitchen, and he could see her a little better.

She wasn't exactly pretty, but she didn't look like anyone else he'd ever seen. Her hair was curly and wild, a strange reddish blonde, and it looked like she rarely dragged a comb through it. Her lips were full and pursed, like she was always evaluating what someone said and found it all to be bullshit.

She had long dark lashes though, and the way they swept toward the ground whenever she was being evasive was taking Jake for a ride. Her eyes were a light blue, and he could see countless freckles dotting her face. She had a thick Cajun accent, but looked like an Irish girl.

She hadn't answered his question.

"I said, what'd he beat the cop up for?" Jake asked.

"Drop it, Jake," Tim said again from the other room.

"You should listen to your friend," she said.

"He ain't my friend." Jake sauntered further into the kitchen. She had stoked the wood stove full of wood and flames crackled brightly in it, the air in the room warm. Their underwear was drying on a rack near the fire.

He still couldn't figure out what she was doing with all the stuff on the counter.

He got closer to her. Despite her unkempt looks, he thought she smelled like lemon.

Her gaze darted over to him, suspicious and wary. Her forehead was creased.

"You gonna answer the question or what?"

"If it ever becomes your business I will," she said. She wrapped something up in cheesecloth.

111

He didn't like the fact she was avoiding the question. She could be lying to them both. Maybe she'd alerted the sheriff somehow when she'd gone outside to fix that damn pen. They hadn't come all this way to be traded to the sheriff easy as pie, and Kelly wasn't thinking. He trusted women too easily and that was his biggest mistake.

Jake reached out and took her by the wrist, aiming to turn her towards him and get her to talk.

Just as his hand closed around her wrist, she shoved him. He saw a flash of metal and leaned out of the way just as she slashed downward with the knife, narrowly missing the side of head.

"What the hell?!"

He grabbed for her, nicking his finger on the knife, but managing to grab one of her wrists. She tried to knee him in the groin, and he twisted her around to get hold of her before she could gut stab him.

Kelly finally got off his ass and got into the fray, but Jake wasn't prepared for what he did. He wrenched them both apart, then socked Jake right in the jaw.

He stumbled back against the counter.

"What the hell did you do that for? She was the one trying to knife me, if you hadn't noticed."

Kelly had an arm out, warding the girl off. She had the knife in her hand, the right way this time, and breathed heavily, her eyes darting side to side, like she expected someone else to jump out of the shadows at any second.

"He's alright," Tim said, his voice low. "Don't worry about him."

"You got a real problem, Kelly," Jake said.

The girl still held the knife, jittery as hell. Kelly talk to her like an injured kitten again. If he had the opportunity he'd just knock her out and call it a day.

"You don't have to worry about him," Tim said. "He's not gonna hurt you. He's just got bad manners."

"Fuck you, Kelly."

Jake was wary as he watched her. Kelly talked to her like he would a scared kid, keeping his voice low. Jake had a sick feeling in the pit of his stomach.

Kelly's voice got like that only once. Jake was at Rett's taking a room for the night and he'd opened up the closet in the room Rett gave him and found Carolyn West holed up in there with a swollen eye.

She hadn't responded to a word he said.

She wouldn't come out, wouldn't talk, and he knew Rett wouldn't be any good at dealing with her. He'd fetched Kelly from downstairs, and he talked to her like he was talking to this girl, his voice low and calm.

He swallowed hard. Like his voice had been when he comforted Ruby after the tornado. Talking down terror.

Carolyn had climbed out of the closet and hung onto Kelly like a little kid. There were rumours about what her home life was like as a kid, and the old man she kept away from. She got fired from almost every job she held, couldn't afford to live on her own and skipped from boyfriend to boyfriend to stay out of that house, and everyone talked about why.

Kelly swept her out of Rett's like it was on fire, and she managed to look Jake in the eye as she left. He wished she hadn't. He'd never forgotten the look in Carolyn's eyes.

Josie's looked like that now, only there was panic there along with abject fear.

"Just put the knife down," Kelly said to Josie.

She hesitated, and Jake took a breath.

"I didn't mean nothing by it," he muttered.

She looked from him to Tim, who nodded at her, and she put the knife down on the counter, staring at it.

"First thing in the morning, I'm outta here," Jake said, feeling sick.

He didn't want to know why her brother was in prison anymore. He knew, and he didn't want to hear it. All he wanted was to get back to Vegas and figure out how to cover his Outfit debt and get back to Darla.

He picked the cigarette out from behind his ear, looked around for a pack of matches and headed for the front porch.

The cabin was empty. Roundtree was relieved.

There was no sign anyone had been here for awhile, and the dogs weren't getting any hits. Hickom was nervous and wanted to head back to the last place the dogs got a hit, but Roundtree was trying to keep him occupied.

"We may as well head up to the Tourgis place," he said. "You know Simeon is always setting out traps, if he saw something it could help us out. This is just the first cabin, they wouldn't be dumb enough to stop at the first one."

"Tourgis don't got a phone either, not like he could call it in," Lee said.

Roundtree nodded. His radio crackled.

"Gimme a sit rep." Roundtree was surprised to hear Warden Striker's voice instead of the Sheriff's.

Roundtree hesitated before hitting his radio. "Clear at the first cabin we checked. Heading on to the next, we know it's inhabited."

"Find those sons of bitches," the warden said. "No one escapes from my prison."

No, no one did. Roundtree suspected plenty of them left, but mostly went straight into the ground. He couldn't handle it if this went the same way.

Somehow it was different—he'd dealt with these prisoners, saw their rap sheets, brought them their food—hell, he'd driven them right to the prison. He could've let them out anywhere along the way and let them find a way back to Nevada, but he'd taken them straight to the lion's den. He should've brought their stuff, given it to them and let them out on the side of the road and told MacGregor they got the jump on him.

The feel of their truck keys in his back pocket encouraged him. He had to make up for it somehow.

They pushed on through the bush, their flashlights cutting a swath through the swampy land. It took about twenty minutes to find the Tourgis place. He could hear a shortwave radio playing inside. Most of the bayou cabins didn't have electricity, and that worked for and against them. It meant anyone who spotted an escapee had to travel somewhere to get access to a phone or radio to let someone know. All that time meant escapees could get further away. Usually that was a problem, but not tonight.

On the other hand, there was no way to warn Josie Landry. She had no radio, no television and no neighbours. She wouldn't have a clue a prison break had even taken place. If those escapees showed up there, she'd probably kill them and anyone else who happened onto her property. If she had a phone, Roundtree could've called and told her to get to safety.

So many "if only's" and not enough results.

"Haven't seen a thing out here, I guarantee," Tourgis said. "Got my traps set, nothing set 'em off, not even possum."

Hickom searched inside, while Lee took the outbuildings, which included an outhouse and a shed.

Roundtree took the chance to figure out a plan. There were other cabins further on.

"Mr. Tourgis, if these prisoners bypassed your cabin, maybe because you were home, where do you think they'd go next?"

"There's a hunting blind," he said. "About twenty minutes due south. It's up higher ground, but big enough for four men. Built real solid. If it was me, I'd go there."

"What if you weren't experienced in the outdoors?" Hickom asked, joining them. "Where'd you go then? Cuz chances are these guys aren't gonna even be able to spot a hunting blind."

He thought for a moment. "Probably to the southwest. There's an abandoned cabin. You gotta take the crick to get there, big gator nesting area later in the year, but clear now. If they took the crick, they'd come right up on it. It's got a boat even though no one live there."

Roundtree was about to mention they could have talked to locals before they left, but he didn't want the deputies to remember they saw Jean René

Landry at the prison work site. If his name got in their thoughts, it would get them thinking about Josie.

"I think the hunting blind's a good bet," Roundtree lied. "These kids are smart, and I bet they'd do some research before they left about where to go. And that boat might be tempting too. Maybe more than a hunting blind."

"The dogs haven't had a hit in a long time," Hickom argued.

"They need a rest, anyhow," Gil said. "Go check your blind, I'll let 'em rest, and we'll track back when you get here."

These guys wouldn't spend hours in the creek, and they'd have no way to get up in a hunting blind chained to each other, but as long as Hickom wasn't putting that together, he didn't mind going through the creek himself.

It was after ten, closing in on eleven. He figured if these guys were smart they'd hole up somewhere. The bayou was no place to travel through at night, even if you were a local. Even so, they'd have to start moving first thing in the morning. He hoped they knew what they were doing.

Josie had put the knife down, but she trembled like a leaf. Jake hadn't helped much by antagonizing her, and Tim was relieved when he heard the screen door bang as he went to the front porch.

"He's gone now," Tim said, his voice low. "Nothing to worry about."

"I'm not worried, cher," she said, her voice shaky and thin.

"I think you are," Tim said. "I think maybe you should sit down."

"I don't need to sit down, I'm just fine!"

He didn't push it. He tried another tack. "I got a sister myself. I woulda done the same thing as your brother."

She looked at him, then at the ground. "Y'all need to move on in the morning, or they'll find you here. They'll come looking."

"What about you?" Tim asked.

"I'll be ready for them."

"Are you sure?" Tim asked. "I mean, you were trying your hardest, but Jake had one up on you. If these guys come, it'll be more than one of them, right? How can you fend them all off?"

She shook, and he saw a tear work its way down her face. She brushed it away angrily.

"I have the shotgun. I'll kill them all if I have to."

She shook more noticeably now, and Tim moved near her. She almost lost her legs out from under her as he braced her arm by holding it lightly. Tim stretched over and pulled one of the little wooden chairs toward her and she collapsed into it, her body shaking uncontrollably.

"Why did you have to come here?" she said miserably. "They're going to come back and they're going to do it again!"

He was quiet for a moment, watching this tough little chick breakdown.

"Think of it this way. If we didn't come here, you wouldn't even know they were out searching, right? They woulda taken you by surprise. Now you got the upper hand."

She looked up at him, her eyes rimmed red and bloodshot. She nodded slowly.

"Go sit down," she said, her voice hoarse. "Rest your leg. I'll have this ready soon."

He was about to tell her to stay put and calm down, but she was already up at the counter, making whatever she was making like nothing had happened.

Tim left her.

Tim went out onto the front porch, striking a match on the door frame to light the mangled cigarette Jake had given him.

Jake sat on an old chair, his bare feet up on the railing. The tip of his cigarette glowed in the dark.

"I think she was raped by those deputies last prison break," Tim said. "No, I don't think. I know. You just freaked her out is all."

"I know it," Jake said morosely. "Fucking cops."

"A girl living alone out here in a cabin and those sheriff's deputies come by. Sure as hell didn't tuck her in and read her a bedtime story."

Jake snorted. Tim watched him, Jake deep in thought.

Tim enjoyed his smoke for a few minutes, listening to all the strange noises in the bayou.

"Which ones do you think it was?" Jake asked.

"She didn't seem to hate that Roundtree guy, my best guess is he wasn't involved. For all I know the sheriff himself could've done it."

"Nah," Jake said. "I bet he can't get it up."

Tim laughed. Jake was probably right.

"They're gonna come here looking eventually."

"Yeah, well good for them. We'll be long gone." Jake looked him up and down. "Or I will be."

"They'll come here, and she'll be here."

"I think she can take care of herself. She'll probably blow their heads off the minute she sees them. She almost got me with that knife, man. They should be worried," Jake said.

"It'll be her against them; I don't think she'll win."

Jake took another drag, then paused and looked over at Tim.

"What are you saying?" he asked.

Tim shrugged. "I'm not saying anything."

"I sure as hell ain't sticking around here like the fucking Lone Ranger and Tonto," he said. "We're taking off first thing and getting the hell outta here. I'm not playing protector to some broad who held a gun on me and tried to gut me. Forget that."

"We don't have to stick around here." Tim took a drag and blew a few smoke rings. "But I don't think she can stay here."

Jake got up. "You're crazy. We are not bringing her with us. No way."

"We don't have a choice, Jake."

"We do too got a choice, and I choose that she's not coming." Jake ran a hand through his hair. "You can't save everyone, you know."

He couldn't save his own sister or mother; he was well aware of that. But he'd helped Lupe, and he thought he could do something about this, and that thought kept him focused.

"Yeah, well maybe you don't get to choose," Tim said. "She's coming."

Jake looked at him. "Then maybe I'm gonna head out on my own. I have a feeling I'll be outta here in no time while you drag Psycho Sally through the bayou."

"Don't be an asshole, Jake," Tim said. "Would you leave Darla here? Would you want someone else to leave her here?"

"Don't talk about Darla. She's dead to me."

"Sure," Tim agreed. "I believe you."

Jake blew a steady stream of smoke out of the side of his mouth, toward Tim.

"Didn't think you were the type to let stuff like this happen."

"Nothing's happened," Jake said. "And nothing will. She'll take care of it. There's nothing we can do unless you want to get caught. You deal with it. I'll be outta your hair in the morning."

Jake stubbed his cigarette out and went back into the house.

12

When Tim came back inside, Josie told him to sit down and put his leg up. He did as he was told.

She held a rag with some chipped ice in it against his leg for a few minutes and then came at him with the bolt cutters, working them between his flesh and the metal. It took awhile, but finally the shackle was clipped off and fell to the floor. He winced in pain as it fell off.

Jake came inside a moment later, glanced at the proceedings and went into the bedroom, shutting the door on them.

"Sorry," Tim said nodding toward the door, "if he's stolen your bed."

"I'll stay on the couch. It's alright."

"He didn't mean anything by it today."

"I know." She sat down on the coffee table and pulled a lantern close.

She lifted his leg up and placed it over a bowl, dousing his leg with clean water and washing out the wound.

When she was done, she dried his leg off, then brought out something steaming in another bowl.

"What's that?" he asked, realizing how hungry he was.

"Poultice," she said. "It'll help with the infection and the pain."

She unwrapped the cheesecloth and showed him the mash of what looked like herbs of some kind. It smelled a bit like orange or lemon, something citrus-like. She covered it with cheesecloth again, then wrapped the whole thing around his leg. It stung.

"What is it?" he asked.

"Bee balm."

"What's that?" He took a deep breath—the smell was really nice.

"It's a plant," she said. "When it's dried it's good for an antiseptic and to help with wounds. Rest for a minute with this on. I'm making a crawfish étouffée."

"What's that?"

118

"Crawfish simmered in a roux."

"What's a roux?"

She smiled. "You really aren't from around here, cher. A roux is a sauce. A dark one. Some onions and oil and flour. Crawfish simmers in it. Pour it over rice, c'est bon."

Tim grinned. "What's that mean?"

"It means it's good."

"I think anything'd be good right now."

She nodded. "It'll be ready soon. How's your leg?"

"Better." He glanced up at her. "Got anything for mosquito bites?"

She nodded, then returned a moment later with another paste, this one a pale green.

"Basil and baking powder mixed with water."

He removed the plaid shirt and turned to the side. She slathered the mixture on the bites, and he felt some relief.

He leaned back and closed his eyes. He was bone tired, and they weren't even close to being done yet. He rested, listening to sounds from the kitchen. He watched with half-open eyes as she took a bowl of food into the bedroom, then came back, shutting the door behind her. Maybe if Jake got some food into him he'd wake up and smell the coffee.

They couldn't leave her here. Those cops would show up, and even if the square one was with them, the guy never stopped to help out him or Jake, so Tim had no faith he'd stop anything that happened to her.

He opened her eyes when he heard her approach. She held out a chipped bowl to him. It was steaming and smelled great. Suddenly he was ravenous.

He hadn't ever had crawfish to his knowledge, but he couldn't remember having anything better. She got him seconds before she'd even tucked in to her helping.

"They don't feed you much inside, do they, cher?" she asked.

"No," Tim said. "Morning meal and evening meal, that's it. Water on the chain gang. It's not human. What they're doing out there isn't human."

He looked at her for a second.

"I got some papers with me you might wanna see," he said. He reached into the waist band of the jeans and pulled out the folded papers he'd rescued from the jumpsuit. Some of the ink had run on one of the handwritten statements he'd taken from the MacGregor file, but the other papers seemed to be okay. He unfolded them carefully—they were still damp and were difficult to unfold.

"What are they?" she asked.

"This is a map of the prison grounds. These markings up here, the x's? I think I figured out what they are. Some of the other prisoners mentioned men that were killed on the inside. I think they were buried here," he said. "See down here, this hallway? Leads to an area I've been told houses a drug operation the warden's running."

"Doesn't surprise me," she said. "He is lower than low."

"I saw him, I think, shoot one of the prisoners one day. A guy that tried to escape. Can't prove it was him, I didn't get a good look. If it wasn't him, it was a guard who did it. Only problem was, the guy wasn't running or anything. He went out in a laundry truck, they caught him and brought him back. The guy was cuffed, and he was shot point blank."

"I tried to write Jean-René best I could. He doesn't get the letters, does he?"

Tim shook his head. "Dunno. Not that he said."

"He sent me a few, but they stopped suddenly a few months ago."

Tim grimaced. "He mentioned it. Was sending them out on the laundry truck. Striker found out."

"What did he do?"

Tim hesitated.

"Tell me," she said. "It can't be any worse than what I imagine."

"He had marks around his wrists. He said Striker hung him from something for a few days. The restraints cut into him pretty bad."

"Torture," she whispered. "It's all men like Striker know. I wish I could feed them all to the gators!"

"These might help you, then," Tim said.

He spread out the other sheets, some of the type faded from the water. She leaned over to try and read them, her fingers splayed out across the pages. She looked for awhile, and Tim realized she was having trouble reading some of the memos.

"They're bank statements and memos," he said. "Striker's been making regular payments to MacGregor. Over here, that one's a handwritten note from MacGregor. The ink ran a bit, but you can still make it out."

"What does he say?"

She concentrated for a few minutes, using her finger to scan the words, and by the speed Tim wondered if she'd gone to school.

"See, right here?" he pointed to the words. "It says campaign contributions. It's a paper trail of money flowing between the two. In some ways what it says isn't important for you, but it needs to get to someone who can use it to blow all this wide open."

"Like a newspaper or a radio or television station?"

"Yeah," Tim said. "That's the idea. Get it to someone who can't help but publish it. Someone in another town, even. You don't know who's in his pocket in Strikersville."

"It isn't so much in his pocket than who thinks Striker is a saviour. When he took over the prison, he expanded it and hired a lot of locals to work as guards and in office positions. He saved the town."

"Now he's killing it." Tim was quiet for a moment. "You ever been to school?"

"Oh, a long time ago," she said. "My mother taught me at home for a long time. She died years ago."

"What happened?"

"A hunter shot her," she said. "We were picking berries. A poacher was trying to get a gator."

"Someone mistook your mother for a gator?"

"You see the same problem I do," she said. "Nothing ever made sense. They questioned the man that did it, but I don't think anything ever came of it. I was young. I don't remember much. Never knew who it was."

"Where's your old man?"

"Prison, north of here. For good reason. When it comes down to it, I suppose Jean-René is there for good reason, too. He's a good brother. He's eight years older, so he's very protective. You won't see anyone more protective, I guarantee."

He thought of Diana. He wasn't quite sure about that. He'd do anything to protect her, but he was failing at it. He understood how Johnny Ray ended up where he did.

"We'll head out first thing in the morning," he said. He hesitated before speaking again. "You should come with us."

She raised an eyebrow. "What on earth for? I live here. Who would take care of this place? Of Gummy?"

"They'll come looking here eventually you know," Tim said. "Why be here when they do?"

"So I can kill them," she said. "I've been waiting for something like this. A chance. I can defend my property."

"You know as well as I do what'll happen," Tim said. "They'll shoot you down in cold blood and paint it like it was all your fault and you attacked them, or they'll haul you in and arrest you, and you'll end up in a prison somewhere. Either way they'll win."

"Either way they'll be dead. No worries for me."

She didn't look likely to change her mind. When morning came, he didn't have a choice, he had to get out and get moving again, or they were going to end up right back where they started.

"Keep these," he said, leaving the papers with her. "Hide them somewhere, then use them when you can, especially if we don't make it out of here."

He held back the files on him and Jake.

She nodded. "You should rest. It's late."

She took the poultice off his leg. It was red from the warmth of the poultice and didn't look much better than before, but it felt better. She bandaged it up and glanced at his wrist.

"I think I sprained it when we fell," he said. "It won't kill me."

She nodded again, then stood up and took their dishes and things into the kitchen, filling a large metal tub with water to soak them. He had no idea how she could survive out here without running water or a shower, but she seemed to do okay.

He got up and walked toward the bedroom door.

"Goodnight," he said.

She didn't reply.

Roundtree was out of ideas.

They searched the hunting blind and another abandoned cabin after reaching it a half hour later. There was no sign anyone had been there in years. The boat tied up at the cabin had sunk, and the dock was so rotted it had given way when they stood on it and dumped all three of them into the water.

It was dark and everyone was soaked to the bone.

"We need to go back where the dogs last got a hit and regroup," Hickom said. "Those little bastards probably went across the river. They could have a whole day on us by now. We'll bring a boat in and go over."

Hickom tried his radio, but it wouldn't connect—the dunk in the river had fried all their radios.

"The river's too dangerous," Roundtree countered. "They'd be stupid to try it, and if I remember right, they're chained together. Those chains could drown them."

"I don't like that they're getting a lead on us chained together," Lee said. "How do you think that makes us look? We ain't chained together, and we can't even find them."

"Maybe they found somebody to take 'em outta here." Hickom said.

"Like who?" Lee asked. "Most folks around here shoot first and ask questions later."

Hickom was poking at the ground with a stick.

"Josie Landry might," Hickom said.

Roundtree looked up, hoping the darkness concealed the panic on his face.

Lee laughed. "Woooo, that is one spitfire of a girl. Left scratches all down my back, I ever tell you that?"

Hickom joined in the laughter. "That little broad sure does hate us. She'd help them in a heartbeat if she knew they were coming her way."

"They wouldn't be dumb enough to cross the river," Roundtree said, trying to steady his voice. "I'm thinking they went south, straight through the night, they're not stopping. They'd know we have dogs out, I bet they're in the water so they lose the scent. They could reach Bellefleur by morning, boost a car and be outta here."

"Man's got a point. Dogs haven't hit anything in awhile."

"Maybe cuz they went across the river," Hickom said. "We can call the sheriff, tell him to get some men down here to go south with the dogs. We can go across the river."

Roundtree was panicked.

"I'll go back and let the sheriff know," he said. "We can't call him on account of the radios. I'll let him know, and we can get a boat in the water."

"There's another cabin about five minutes from here, we'll check it then meet you back where Gil Pender is at the Tourgis place. We can all go over," Hickom said.

Roundtree nodded, unsure if the men could even tell that's what he was doing, and he turned and began the walk back toward the Tourgis place. As soon as he was out of sight of the cabin, he began to run through the bayou, not caring what was out there.

He had to reach the other side of the river first.

Tim slept for an hour, maybe two, and was woken by something—maybe Jake snoring. Maybe it was the sound of everything out the window, frogs croaking, crickets chirping, the groan of that damn alligator. Everything sounded alien to his ears.

Maybe it was the knowledge the sheriff was on his way that woke him.

He knew they were searching, and he knew they weren't going to give up looking for them. He hoped they'd bring those dogs with them—you could hear them before you saw them, and that gave them valuable time.

He saw a light move under the door, and heard the couch cushions creak.

He wouldn't be able to sleep the rest of the night. As soon as the sun started to rise, they needed to move.

He tossed the covers off and stood up, wincing at the pain in his ankle. He limped toward the door and opened it, glancing back at Jake's sleeping form. That asshole could sleep through a tornado.

Josie sat on the couch, a blanket in her lap, and the shotgun on top of it. She glanced up when the door opened. He limped out and shut it behind him.

"Your leg," she said.

He shook his head. "Dunno what's wrong with it."

She cleared a place on the couch and he sat down, swinging his leg up onto the table. It hurt like hell.

She rolled up the pant leg. He'd slept in the jeans, just in case they needed to make a quick getaway in the night.

"Infection is coming out," she said. "Always gets worse before it gets better. I'll make another poultice. Plantain, bee balm and lemon balm I think this time."

She went to work in the kitchen, stoking the fire in the small wood stove and preparing things. She reminded him of a witch; all she was missing was the pointy hat and cauldron.

She brought the warm poultice for his leg again, and he winced as she put it on.

"You may not be able to go far today," she said. "Will your friend leave without you? I heard him say he would."

"He's not my friend. And yeah, he probably will."

"Why isn't he your friend? You must have been traveling together if you got thrown into Strikersville together."

"We were . . . doing a business deal. He needed money, I needed the product, and . . . well, it just happened."

"What kind of business?" she asked, giving him the side eye.

He smiled. "The kind that's on the wrong side of the law, but I think you figured that out awhile ago."

She hid her smile. "You two don't like each other much."

"What gave it away? The swearing or the name calling?"

"Neither," she said. "He resents you, and you hate him. I see it on your faces. Yet . . . you worked together to get this far. It's interesting."

"I have good reason to hate him."

"What did he do?"

He looked over at her and then stared into the kitchen. "He . . . he slept with the girl I was seeing."

"You should hate her too. But you don't."

"I want to."

She nodded. "So do you do these illegal things together? Or on your own?"

"I have some guys that run with me."

She pursed her lips. "Not like the gang of sheriff's deputies that run around here I hope."

"Nothing like it," Tim said.

She smiled at that.

He noticed his leg felt better, even though the swelling was worse, probably from the heat.

"So he needed your money, and you didn't trust him to go alone."

Tim nodded. "That's about the size of it. I thought he'd robbed that gas station, but I know he didn't now."

"Tommy MacGregor?" she asked. She shook her head when Tim nodded. "He's weak. They'll use him for whatever they need. If you hadn't stopped, maybe you wouldn't be sitting here right now."

"Yeah, and I'd have the truck and the load we were hauling home. As it is I'm out a grand."

Her eyes widened.

"And Jake?"

"Out just as much."

"So you're cut from the same cloth and have the same problem now."

Tim looked over at her. "He's nothing like me."

"I don't suppose many people are."

She still had a hand on the shotgun.

"You sleep with that thing every night?" he asked.

She smiled, but there was nothing happy or light about it. "Yes. I'm waiting. Always waiting."

"Hell of a way to live," he said.

"What else would you have me do, cher?" she asked. "I was caught once not ready for them, it won't happen again."

She got up as a kettle began to whistle and came back with a steaming cup of coffee, black. She handed it to him.

"How'd you know I take it black?" he asked.

"I can't imagine you with sweet coffee, cher."

He sipped it, burning his tongue on the first sip.

She resumed her place on the couch, the gun in her lap. Her coffee was light, more milk than coffee.

"How long ago were they here?" he asked.

"Almost a year," she said.

"Did you ever tell anybody?"

"Just Jean-René. You see how well that turned out."

"You didn't go to a hospital or anything?"

"And say what, cher?" she asked. "Tell them two deputies raped me in my own house? Tell them the three prison escapees didn't scare me at all, but the police who live in my town do? No one would have believed me. No one would have done anything. Don't you understand? There is no one to tell."

She was probably right. He remembered seeing a few cops beat a guy in one of the holding cells so bad they'd broken his jaw. One of the guys in the drunk tank had complained to high heaven, and he'd been silenced with a night stick. The cops all stuck up for each other.

"You should come with us," he said.

"I can't, I told you, cher," she said. "I've been waiting for this for a long time."

"It's not going to fix anything, Josie," he said. "You blow holes in every one of them and turn them into gator chow, it's not going to make a lick of difference in how you feel. Maybe for a little while, but not for keeps. You'll still be hurting, your brother will still be in prison, and you'll be locked up with nothing but a lot of time to think over what happened. It's not going to fix anything."

"Running away with you, that will?" She looked over at him and pulled on her hair. "I was too scared then, and this time will be different."

"This time they can still hurt you. Don't give them the chance."

"It's funny a man like you is telling me to run."

"I'm not saying run for keeps. Just come with us until we know it's safe."

She looked at him, her eyes narrowing. "You only want me to come to show you the way out of here, get you somewhere safe, save your own behind."

"The thought occurred to me."

"You're just as bad as they are."

"Hey," he said, his voice sharp. "That's not a comparison I think is fair or right. Fact is, we'll find our way out of here with or without you. It'll be faster with you. But I'm not the one headed here with bad thoughts on my mind. I'm not the one you gotta worry about."

She turned and looked straight ahead, almost caressing the gun.

"Josie, don't let them beat you like this."

"Go to bed, Tim," she said wearily. "The sun will be up in an hour or two. You'll need to be rested when you leave."

She got up and took the poultice off his leg. He watched her for a minute, her back to him, then he limped back to the bed. He stared at the ceiling until the sun began to rise.

Tuesday, March 28, 1967

Jake woke up to the sound of some kind of bird screeching outside. He'd slept okay—better than crashing out in a barn or a car somewhere—but a part of his brain hadn't let him sleep too deeply in case they had to run.

He looked over at the other bed, and Kelly was curled up like a little kid. He knew Kelly wasn't going to drop it about taking the chick with them.

Personally, Jake thought she'd do just fine on her own. She was ornery, like Midnight Bandit when Rett first brought him back after he won him in a card game. He could see she'd probably blow those cops' heads off the minute they got close.

Even if the cops got the jump on her, she wouldn't let them leave this place still breathing. She'd be just fine on her own.

Kelly was the bigger problem. He could see plain as day he was in bad shape, but like the asshole he was, he was playing it off like it was nothing. They'd get into the brush and Kelly would start to slow and keep them both from getting away. They'd be killed or thrown back into that prison and never see the light of day again. He was a selfish bastard.

Kelly couldn't admit he was toast, and that was going to screw them both over.

There was a reason he always kept to himself and didn't trust anyone, and that was because trusting someone meant you were beholden to them. You were tied to someone else and they had the power to change the direction of your life.

Kelly had that power now, and it burned him. If Kelly was any kind of a leader he'd let Jake go, tell him to find his way to help of some kind, and take what was coming like a man.

Jake turned away from the window.

Of course, the cops probably weren't going to let Kelly get more than two steps without shooting him dead.

He shouldn't have a care in the world about what happened to Kelly, but some terrible part of him knew this was all his fault. He hadn't done anything to get the sheriff's attention, but the fact they were out this way at all was because of his Outfit debt and his need to be with Darla, and Kelly didn't have anything to do with that.

Kelly probably should've just murdered him on the spot and got it over with, but he'd thrown in money and jumped on board with Jake. He wouldn't have done it if their positions were reversed.

Still. Kelly should know better—at least one of them had to get out of here, or it was all a waste. Kelly couldn't play hero to everyone, and that's all he seemed to be interested in doing.

Jake stoked the fire of his anger enough to convince himself leaving was the right move. He tossed back the covers. Josie had left their now-dry underwear on the dresser, and he pulled his on, then the borrowed jeans and shirt. It looked like the sun had just started to rise, and he could better see what was around the cabin. It looked like she'd been telling the truth about no phones or anything.

He opened the bedroom door and saw Josie asleep on the couch, a shotgun in her hand.

"Hey," he said. "You awake?"

He hung back near the door, watching her stir and a little afraid she'd go bonkers and fire the gun.

"I'm awake." She struggled to a sitting position. She lay the gun across the coffee table. "I can make coffee. Before you go."

He nodded. He'd need something to keep him awake. "Food too, if you got it."

She nodded and went into the kitchen, and he sat down on the couch.

His entire body ached. There was stiffness in his muscles that was different from the stiffness he felt working on the chain gang. It was worse than the aches and pains he got from rodeo riding, too. They used so many other muscles running he felt like there were ones he didn't even know about hurting.

His thigh was badly bruised on one side and his own ankle was chaffed from the shackle, but overall he couldn't complain.

He wandered into the small kitchen, watching her set the kettle down on the woodstove. She made him nervous. He had no idea what to say to her.

"You always live out here?"

She nodded. "Was born here."

She worked efficiently, never looking back at him. He needed her to look at him.

He got in her way when she moved to the woodstove. She looked up at him, her eyes large and mistrustful. He made sure not to touch her, afraid of what her eyes would say if he did.

"Didn't mean anything by it."

She looked at him, sizing him up. The corner of her mouth quirked up—he couldn't really call it a smile. "I know."

He nodded at her, then moved out of her way. Something about her odd smile reminded him of his mother suddenly, and it made him angry.

"You should stick together," she said. "It's your best chance."

Jake snorted. "Kelly's on his own. At least if one of us gets out of here, the other has a chance. If he slows me down, we'll both be caught. No good in that. It'll be harder for them to track the two of us apart."

He left out the part where he knew Tim would drag her along, and he couldn't stand to look at her. He didn't want to risk that thing—that look in her eyes—chasing him all the way out of the bayou. It took him long enough to forget Carolyn's eyes that day.

He wandered back to the living room.

The bedroom door creaked open, and Kelly limped out. Jake noticed right away, although it looked like Kelly tried to hide it.

"Don't tell me you're crippled," Jake said. "Because if you are, we're definitely going our separate ways."

"What time is it?" Kelly asked, ignoring Jake.

"Five-thirty," Josie said. "It'll be light enough for you to move in an hour. For now, stay indoors."

"We really gotta move," Tim said. "I can feel they're coming."

"I ain't going nowhere with you until I see what's up with your leg. I can see you limping, Kelly."

"It's nothing."

Jake looked at Josie who just shrugged and went back to the kitchen.

Kelly sat down on the couch.

"I ain't kidding," Jake said. "If you can't move, then you're the thing that's gonna get us caught. The dogs'll be on you in a hot second. If I can get out of here, I can get you out."

"Right, because you're gonna come back and tear that place apart to find me?" Tim asked. "Fat chance."

Jake grabbed for Tim's leg.

"You wanna keep your hands to yourself?" Kelly asked.

Tim rolled up the cuff of his jeans and Jake cringed. The skin was swollen and an angry red. The shackles had rubbed Kelly's skin raw and the wound oozed.

"It's fine."

"It's probably gangrene," Jake said.

"Fuck you."

"It's not gangrene," Josie said. "But he needs to be careful. He needs to stay out of the water."

"No can do," Tim said. "We gotta get outta here. If they bring the dogs to this side, we're in trouble. Staying in the water's the best way to avoid them."

"Best way to meet a gator, too," Josie said.

"Which is why you could be of help to us," Kelly said. "You know this place, it'll be faster with you."

Jake took the cup of coffee Josie offered, and took a bite of buttered bread she gave him. He drank his coffee with a bunch of sugar, but he didn't enjoy it. Josie hadn't responded to Tim's offer either way, and that was the only hope he had.

Kelly would mess everything up. First he convinced him to run off the chain gang when working for Striker would've been the better deal, and now Kelly was crippled and barely able to walk. He was going to screw up everything for them. There wasn't a chance in hell Jake was going to walk through a Louisiana bayou with Tim Kelly on his back. They'd both be back in that prison in no time, so he had to make it out first.

He had to make it out alone. She was not coming with them.

"You can't even walk," Jake said. He finished the last of his coffee. "You're gonna slow me down."

"Your brain slows you down," Tim said. "We gotta stick together. It's the only way we're gonna get out of this."

He stared at the girl when he said it. Trust Tim to be thinking about playing rescuer to some girl when they had a posse on their tails. He needed to focus on the fact he was a liability and bringing her along was going to make things worse.

"If we stick together, we're gonna get caught," Jake said. "It's better if at least one of us makes it back. We can blow the lid off this place and everything's fixed. We don't need any help. I get out of here, and I'll wait around 'til they haul you back and run their cars off the road."

"With what?" Tim asked. "You really think they're taking me back? Dammit, Jake, we need to stick together."

Jake tried to pace his nerves off. There was no way in hell he could tell Kelly the broad creeped him out. If the asshole would just drop the Lone Ranger routine, then maybe he could stand trying to help Kelly through the bayou, injured as he was. They might not have to go their separate ways. The girl would shoot those deputies, and they'd be home free.

"So that's it, huh?" Tim asked. "You're gonna leave me here?"

"I don't got a choice, you're lame, and I can't drag you through the bayou. I told you how things were. You could've changed your mind."

"I can move just fine," Tim countered. "I'm not lame."

"You can't even swim!" Jake countered. "You'll drown before you get two feet into the water."

"This is a mistake, Jake. You ever wonder why your life always goes to hell, it's because you can't make the right decision to save your life."

"Try and convince me you're not a liability," Jake said. He looked over at Josie. "We don't need another shackle trapping us here. I'll see you in Las Vegas, Kelly."

Jake got up and headed to the door, letting the screen bang loudly. He was angry at Kelly. They didn't need to be dragging the girl through the bayou. They needed to get the hell out of here, and Kelly was all about playing Lone Ranger. He was going to lose his chance with Darla, he was going to be on the Outfit's radar until he died . . . all of it was going to hell.

Jake took the path to the right and stalked through the bayou, aiming to make it out of there before noon. Kelly and the chick could fend for themselves.

13

The sheriff paced at the entrance to the woods where they'd set up a command centre of sorts. He hated coming out in the swamp during the night. It was a pain in the ass conducting a search in there anytime of day, but the night was the worst.

He knew Gil Pender probably had his stupid dogs resting—he treated those dogs better than he did his own family—and he was getting impatient.

Striker was on his ass every five minutes, asking him why the hell no progress had been made and where the hell were those loser hoods?

He'd sure like to know where his deputies were. He couldn't raise them on his radio. He didn't think anything had happened to them—those hoods weren't strong enough to take out three sheriff's deputies—but things in the bayou were unpredictable. Someone could've been hurt or injured, the equipment could be down, or they could be in the midst of a major chase through the woods.

Either that or an alligator got them.

He sighed, looking up at the lightening sky. Striker was seething they didn't have them in custody. How two men chained together could outrun and hide from an entire search group was beyond him.

Striker suddenly appeared, manoeuvring around an oak tree.

"Any word?"

"Nothing yet."

"It's been 'nothing yet' for the past four hours," Striker said. "I need these guys captured, and I need it now."

He lit a cigarette and puffed out smoke for a few minutes. MacGregor hated it when the man went to cigarettes. A cigar-smoking Striker was one that was more easily placated. The cigarette smoking version was a bundle of nerves and anger.

"You get these guys," Striker said. "I don't care if you take an M1 Garand and mow 'em down in the middle of the bayou. I want their heads on sticks!"

"We'll find 'em," MacGregor said. "No need to get so excited. They're just like any other escapees."

"No, MacGregor, they're not," Striker growled, moving closer. "One of them—I think the dark-haired one with the messed up face—was left alone in my office. I went over the tape recordings the other day, and it sounds like he searched my desk. So I checked, and he took some files. You wanna know what file? The one with your name on it. That hood ran off from my prison, and he's got fucking insurance. You know what that means?"

It meant that kid could bury him. MacGregor shifted his weight, feeling like his duty gun and belt were going to weigh him right down into the centre of the earth.

"It means we gotta find them hoods," he said, his voice low.

"They get out of this bayou alive, and we're gonna lose everything," Striker said. "Everything!"

MacGregor got on his radio again, but there was no answer. A moment later he spotted Hickom and Lee walking toward them. Behind them came Gil Pender and his exuberant bloodhounds.

"Where the hell have you been and why aren't you answering your radios?"

"We got dumped into the crick back past the Tourgis place," Lee said. "Shorted out the radios. We couldn't radio back, but Roundtree said he'd let you know."

"When? He hasn't been back," MacGregor said.

MacGregor caught the look Hickom and Lee shared.

"We sent him back hours ago," Hickom said. "He said he was coming back here to let you know we didn't find nothing at the Tourgis place or the abandoned cabin, and to get a boat to meet us down river. When he got back we were going to go across the river. We waited on him as long as we could then decided to hike back here and see what the hold up was. Pender needed to feed the dogs anyway."

"He never showed up," MacGregor said.

He sighed and looked at the trees, wondering what the hell Paul Roundtree was up to.

"Where would he have gone?" MacGregor finally asked. "Maybe he found some kind of a clue and took off after them?"

"He probably went across the river," Lee said. "I bet you anything he wanted to go over there and get all the glory for himself."

"He's been gunning for a promotion, hasn't he?" Hickom asked. "Dammit, I knew we shouldn't have let him go. Hell, we shoulda forgot about coming back here and just got over the river ourselves."

MacGregor shifted his weight and then looked over at Striker, who saw the deputies and was coming over for an update. This wasn't going to go well.

Paul Roundtree was going to pay for whatever he was up to—unless he came in with those hoods at the end of a rope.

Tim watched the door after Jake left and sighed.

"He's such a stupid son of a bitch." He took the cup of coffee Josie offered.

"I scare him," Josie said, her eyes focused on the door, her expression understanding.

"Jake's faced things a hell of a lot scarier than a redhead with a shotgun."

He looked at Josie's face, her expression odd. He was reminded of sitting down on the edge of the old mattress in the warehouse, Carolyn asleep on a sleeping bag he'd stolen from the outdoor supply store. Jake had found her at Rett's and didn't speak to him for two weeks after that. Jake never talked to Carolyn anymore, and Tim never realized why until now. He wondered why it bothered Jake so bad. Maybe it reminded him of all the high rollers pawing at Darla.

"He doesn't know what to say," Josie told him. "I see in his eyes he feels . . ."

"Yeah," Tim said, cutting her off. Powerless, angry, sick. He knew it. He didn't know why Jake couldn't face it, and he wasn't going to try and figure it out.

"What are you going to do?" Josie asked. She sat down on the edge of the coffee table and handed him a thick slice of buttered bread.

He shook his head. "Don't know yet. Guess I'm on my own, unless you come with me. I'll move east—where'll that take me?"

"You're between the arms right now. When the water is high, this area is like an island. The water is high on the west arm side right now; it is most of the year," she said. "If you go east you'll reach the east arm. You might think crossing is the best option, but it isn't. You'll be stranded once you reach the Atchafalaya unless you have a boat. Easiest option is reach the arm and follow it south. It meets up with the west arm and then Guidry flows southeast toward the Atchafalaya. Where the arms meet you can swim across and be at the road."

"But no chance to find a car."

"No," she said. "Likely not. I'm not sure anyone would stop to pick you up, either. The good news is Duchenes is close, and that's where they would have taken your car."

"Truck," he supplied. She was probably right about no one picking him up. He didn't look like the most easygoing hitchhiker in the world.

"What about crossing the east arm and going down the Atcha . . . whatever you called it?"

"You'd need a boat. It's a big river, lotsa gator. Not safe for you on a good day and downright stupid with your leg like that. Crossing the east arm won't be much safer. Lots of gator nests that way."

"And if I went back the way we came over?"

"You'll run into them I suspect. Your only chance is go east and south and cross over before they get there, cher."

"What's that mean, anyway? Sha?"

"Cher is a Cajun word, from French, chérie. It's a term of endearment, like honey or sweetie."

Tim huffed out a laugh. "Been a long time since I've been called anything like that."

"Too bad for you," she said, the hint of a smile on her face.

In the light, he could see her hair was a wild mess of strawberry blonde curls and tangled knots. Freckles thickly covered her nose and cheeks, a smattering covering the rest of her face. She still had bare feet, the soles dirty, and Tim wondered if she owed a pair of shoes.

"You're staring," she said.

"How long have you lived out here?" Tim asked.

"Always," she said.

"How long did you stay in school for? You said you went."

"When I was small," she said. "The kids in town, they don't like those of us that live out in the bayou—swamp kids, they call us. They teased us in school. I didn't do so well in class. I can't stay still long enough for anything to reach my head. I'm smart—my mother said so, she taught me and Jean-René at home before she died. I'm not stupid, even if I didn't go to high school."

"Never said you were," Tim said. "I made it through, but barely."

"Really?"

"I know you figure someone with my high intellect probably graduated top of the class, but you'd be wrong."

He could've done better in school, if he'd tried. But he already knew his future didn't lie in academics, so there was no use in it all.

"I like it out here," she said. "I don't like the town. The town is full of poisonous people. The bayou is just filled with gators and snakes. They're easier."

"Amen to that," Tim said.

He laced the prison-issue sneakers. They still squished and his socks were soaked through a moment later.

"You're going now?" she asked.

He thought she sounded regretful about that, and he wondered how often she saw other people.

"There any neighbours around here?"

"Not for miles," she asked. "A few other cabins, but only one inhabited full time. An old hermit, he doesn't do much but stick to his own area. He wouldn't bother you if he saw you, I say you should do him the same courtesy."

"You're sure that boat of yours wouldn't help?"

She frowned at him. "Your leg?"

He nodded. "Jake may be an ass, but he's right. I'm gonna be a little slow. Gotta think about any advantage I can get. He was right to go. If one of us gets out, there's a chance for the other."

"The last prisoners, they took the boat. Sheriff caught up with them pretty easy." She shifted and stared at her nails for a second. "It won't get you far anyway, engine is almost done for, and you'd have to paddle. They spot you on the water, and you're a sitting duck. They probably have a boat waiting down river anyhow."

"I figured as much. Then I guess I better head out. Sure you won't come?"

He put his coffee cup down and stood up, trying not to wince at the pain. She looked conflicted, and a little bit sorry he was leaving, but she didn't say anything about leaving with him. Jake probably left him behind for nothing—if he was scared of Josie, he didn't have to be. She looked stubborn as a mule about staying put.

"How will I know you made it out of here?" she asked. "And what am I supposed to do with those papers?"

"Hide them," he said. "In case they come by. If you get a chance, hightail it to another county and take the papers to their sheriff."

She eyed him warily. "Another parish, you mean. Doubt that'll do anything."

"Well, you may not have to worry," he said. "You know, after killing them and all."

He walked out onto the porch and saw the alligator in the light for the first time. He was an eerie yellow-ish white, and sat there with his mouth hanging open. He sure as hell was glad the thing wasn't hungry last night.

"What's he do that for?" he asked. "Hang his mouth open like he's waiting for a snack."

"Gator's do it to regulate their body temperature. Gummy likes to bask in the sun, but he burns easy, overheats. It helps them keep cool."

"So it doesn't mean anything?"

"Nothing but they're trying to air condition."

He buttoned up the shirt she'd given him.

"You should let me bandage your leg up," she said.

"No time." He looked back at her. "Come with me. Don't let it happen this way."

"Be careful out there," she said.

Tim looked at her, then nodded. She was determined, that was for sure.

"Don't think I'll be by these parts again. You take care of yourself, Josie."

"You do the same. I'll look over the area and get rid of your footprints. I'm sure you and your friend left a ton of them."

Tim cracked a small grin, and then nodded his goodbye.

He went down the stairs and off to the right, heading through the bushes, trying to make every step look normal, the pain burning in his leg.

Jake had been moving through the brush for a half hour by his calculations. He hadn't heard any dogs or the crackle of police radios, but he did hear all kinds of creatures. He was beginning to go crazy with all the noise and how it reminded him of Alabama and things he didn't want to think about.

He went through a small creek a little for awhile. It dried up and then he saw more slow moving water in the distance. It wasn't large, but enough he'd have to swim across, and he wondered if this was the east arm. He debated going through it to try and get rid of his footsteps and scent, but saw more than one gator and kept himself up on land to avoid them. He tried his best not to leave footprints by stepping lightly, but there was no way to erase them.

He wasn't really fond of the woods, and this bayou was like the woods amplified. Everything seemed older, creepier, dirtier and more complicated than a simple stroll through some trees.

He was beginning to feel like a shit for leaving Kelly and the girl behind, too.

He figured he'd get out and go to Kelly's rescue once he had a car and a way out of town, but the more he thought about the warden, the sheriff and those deputies, the more he knew they were going to overpower that girl easy as pie, and then go after them. And they weren't going to put them back in prison. They'd shoot them the minute they spotted them, and that made Kelly a sitting duck.

"Fuck," Jake swore. He stopped and looked up at the sky.

He wasn't a rat.

You couldn't get by in Vegas if you were a rat, and he'd never been one. It was a good way to end up dead, and you'd have no reputation if you got one for squealing.

It wasn't ratting him out to leave, but it was a candy-ass move.

Jake kicked at the ground and swore. He was probably going to regret this.

He turned around.

Jake started following the trail back upstream to where he thought Josie's cabin was. Maybe he'd run into Kelly and they could figure out a way for him to move faster. If he had a log of some kind, maybe they could float down the river so Kelly wouldn't have to walk.

If the girl was with him . . . well, he'd just let her do her thing. She could lead, they could follow. He could stand looking at the back of her head for a few hours.

He paused and went down to the edge of the water, wondering if it was safe to drink. He'd never asked the girl that, but he figured maybe she got her water from a branch of the river. She had no working plumbing so it had to come from somewhere.

He leaned down at the water's edge, then heard a strange noise. Glancing to the right he spotted the gator, and a second later it lunged, charging up through the shallow water, its jaws open and a bellow coming from it.

He scrambled backwards, slipping on the bank and almost falling. He moved back as quickly as he could, just waiting for the jaws to snap down. He felt his back hit a fallen log, and he pushed back against it.

The gator was about five feet away, frozen in place, its mouth closed. He wasn't sure what the hell it was doing, or what it thought he was doing. He didn't know whether to move or not.

He waited for a minute, not moving a muscle. The gator did the same. He felt around behind him at the size of the log. He could jump over it and give himself a little more safety between him and the gator.

He placed both his hands behind him, counted to three in his head, then swung his legs over. The gator lunged forward briefly, but half heartedly, like it had realized he was going to be too hard to catch without some effort.

Jake let out the breath he was holding. Christ, he didn't realize how much he missed horses and prairies, desert and dry heat. Cars, guns, pool tables, rodeos, diners, traffic, cigarettes and loud obnoxious women at the craps table. That's what he needed. Not alligators and all this bayou shit.

The gator turned slowly, approached the water's edge and then turn again, sliding around on its belly, still watching him.

It was as good a sign as any to start moving again. Instead of following the water, like he had when he walked down here, he'd move inland a little. As long as it wasn't gator territory, he'd be happy. With any luck he'd run into Kelly and they could start to move.

He turned around, walked three steps, and then screamed as the world tilted and everything changed.

Tim hadn't gotten far. He stopped seeing Jake's footprints and figured they'd diverged paths somewhere along the line. All he had to do was keep going until he got to the point where he had to decide between going across the arm or finding his way down to the point the arms merged. He'd be safe and Jake could go to hell.

The only problem was Tim knew he wasn't going to make it.

His leg was swollen and the pain was immense. Each step got harder and harder. He figured by the end of the day, if the cops hadn't caught up to him, he'd barely be able to take a step. The poultice she'd used had certainly pulled out the infection, but his leg was in need of medication—antibiotics for sure. His wrist ached with sharp pains stabbing up his forearm and bicep whenever he took a particularly hard step. She'd wanted to bandage both wounds and he'd said no, more from stupid pride than anything.

He slumped against a tree, trying to get some weight off his leg. His bad shoulder ached from the cool temperatures. He was falling apart.

The search party would spot him and open fire. There was no going back to that prison.

He slid down the trunk of the tree and rested. He was having a hard time catching his breath, and wondered if he was just overly tired from moving or if the infection was affecting his lungs.

He closed his eyes, feeling the long day before catching up to him. He hadn't been able to sleep the night before, but he could sleep for at least eight hours lying against this tree. He let his mind drift, images of Las Vegas in his head. He didn't care about the truck or the cigarettes or the money he'd lost. He just wanted to be somewhere familiar.

Rett's maybe.

He'd sit at that table that faced the big window, Carolyn next to him, running her hand up his leg. He'd take her upstairs and spend the night twisted in the sheets with her.

He imagined her riding him, his hands planted firmly in the curve of her back, her back arched and her head tilted back. Her face turned into Ruby's and he froze, remembering the feel of her skin. It was over. It was dust.

Wasn't it?

A twig snapped. His eyes flew open—it was somewhere close.

His heart pounded. The blood rushed in his veins, and all thoughts of the pain in his leg and the fantasies about Ruby were gone. He listened carefully, hearing nothing but the occasional bird, or a little splash in the water.

He wished he had a rifle or a gun or something. The search party could show up and shoot first, nailing him against the tree. They'd either kill him or drag him back to that hell hole, and he didn't know which he wanted to happen less.

He looked around again, then braced himself against the tree and tried to stand. It was painful to put much weight on his leg, and he thought maybe he could find a sturdy branch to use as a crutch.

"You're nothing more than gator meat out here with that leg, cher."

Josie stood in the clearing, a rifle over her shoulder and a shotgun in her hands.

"Was that you?"

"Stupid. Stepped on a twig, it snapped like I'd fired the shotgun. I was hoping to sneak up on you like those deputies will."

"To prove what?" he asked, sliding back down the tree trunk. "What are you doing here, anyway?"

"Following you." She put a worn cloth bag down on the ground near him. "Your friend was right, you're going to be captured with your leg like that."

He sighed. "Infected."

She nodded. "That's why I brought this."

She opened the bag and crouched down, opening up the tied flap. Inside he saw gauze, salve and a bottle of something. Prescription.

"Antibiotics, left over. There's not too many left, and I don't know how good they are for blood infections, but I got bronchitis real bad before Christmas, and the bayou doctor I saw gave me that. I never finished them."

Tim popped a couple of the pills, dry swallowing them. She uncapped a canteen.

"You hurried out so fast I didn't get to give you all of this."

She handed him the canteen, and he took a long drink.

"I never asked where you get your drinking water."

"There's a well about a quarter of a mile down river," she said. I take as many containers as I can, fill up every other day or so. When Jean-René was here, he would come back with so much. It's hard without him."

"He's a lot older than you."

She nodded. "I was a mistake. A happy one, said my mother, but a mistake nonetheless."

She took the tube of salve and squeezed half of it on Tim's wound. He winced at the pain.

She unrolled the gauze and wound it up around the wound, tucking the ends in tightly. It already felt more stable, but the pain was still there.

"I erased your footprints from around the cabin," she said. "I also took the uniforms and the cuffs and shackles and buried them inside Gummy's pen. No one will look there. There's nothing to show you were there."

"Smart girl," he said. He should've thought of that, but she seemed to be one step ahead of him, and he blamed it on the infection.

"I brought aspirin too," she said, handing him a few tablets. He swallowed these with water, although they disintegrated on his tongue almost immediately, leaving a bitter, chalky taste in his mouth.

She held out something. A peppermint.

He smiled. "Guess I did kind of rush out."

"You won't be able to make it far on your leg; I saw how you tried to hide the limp from me when you left."

"You didn't want to come."

"I still don't," she said. She looked into his eyes. "But I know I have to. Not to run from them, but to help you. We can catch up to your friend. He may be a southern boy, but he's no good in the bayou. Not many people are."

"Where'd you put the papers?"

"I brought them with me." She pulled them out of her back pocket, showed him, then tucked them back in again.

Tim sighed. He was not going to admit how glad he was to see her, not just because he needed help getting out of here. He was relieved she wouldn't be anywhere near that cabin.

She leaned down and moved hair off his forehead.

"You're sweating from the infection," she said. He took in a breath at how tenderly she moved the hair away from his eyes. "You're a mess."

"You can say that again," he said.

"What happened to you face?"

"Got introduced to a baseball bat."

She raised both eyebrows.

"I probably deserved it," he sighed. She brushed hair off his forehead again and looked at him. It surprised him when women looked past the scars.

"Jake's better looking," he said.

She nodded. "He doesn't look real. Like a face in a magazine. It's creepy."

He laughed, his head swimming. He put a hand on her arm, seeing fleeting alarm in her eyes. As she relaxed, he ran his hand up her arm to her shoulder and into her hair. Her hair was soft.

He pulled her down to him slowly, waiting to see if she'd pull back, but she didn't. Her hair smelled like lemons up close, and he supposed she did drag a comb through it now and then.

He touched her cheek, running his thumb over her freckles. He brought his hand around to the back of her neck.

Her lips were soft when they reached his, and he wondered if the deputies were all she knew about men. She kissed him, flicking his lip with her tongue and decided they probably weren't. She braced her hands on his shoulder, and he reached up, trying his best to get his arms around her. They tumbled over onto the ground, and she began to laugh.

"Clumsy, huh?" he said, his eyes full of mischief.

She ran her fingers along his lips. "Not so clumsy, cher."

He wondered why he always found women in bad circumstances. Lupe, now Josie . . . hell, maybe even Ruby. Her wounds hadn't been as visible as Lupe's or Josie's were, but maybe they ran deeper in some ways.

He put it out of his head and kissed Josie again, pulling her tightly to him, feeling cypress needles poke into his arms.

Roundtree approached the cabin slowly, shivering. He crossed the arm in the dead of night, freezing to death when he reached this side, and not sure where to go.

He breathed a sigh of relief when he spotted the chicken wire fencing. He was about to step over a section of it when he spotted the gator.

He held his gun on it for a minute, marvelling at the sight. There were rumours around town the Landry's had a gator around their homestead, but he never would've believed it if he wasn't staring at it.

He'd never seen an albino alligator before, but he'd heard about them. They were pretty rare, and it amazed him Josie Landry kept one as a pet.

He noticed the pen only went up to the side of the house. She would've been better off making the pen around the whole house to keep people out.

He skirted the edge of the fence, went past an outhouse, and looked around for clues. There wasn't a single footprint around except the small, barefoot impressions in the mud he assumed were Josie's. She'd never worn shoes any time he'd seen her, and he had no idea how she managed to navigate around a dangerous bayou without something protecting her feet.

He got around to the back of the house, but the windows were up too high since the place was built on stilts. Parts of the bayou still flood badly certain times of the year, and most of the cabins out here were prepared for it.

As he circled around the house, he wondered if Sheriff MacGregor had figured out what he'd done and where he was. He'd floated across the west arm on a makeshift raft that probably wouldn't have earned him any Boy Scout badges. He was wet up to the thighs, but his gun was dry.

Hickom and Lee would know where he went; they'd be on his tail. He had to make this quick.

He went up to the front porch and looked inside the window, but didn't see anything astray. He knocked on the door.

"Josie! Josephine Landry, this is Paul Roundtree," he hollered. He paused. "Don't shoot me!"

There was no telltale click of a gun or booming shot. In fact, it didn't look like anyone was home.

He knocked again, then tried the knob. The doorknob turned, and the door opened.

He wasn't shocked. Most people in the bayou left their doors unlocked, and Josie had an alligator keeping watch that would scare off most people. He didn't think the two escapees were most people though.

He called out a hello, but there was no reply. The cabin wasn't very big, and he searched it quickly, not finding anything out of sorts. Dishes were clean in their cupboards, food was in an icebox, and everything seemed to be made up and in its rightful place. He was starting to wonder if they had come through here at all.

They had to have, he thought. He could not have just thrown away his career on a gamble that didn't pay out.

He went outside the cabin and shut the door behind him. He went down the stairs and to a little trail down the right hand side, following the creek. Her boat was tied up at the makeshift dock.

He followed a barely visible trail along the edge of the water until it dried up. He continued east until the creek bed got damp again.

About a half hour later, he heard voices and crept into the brush as quietly as he could. He leaned around a tree and spotted Josie leaning over a man. It was the dark-haired one, Kelly.

At first he thought maybe she'd shot him, but the way she tenderly brushed his hair out of his face told him otherwise. He was hurt somehow though. Paul had seen that sheen of pain on too many faces.

He felt like an intruder as he watched Josie kiss him. A part of him was relieved she was okay, she wasn't irreparably damaged by Hickom and Lee. She trusted someone. It wasn't him—it shouldn't be—but it was someone. Even an escaped prisoner was better than nothing.

They fell over onto the forest floor and laughed, and she kissed him again for a few moments, before they righted themselves.

She had a rucksack with her and helped him to his feet. He favoured one leg. Paul had no idea where the other prisoner was. Maybe they had parted ways the minute those chains came undone. Maybe the other one had hurt this one.

Josie found him a stick to use as a cane, then let him lean on her as they moved.

He couldn't let them go. He pulled his gun from the holster and cocked back the hammer.

14

Tuesday, March 28, 1967

His leg was worse now that he was upright, but Josie seemed strong—she was supporting a lot of his body weight anyway.

They hadn't gone more than a few steps when a voice rang out.

"Josie Landry!"

Her head whipped around, and she had the shotgun up and pointed at a tree. He tried to balance, thrown off by her sudden movement. He wished he'd asked to carry the rifle she had slung on her back.

"Josie, this is Deputy Roundtree . . . this is Paul. Paul Roundtree."

"Shit," Tim swore. There was no way he could run with the cops this close. For all he knew, they were surrounded.

Roundtree slowly stepped around a tree, his gun drawn and pointed at them. Josie stepped in front of Tim and trained the gun on the deputy. He stared at the back of her head, surprised she put herself between them. Although maybe it was just to get a better shot.

"Josie, put the gun down," Roundtree said.

"No," she said. "I'll go to hell before I do that. You put yours down."

Tim stared at the cop for a moment, looking at him hard. He was alone. That much was certain, because MacGregor and his cronies, especially the warden, wouldn't have been able to stand being hidden this long. They'd want to come out and gloat.

"I think he's alone," Tim whispered. "And I don't think he's come to shoot us."

She still had the gun trained on Roundtree, and Tim saw the gun didn't move. He knew when push came to shove she'd fire, and she'd hit Roundtree. She struck Tim as being a decent shot.

"Put the gun down!" Roundtree said. "Now!"

"I think you oughta put your gun down," Tim called out.

Josie's breaths were coming faster and faster. The longer Roundtree held the gun on her the longer she had to remember, and it wasn't doing Roundtree any favours.

Tim turned toward Roundtree. "Put it down. You owe it to her."

Roundtree looked at him, then Josie, then nodded and slowly holstered his weapon.

Josie held her shotgun on Roundtree. Tim reached out his arm alongside Josie's.

"Put the gun down," he said. "He's not gonna hurt us."

"No!" she said, her voice animalistic. "No, he won't."

"Was he one of them?" Tim asked.

"No." Her voice faltered.

"Then don't make him pay for the mistakes of others," he said. "Come on now, cher, put the gun down."

Maybe it was the use of the word that distracted her, but she wavered enough to let the barrel drop, and Tim closed his hand around the stock and took the gun out of her hands. He pointed it at the ground, but kept it at hand.

"Where are they?" Tim asked.

"Coming," Roundtree said. He approached them slowly. "Hickom, Lee, and if they've figured out I ditched them to come over here, probably the sheriff himself, along with warden Striker."

He heard the sharp intake of breath from Josie. "I'm ready for them."

"I'm not," Tim said. "I gotta get outta here."

"You both have to, and your friend too, wherever he is," Roundtree said.

"Don't know. We parted ways."

"They'll bring dogs."

Josie groaned. "They'll smell that wound right away. Gil Pender keeps bloodhounds for searches."

"They lost your scent last night in the river," he said. "I suspected you two might have come here, Jean-René thought you might."

"Is he okay?" Josie asked.

"Yeah, he's fine," Roundtree said. "But you need to move."

Josie looked from Roundtree to Tim.

"She doesn't wanna go," Tim said. "Not when she could stay behind and blow some heads off."

Roundtree nodded. "I know."

"This isn't fair," Josie said. "I'm not running from them."

"You aren't a runner, Josie, I've seen that," Roundtree said. "You're a strong person. A strong woman. Maybe it's just today isn't the day to make the stand."

"Or you make it another way," Tim murmured.

Josie looked back at him, and he looked at Roundtree.

"She's got some papers," Tim said. "Ones I stole from the prison. Enough to turn that place on its ear and oust your sheriff."

"That true?"

Josie nodded, then looked back at Tim. He nodded at her, and she pulled out the papers. Roundtree approached and took them, giving them a quick read.

"Jesus Christ," he whispered.

Josie took them back, stuffing them in her rucksack.

"That ought to be enough," Tim said. "Now help us out."

"The truck you guys drove in with? It's in an impound lot just on the outskirts of town, not too far from the river," Roundtree said.

"Duschenes place," Josie said.

Roundtree nodded. "All they have for security is a fence and a chain lock. If you can take care of those shackles, you can take care of the chain lock." He held out his hand. "Your keys. The rest of your things are in my pickup, it's a 1962 Ford. It's at the bridge site."

Tim took the car keys wordlessly.

"You need to stall them," Josie said. "We need to find his friend, and he needs help getting out of here. We need time."

"I'll do the best I can," Roundtree said. "I'll go back to your cabin and stall them as much as I can. They'll be angry—I was supposed to report back to the sheriff so Hickom, Lee and I could get over here last night. I came over on my own, and I suspect they went back to the sheriff to see where I was. They'll have figured out by now I came here instead."

"What about your radio?" Josie asked.

"Fell in the river back past the Tourgis place, shorted all our radios out. You won't be able to hear them coming."

"Then we should move," Josie said. She sounded resigned to her fate helping him limp through the bayou, but he couldn't feel sorry about that.

"Look, if you manage to get them taken care of and you come looking for us, we'll need a signal so we know it's you," Tim said. "Or else she's liable to shoot first."

"Whistle like this," Josie said. She whistled a high-low-high note.

Roundtree nodded. "Find your friend. If they only come upon one of you . . . well, they won't be happy. Find him, or else he doesn't have much of a chance of getting out here alive."

Tim moved with a bit more speed in his step after Roundtree let them go. His leg felt like fire, his breathing was hard, and he felt sick and dizzy at turns, but he had to move. He knew where the truck was and had the keys, now he just had to get to it.

"We need to find Jake," Josie said.

"I'm going to kick his butt for taking off."

"You can't kick anything with that foot. Anyway . . . he didn't want me coming with y'all," she said. "I could see that plain as day if you couldn't. But if they find him first they'll kill him. You heard Roundtree. Do you really want that?"

"Some days . . . some days I'd like to pull the trigger myself," Tim said with a laugh.

"I saw his footprints over here. He came this way. We need to find him, and thankfully he's not unnoticeable in these woods. The University of Alabama chose their mascot well."

"Why's that?"

"It's an elephant. Your 'Bama boy crashes through here like one."

Tim couldn't help the chuckle. "Jake isn't much for finesse. As most girls could tell you, I'd guess."

"You argue like brothers."

"I have enough on my plate with a sister," Tim grunted, his foot aching. "And a brother wouldn't do what Jake did."

They travelled for only a few minutes more, when Josie stopped him.

"What?"

"The tracks reverse." She stared at the ground, concentrating deeply. She smiled a minute later. "He turned around. He was coming back."

Tim lifted an eyebrow. "You sure about that?"

"Come on," she said. "This way."

They walked about five minutes near the shore, and then she stopped him again.

"Over there."

He looked over, half-expecting to see Jake's body floating in the bayou, but instead saw a huge gator on the bank nearby.

"That's the big gator." Josie's voice was low. "She had babies with her through Christmas. They have their babies in the spring and summer and stay with them for about a year, through winter. This one's always been awful aggressive. We'd best steer clear."

"Yeah, you'd best do that," a voice said.

Tim looked around, trying to spot where Jake's voice had come from.

"I want you to shut your fucking mouth. I'm up here."

Tim looked up, and Josie yanked on his arm and pointed. Hanging upside down from a trapper's snare about twenty feet away was Jake Wheeler.

He bit the inside of his cheek, but couldn't stop the laughter.

"Come on," Josie said. "You're aggravating the gator."

Josie pulled Tim inland, past an old fallen tree, until they were underneath Jake in the snare.

"Fancy meeting you here," Tim said with a grin.

"Shut the hell up and get me down."

"How long have you been up there?" Josie asked.

"I dunno," Jake said. "Awhile, I guess."

"Jake, I don't know," Tim said. "I might slow you down if we get you down from there."

"Fuck. You." Jake tried to move, but the snare had him tight. "Just get me down! I got tangled up here coming back for your sorry ass."

"Quiet!" Josie said. "The gator will get over here and eat us alive just to shut you up. And we have no idea how far out the sheriff is."

"Sheriff?" Jake asked.

"Remember that cop that drove us to the joint? He came after us to warn us. To warn Josie. Those deputies and the sheriff are on their way here. He told me where the truck is and gave me the keys. It's not far off the river. We just have to get downstream further and cross the river, then we can get the hell outta here."

Josie laid the two guns down and took a knife out of the rucksack. She climbed nimbly up the tree the snare was in. She shimmied out along the branch and cut the snare. Jake tumbled to the ground unceremoniously.

"Goddammit," he swore. "You couldn't have been a little bit gentle?"

"There's no time." Josie hung off the branch and dropped to the ground as quiet as a cat. "We have to move if we want to get you both out of here."

"Kelly's leg's a mess."

"And yet *you* were caught in a snare," she said. "Do you want to continue to argue? If you forgot, I have two guns. Let's go!"

Jake and Tim exchanged a look, then moved ahead with Josie.

MacGregor crossed the river on a small skiff the guards had made the prisoners carry down the bayou to their location. Striker had yet to take them back to the prison, making the prisoners sleep on the bus as punishment for the chain gang break.

Roundtree was going to catch a lot of trouble when they caught up with them. Maybe he wanted all the glory of capturing the prisoners . . . or maybe it was something else entirely. It was that something else that was sitting in his gut making him sweat.

They moved through the bush on the other side of the river, slashing at the branches with machetes. It was still early in the year, but it had been a warm winter and things were budding and flowering early.

MacGregor stopped the group when they got to the pen. Striker was right behind them, and he likely spotted the cabin over the alligator. Striker stepped over the fencing without bothering to look around.

"I'll wring that little whore's neck if they're in there," Striker said.

MacGregor stopped dead in his tracks.

"Come on, you son of a bitch," Striker said. He turned around, looking at MacGregor, Hickom and Lee. "Let's go!"

MacGregor nodded to his left, and Striker turned to face the alligator.

"Holy shit!"

Striker fumbled with his gun and fell over as the alligator lazily rushed him. MacGregor didn't even think to get his handgun out.

Lee fired off a few shots, but missed, and the gator slunk back toward the water.

"Didn't anyone ever tell you to go around an alligator pen?"

They looked ahead and saw Roundtree standing on the front porch.

"Where the hell have you been?" Hickom asked. "We spent half the night waiting on you."

"When I passed by the river, I thought I heard some commotion on this side, so I got myself over here. Found the cabin a little while ago. Met the gator, too."

They all skirted the enclosure and came up onto the front porch.

"Where are they?" the sheriff asked.

"Not here," Roundtree said. "Don't know where they are. The place is empty, and it doesn't look like anyone was here. There's no clothes or shackles or anything. Maybe they skipped past or went down the river."

The sheriff took a good look at Roundtree. He hadn't been there the night of the last big escape, but it damn well looked like he knew what happened. He glared at Hickom and Lee with barely contained rage. MacGregor moved past Roundtree into the cabin, looking around himself. There was little furniture and it took seconds to realize the place was empty.

"She harboured some fugitives awhile back," the sheriff said.

"I heard it another way," Roundtree said.

"You're headed on a good path, Paul, don't ruin it now," MacGregor said. "I thought you might be worthy of working alongside Mr. Striker here."

"He isn't fit to shine my shoes," Roundtree said.

Striker burst through the crowd to get to Roundtree, and MacGregor let him and Roundtree go at it for a minute, until he saw Roundtree was getting somewhere. He'd bloodied Striker's nose and ducked almost every punch that came his way.

MacGregor watched a moment, noticing Striker wasn't all that comfortable on the offense, never mind the defence. He probably hadn't needed to fight in a long time.

"Get them apart!" MacGregor said, ordering Hickom and Lee into the fray. A moment later all that you could hear in the cabin was heavy breathing.

"What are you doing, Paul?" he asked.

"What I should've done the moment I heard these assholes raped Josie Landry," Roundtree said. "I'm taking a stand. I'm not doing this anymore. That girl was ready to shoot your brains out if you showed up here. Not that I'd mind, I want to get that clear. But I mind her going away for something like putting a lame dog down. I'm not gonna let this happen."

"You don't get to make that choice, Paul."

MacGregor turned to Hickom. "Go tell the officer outside to radio word to the command centre. Tell them to bring Jean-René Landry out here. I saw him on the bus back at the work site. Bring him on down."

"What are you doing?" Roundtree asked.

"Stacking the odds in my favour," MacGregor said. "I always do. You said she was ready to shoot us. So that says you saw her. It's a shame, Paul, you could've been something. There's a good chance they all headed south— it's pretty much the only way out of here that gets them near civilization. We'll get down to where the arms merge since they'll try and cross back over at that point I think, it's the closest to the road. I don't think they'd try the Atchafalaya. Get Jean-René Landry to the Guidry, and we'll meet up and cut them off. I'm pretty sure Josie won't have much to say when we got a gun to her brother's head. She'll put her weapon down, and she'll give those boys up pretty damn fast."

Roundtree looked properly horrified.

"Lee. Take Paul for a little walk in the woods. Strip him of that badge and gun. A man like this ain't fit to be a sheriff's deputy."

"Yes, sir," Lee said, grinning like a maniac. He grabbed Paul's gun out of its holster, then yanked the badge off his chest.

"We have to keep moving," Josie said.

Jake huffed out a breath, tired from Tim leaning on him the last while. Josie led them through the bush at a good pace, but Tim couldn't keep up and Jake was the only thing keeping him upright.

Kelly's limp was so bad he barely put any weight on his foot, and Jake was tired from hauling Kelly so far. But Josie kept moving, so Jake kept up with her, but he was slowing down with Kelly on him.

For once, he didn't run his mouth about it. Kelly had lapsed into a sullen silence as they moved. Kelly was taciturn on a good day, but it unnerved him that Tim wasn't getting on him about being caught in a snare. On any other day Tim would've been running his mouth non-stop about it, and he hadn't said a word since they left the snare.

"I'm moving as fast as I can," Tim said, as if he'd heard Jake's thoughts.

"I know," Jake huffed, his breathing heavy. "They're gonna kill us. Ain't gonna take us back to any prison."

"Yeah."

Striker's whole deal had probably been bullshit, too. He knew it then, somewhere deep in his mind. It had seemed like a good gamble to make at the time, but if he'd really believed it, he wouldn't have run with Kelly off that chain gang. Striker had a decent poker face, but Jake hadn't lived in Vegas for as long as he had without learning something about reading people. No matter how much he might delude himself.

Somehow, moving through the bayou, sweating and in pain, it had been hammered home pretty hard that Striker was going to kill them, and the sheriff would go right along with it. Jake knew Kelly had realized it too—it might not account for his quietness, but it explained why Kelly kept moving, pushing ahead even though Jake was doing most of the work. A gun sight on your back sure sped things up.

He thought about Darla. He pictured her blonde locks, those blue eyes and that smile that could grind his gears more than anything. He'd cut off his arm to be with her right now. This was all happening because he wanted to be with her.

Damn her. Damn her to hell.

Josie stopped up ahead and waited for them to catch up. She handed Jake the canteen, and he took a cursory sip. He passed it to Tim, who drank in choking mouthfuls. His lips were cracked.

"If I don't make it—" Kelly started to say.

"Shut up," Josie said.

"I mean it, if it doesn't look good, leave me here and get Jake out of here. Get yourself out of here to another county and get those papers to someone."

Jake looked over at him, his hard eyes narrowed. So he'd given the papers to Josie.

"It's a parish, not a county. And shut up. Don't be such a wimp now, cher," she said. "We don't have much farther to go."

Jake looked over at Kelly, his face thoughtful. At least Kelly knew the score. He nodded at him. "Come on, I ain't dragged your ass this far to drop you now."

They moved on through the bayou, past swampy ponds, and dry copses of trees.

Awhile later Jake called Josie to a stop. Kelly was sweating up a storm, his leg barely able to support his weight. Jake sat him down at the base of a tree and handed him the canteen. It was almost empty.

Tim closed his eyes as Josie yanked up the pant leg. Jake looked at it—the infection was worse. He watched Josie change the bandages and cringed at the pus in the wound surrounding Kelly's ankle. There were red spider-like streaks midway up his calf and those hadn't been there that morning.

Kelly breathed heavily, a sheen of sweat on his forehead. Josie rewrapped his leg after covering it in salve, then wiped his forehead with a bandana. Her gaze was guarded, and her forehead wrinkled.

She took the rifle off her shoulder and handed it to Jake, then slung the shotgun over her shoulder.

She stood up and looked at Jake, subtly nodding to the side. He followed her away from Kelly, the rifle on his back.

"He's in bad shape," Jake said, his voice low.

"He needs a hospital," she stated.

Jake sighed. "Even if we get outta here, we ain't gonna be able to walk into any hospital."

Josie looked over at Kelly, then back at him. "I know a doctor. She treats a lot of us here in the bayou. She keeps her mouth shut real good and can help him. We need to get to the river's edge, where the arms meet, and cross over. Roundtree said your truck was at Duchenes' place. After we make it across, it's a fifteen minute hike on the road to Duchenes."

Jake looked back at Kelly. "What're his chances?"

"With a doctor, good. Without, he's going to die," Josie said. "He's got blood poisoning."

"You're sure?"

"They got the bullet out of my mother at the hospital. She was gut shot. Bullet didn't kill her, it was the infection afterward. Took her four days to die. I'm sure."

"Well, he ain't gonna die," Jake said, glancing back at Kelly. He looked back at Josie whose worried gaze was on Tim.

"You were eager to leave him before," she said.

"But I didn't."

"He said we should leave him if it gets bad. Will you go then?" she asked. Her gaze was still on Kelly.

"They'd kill him, you know it as well as I do."

"He said you betrayed him."

"Yep," Jake said.

"So why are you sticking your neck out for him now? To make up for it?"

Jake shrugged. She had good questions, and he had no answers. Maybe he didn't want to owe Kelly, and after realizing he hadn't slept with Darla—he bet his hat Jimmy Lewis had—maybe this was making up for it.

"I'm not gonna let him get off easy sitting on his ass the rest of the day while we hike around here," Jake said. "I leave him behind I'll never hear the end of it. Best way to keep his fat mouth shut is drag him along."

Josie looked up with him, a slight smile on her face. Her eyes were clear, nothing haunting them. They just looked determined. "He said you weren't friends. I believed him until now."

"Best not to think too hard on the two of us, we'll give you a headache after awhile," he grinned. It faded as he looked at Kelly. "Anyhow, he didn't have 'croak in the bayou' in his plans, and Kelly always sticks to his plans."

Josie nodded, gave him a terse smile, then headed back to Tim. Jake followed a minute later. He hauled Tim up, ignoring the groan of pain he made and started dragging him through the bayou a little faster.

15

Lee marched Roundtree down the trail to the right of the cabin, through the bayou and away from any chance Paul had to stop this. Lee seemed nervous, his hand quaking every time Roundtree looked over his shoulder and saw Lee holding Paul's own service weapon on him as they moved. They skirted the water and Roundtree figured the man might not have the heart for coolly dispatching him the way MacGregor wanted. Roundtree knew he had to do something before they got to a place where Lee decided they were deep enough in the bayou to do this.

He knew the sheriff and his cronies would head back to the water's edge on the other side to wait for Jean-René to be brought down. They'd sail down the river and cut them all off. Josie would go that way because it was closest to Duchenes, and maybe MacGregor realized that. He knew they wouldn't try the Atchafalaya, not without a boat, and hers was still there. He didn't want to think about what would happen to Josie once the posse caught up with them.

As they walked, Paul kept his eyes open for anything that could help, a stick, a rock, anything. Lee had taken his baton and revolver, and Paul had nothing on him that could help.

"How could you do it?" he asked. "She was a kid."

"She was legal," Lee muttered. "She was asking for it, too. Short shorts, low cut top, looking at us the whole time. You can't tell me she didn't give it up to each one of those escaped cons that came through her place that night. Come on now, you ain't that stupid."

"It's too bad you are," Paul murmured.

He saw the gator before Lee did. A big one along the side of the water, basking on a log not too far from where they were heading. She was frozen in place, mouth gaping open. Paul thought for a few seconds about whether he could do it or not.

"Okay, that's far enough."

Paul stopped and Lee marched past him, then turned around, his back to the gator.

Lee had Paul's own gun pointed at him. Somehow it seemed worse that it was his own gun.

"On your knees," Lee said.

"You're not serious, are you?" Paul asked, hoping to hell he could talk him out of it. "You're gonna shoot me here in the middle of the bayou? What are you going to tell everyone? What are you going to tell my wife?"

"Prisoners got the jump on you, grabbed your gun, shot you. Simple as that."

"I don't believe you."

Lee had the gun pointed at him, but it was angled more toward his feet. Paul looked the man in the eye. Carter Lee was someone he'd worked with for the past few years, had lunch with at the diner every Friday and saw him in church on Sundays. This time Paul really looked at Lee for the first time and didn't like what he saw. Carter Lee was going to kill him.

Lee was a slow shot. There was time.

Paul rushed him and pushed Lee as hard as he could, using everything he could remember from his days as a defensive end. Lee flew through the air and landed with a whump at the edge of the water. The gun flew out of his hand when he landed, tumbled butt over barrel about five feet from Lee's left arm.

The gator roared, lunging off the log and toward them both. Paul scrambled up and jumped back up the bank, leaping at the gun, grabbing it and rolling away from the water. Lee, the breath knocked out of him, tried to scramble to his feet.

Lee reached for his own gun in its holster, but the gator was on him.

The gator clamped down on Lee's leg, and his screams echoed through the woods. Paul turned away from the thrashing water, turning red with blood, and scrambled toward a stand of trees. A few feet from where the gun landed Paul saw his badge. He picked it up and stuck it in a pocket.

Lee's gun fired once, then there was an ominous click.

Wet powder from falling into the creek was his guess. Roundtree heard the screams again, the bellowing of the gator, and he turned away. He got up and leapt through the bush and trees, running as fast as he could, putting the image of Carter Lee out of his head.

He had to focus on getting to the escapees before anyone else.

He just had to figure out which way they'd gone first.

Tim had never been so relieved in his life when Jake reported he could see the river. He was feverish and sick, and he knew it wasn't good.

"Stay down," Jake said. "They might have lookouts along the other side of the river, just waiting to spot us."

Josie nodded. "We need a way across. Tim can't go in the water with his ankle like this."

"Kelly'd drown even if he wasn't laid up, he's a lousy swimmer."

"We need to make a raft."

"Jake can make a raft," Tim murmured. "He was in the service."

"Yeah, the Air Force, dumbass," Jake said. "They didn't teach me a lot about raft making, and I ain't no Boy Scout."

"I know how," Josie said impatiently. "I need some small tree limbs, and some reeds and branches. I've got plenty twine in my bag. Take this and start collecting. And by God, hurry."

She unfolded a small knife from her rucksack and handed it to Jake without a second thought.

Josie laid Tim down next to a big felled tree, butted up against a rocky outcropping. Tim was sluggish and tired, and felt pretty stupid that he couldn't help. Jake and Josie managed to get the raft about two feet across and six feet long when she stopped.

"That's enough." She moved it toward Tim. "Just enough for him."

"What?" Jake asked, following her and sitting behind the huge tree next to Tim.

"We don't have time," she said. "We'll get in the water, hold the raft and swim across with it."

"Jake's a strong swimmer," Tim piped up, the effort it took to talk surprising him. He was in bad shape.

"Better than you, that's for sure. You could drown on the raft the way you are in water," Jake said.

Tim chuckled, and had the vague realization he should be worried about something.

"Come on. Help me get him on the raft." Josie wasn't listening to him.

Tim lay in a depression in the ground, a giant tree trunk next to him. He was tired and not in the mood to float across the river.

He just wanted to go to sleep.

Jake moved the makeshift raft next to Tim, and was going to haul Tim's ass onto it whether he liked it or not. If it held together long enough to make it to the other side, he'd be surprised. He didn't know what it would do to Kelly's leg to get it wet again, but he was going to have to suffer.

"Hand me my bag," Josie said. "We'll have to drag this thing down to the water with him on it."

Jake scooted over to the rocks where she'd left it and grabbed the bag.

"Josephine Landry!"

Jake scrambled over to her and yanked her to the ground, shoving her next to Kelly behind the felled tree. He swung the rifle around in front of him, keeping his head low.

"Where the hell did that come from?" Jake asked.

"We're fucked," Tim muttered.

"Over there," Josie whispered, pointing on the other side of the log.

Jake scooted up and dug out the depression next to the log until there was a hole at the bottom he could see through. About twenty-five feet away he could see the warden, the asshole cop, and the sheriff standing at the shore, a boat behind them. They weren't alone.

"Shit!" Jake spat.

"What?" Josie asked.

"It's the sheriff. And he's got your brother."

"What?" Tim asked, suddenly more lucid. He struggled to sit up, and Jake shoved a hand on his shoulder, pressing him back down. They may have seen him and Josie, but they may not realize Tim was with them.

"Don't get us fucking shot, Kelly," Jake whispered. "Shut up."

Josie's eyes widened, and she wriggled near Jake to look under the log. Josie quietly pumped the shotgun next to him.

"He's got your brother," Jake said again.

Jean-René Landry was blindfolded, standing with his hands cuffed in front of him and his ankles shackled. One of the sheriff's deputies had a gun on him. He knew the other had to be nearby. They were probably flanking them now. Jake's finger rested on the trigger.

Josie made a move to get up, but Jake grabbed her and wrestled her back to the ground, tucking her in between him and the log.

"What are they doing? Why do they have Jean-René?"

"Why do you think? He's the bait," Jake said.

"Oh my God," Josie said.

"Josie, we know you've been helping these escapees, and that's a pretty big felony, aiding and abetting," Sheriff MacGregor said. "We ain't so sure your brother approves."

Jake heard Jean-René struggling to speak through the gag they had on him.

"Don't give in," Jake growled. "No matter what he says."

"They're going to kill him!" Josie whispered, her voice hoarse. "I never should've come, I should've stayed at the cabin, I should've—"

"Shut up," Jake said. "You did come, now he's here. We gotta figure something out."

"You got 'til the count of ten to throw out your shotgun, or Jean-René ain't long for this earth. You hear me, Josie? Count of ten. Then I want you and those prisoners to put your hands up and walk out from there so we can take you in."

Jake heard Jean-René's protests again. He, probably better than anyone, knew that taking them in meant putting them six feet under.

"He don't know about the rifle, I don't think," Jake said. He moved with Josie, so he could see better. He was afraid to let her go—she was shaking, and her hand was on that shotgun. She couldn't fire it without risking buckshot hitting her brother, and he hoped she knew it too.

Tim turned his head, looking away from the log.

"We are so fucked," he said again.

"Shut up!" Jake hissed. If they didn't know Tim was there, they might have a chance. A chance of what, he didn't know. Kelly didn't look like he could handle remembering his own name, forget about firing a rifle.

He looked at Kelly and frowned. He was staring off into space.

"Leave me the rifle," Tim said. "You two make a run for it, behind us. Get behind the trees."

Jake looked over at him, nodding, a measure of respect in his eyes.

"I'll give you the rifle," Jake said. "Long as you promise not to shoot us."

Kelly smiled weakly. "I'm tired, but I'm not stupid. I'm a good shot."

Jake peered down under the log again to get a better view.

Striker and MacGregor, both armed to the teeth, and one of the deputies—he thought it was Hickom—were holding the gun on Jean-René. The other deputy was missing and that worried him.

Josie was still pressed against him, her breathing ragged.

"The trees, Jake," Tim said.

"Gimme a minute," Jake said, trying to get the rifle strap off him. "Josie, when he fires, you run."

"I'm not going anywhere!" she said. "They have my brother!"

"Jake, the trees," Kelly said again. "Look."

Jake glanced over at him. Kelly was pointing.

Jake looked into the trees and caught the glint of something bright. He squinted, trying to make it out. The sun flashed on it again a second later.

It might be the other deputy, flanking them from behind. He suddenly had visions of catching a bullet in the back of the head and shuddered involuntarily.

A whistle sounded. The note was high, then low, then high. Too practiced to be a bird.

"What the hell?" Jake asked.

"It's Roundtree," Tim said. "We told him to whistle."

That pretty boy cop sure as hell better be on their side.

Jake peered towards the sheriff and warden again, the boat behind them, bobbing in the river.

They needed that boat, and the only people he had to rely on to get it were a Cajun girl, a crippled gang leader and a cop. What a fucked up day.

There was no way Roundtree was going to take these guys out. He was a cop, and like it or not, the guy was going to want to bring everyone in nice and easy and all wrapped up with a bow like a good little boy.

"I'm giving you to the count of ten, or he gets a bullet in the brain," Mac-Gregor said. "One, two—"

"No!"

Josie scrambled up, and Jake swore as she leapt over the log, the shotgun held in her outstretched hand.

"Lay down your weapon!"

"Let him go!" Josie yelled.

The sheriff laughed. "You want me to let him go? Honey, he beat up one of my deputies pretty bad. This one right here in fact, the one holding the gun on him. I don't think your brother is going anywhere. Put the gun down."

Josie moved closer to them, laying the shotgun down on the ground.

"I might be persuaded not to kill him, though."

"Anything. Just don't hurt him," she said.

Jake could hear her brother screaming behind the gag. Josie offered herself up like a lamb at slaughter.

The deputy, Hickom, began to laugh. "Looks like it's my lucky day."

Jake held onto Josie's rifle. He couldn't fire now—she was right in his line of fire, and Hickom had a gun on her brother. MacGregor and Striker had guns on her. If he shot at one, the other could fire and kill her or her brother.

Hickom told her to walk toward him, and Striker moved over to hold a gun to Jean-René's head. Jake could read this like the ending of a bad novel—Josie'd be raped again, and Striker would still put a bullet in her brother's head and maybe hers, too.

Jake looked at Tim.

"Roundtree's out there," Tim said.

"You sure he's not gonna shoot us?"

"Yeah," Tim said. "Don't fuck up his shot."

"You think he's gonna shoot another cop? You're out of your mind, man!" Jake said. His hands closed around the stock of the rifle.

"Just wait it out," Tim said.

"You get those prisoners on out here," MacGregor said.

"I only got one," Josie said. "The other one got hurt, bad. We had to leave him behind."

Jake let out a breath. At least she hadn't given up the entire farm.

Her voice got further away as she moved toward the sheriff. A minute later he heard her screams of protest. He looked under the log and saw Hickom dragging her toward the boat. Striker and MacGregor laughed.

"Stupid," Striker said. "Like they all are."

Striker pulled back the hammer on the pistol at Jean-René's head. Josie, seeing her sacrifice had gained her nothing, screamed and fought Hickom, who had a good grip on her.

"Ah, shit," Jake said with feeling. He counted to three in his head, then popped up from behind the log, aiming to take out Striker and save Jean-René. Somehow, he knew Josie would think it was the right decision over shooting Hickom.

He took in a measured breath and fired.

Josie screamed.

Tim struggled to get up and see what the hell was going on. He scooted over and peered under the log.

Striker was on the ground, grasping his leg, and Jean-René had stumbled against a tree trunk. Josie, screaming, broke free from Hickom and ran towards Jean-René.

Jake had run to a nearby tree that couldn't hide him completely. He had the rifle trained on MacGregor.

"I'd put that down if I were you," Jake called out. "I'm a real good shot."

Hickom unholstered his gun and had it on Josie. Tim wished like hell he had a gun. He struggled to move down toward the other end of the fallen log and towards the rocks, away from Jake, aiming to make a distraction.

If he could make them think he had a gun too, they might be able to distract them.

"Throw it down!" Tim yelled, popping up from behind the log. Another shot rang out, and Tim ducked down as the wood splintered near his head. Shots rang from behind him, and he heard the repeat of the rifle Jake had from his side. Josie screamed again.

A moment later Roundtree charged out of the bush and toward him. He crouched behind the log, not far from Tim, firing two rounds.

Roundtree wordlessly pulled out another gun from an ankle holster and handed it to Tim without a second thought. Tim cocked the weapon and then cautiously peeked up. Josie was in Hickom's arms again, a gun at her head.

Tim saw a flash of grey out of the corner of his eye and saw MacGregor disappear into the bayou, racing through the trees way faster than Tim expected a man of his size to move.

Jake fired the rifle twice at MacGregor, then swore.

"He's getting away!" Jake said, charging after MacGregor. Hickom fired a wild shot after Jake.

Josie struggled with Hickom and his gun. Tim ducked as Hickom's weapon discharged his way. He tried to aim, but Josie and Hickom were too close together.

Roundtree stood up and yelled at Hickom to put down the weapon. Hickom had his hand on Josie's throat, the gun at her head. Tim braced himself against the log, trying his best to hold his shaking arm steady and get a bead on Hickom's head. One wrong move and he'd kill her by accident.

Josie grabbed the gun and tried to turn it around on Hickom. They both moved too much for him to get a shot.

He blinked to try and clear his vision.

Before he could fire, Hickom and Roundtree fire toward each other at the same time. Tim ducked down, trying to look out from below the log.

Josie was screaming, sprawled on the ground next to Hickom's body. There was a neat hole in the middle of his head. She scrambled to retrieve Hickom's gun and then scooted back and pointed it at Hickom's body.

The bayou was silent.

"I didn't even get to shoot him," she said.

Tim looked around and saw Roundtree, lying on the ground not too far away, blood blooming on the front of his uniform. Hickom must've hit him, but Roundtree had returned fire just in time.

Josie whirled around, looking for all of them. She saw her brother was okay, leaning up against a tree, the blindfold pushed up on his head. Striker was nearby, grasping his wounded leg, and not bothering to try and move. Josie saw her brother was safe, then rushed toward Roundtree. Tim got up and crawled toward him, too, his leg burning with pain.

Josie held pressure on the wound in Roundtree's chest.

"Sorry," Roundtree gasped. "I couldn't . . . couldn't let you shoot him."

"It wasn't your fight," Josie said, tearing up.

"Wasn't . . . yours."

Tim saw the gun in Roundtree's hand. He looked from Roundtree to Hickom. He didn't think the cop had the guts to do it, but he'd killed one of his own.

"We gotta get him to a hospital," Tim said, his breathing laboured.

"He's not the only one."

Tim flopped onto his back, and Jake loomed in front of him.

"He got away. Fucking fat bastard sheriff runs like a jack rabbit. I lost him," Jake said.

"Where's Lee?" Josie asked.

"Gator," Roundtree coughed and spraying blood.

"Get him into the boat," she said. "Come on."

"I'll stay here with Striker," Jean-René said. "I'll keep an eye for Mac-Gregor. Leave me the shotgun."

Josie hurried over and took the keys from Striker's belt, unshackling and cuffing her brother. She hugged him, then passed him her gun. Jake and Josie prepared to move Roundtree.

"I don't normally help out cops like this," Jake grunted. "You owe me."

Roundtree grunted out a laugh, his breath coming in a wheezing gasp. Tim watched them move Roundtree to the boat, struggling with his weight. Josie stayed with him while Jake came back for Tim.

"I told you to leave me," he said.

"Yeah, when do I ever listen to you?" Jake asked. "Stop whining."

Tim laughed, feverish and hurting, smelling blood and gunpowder in the air.

He was in the boat next to Roundtree a few minutes later, the whir of the outboard sounding much farther away than it should. He watched the sky shift as the small boat moved across the river, toward the far shore. Birds wheeled in the sky, and at some point, it all went black.

16

Jake didn't know who was worse off—Tim with his deadly infection or Roundtree with a hole in his chest.

Josie piloted the small skiff across the river, and they both hoped no one was on the other side. They were relieved to hear nothing but the croak of frogs.

"We don't have much time," she said. "They'll have men coming here looking for the warden."

She jumped out of the skiff and pulled it to shore, then scrambled up the bank.

"Get them out," she said. "I'll be back."

He hauled Roundtree out first, and laid him down on the ground. It was spongy and wet. He was semi-conscious and still bleeding. He looked like death warmed over.

Tim came next. He was unconscious and dead weight. Jake strained to get him onto the bank.

He put pressure on Roundtree's wounds, trying to stem the bleeding. He looked around, seeing no sign of Josie. This guy would die soon if she didn't return, and he couldn't save both of them.

A moment later she came crashing through the trees, making no effort to be quiet.

"I got . . . truck," she said, choking out the words.

"What?"

"We're close to . . . Duchenes." She couldn't catch her breath. "Took it . . . from the lot."

She looked at Roundtree, then around the area and dashed off toward some plants. She picked a bunch and came back over, laying out cloth from her bag and putting what looked like moss between it. She folded it and press it to Roundtree's chest.

"We have to move." She looked from Tim to Roundtree. "If you help me with him, can you move Tim yourself?"

Jake nodded. He helped haul Roundtree to his feet, and he groaned in protest. She kept a hand plastered over his sternum, holding the moss concoction to his chest. They moved as fast as they could to the road, and he saw she had a small pickup idling there. It took some manoeuvring to get Roundtree into the bed of the truck, but he managed it, then dashed back to Tim while she tended to the cop.

Tim was still out. Jake managed to get him over his shoulders in a fireman's carry and hauled him through the trees, reminded of basic training in the Air Force, carrying sandbags around as punishment.

He reached the truck and tossed him into the bed, Josie catching his head in time to prevent it from smacking the truck bed.

"Where to?" he asked.

She pushed him out of the way and got in the cab.

"Get in back. I know the way."

He would've argued, but she had a point. He climbed into the truck bed.

"Put pressure on his wound. Don't take the moss off."

She stepped on it, shooting past a tow yard, where he noted with satisfaction their truck sat.

Josie screeched toward a scrim of bushes, and Jake thought she was suicidal until they broke through, driving on a barely visible trail, branches and leaves hitting the truck as they passed by.

A cabin arose out of the trees a moment later. It was rundown and shabby, but smoke rose from the chimney. Josie jumped out of the truck cab and ran to the door.

The woman that came out of the cabin was Negro, likely in her forties. She looked at Roundtree and checked the wound, nodding at the moss.

"Get Roundtree to the hospital," she told Josie. "I'll take this one."

Jake scrambled out of the truck bed and hauled Tim out. Josie didn't wait and took off into the ether with Roundtree in the back of the truck.

The woman got on one side of Tim, and Jake the other, and they dragged him into the cabin.

It was dark inside, three beds against one wall, a kitchen along the other. A fireplace burned bright and a woodstove was going, a kettle whistling.

The woman walked past the beds to a bedroom. Jake was shocked to see it looked like an operating room. There was a gurney, medicines and all kinds of things like blood pressure cuffs and other medical equipment.

He loaded Tim onto the table.

"How long has it been since he got sick?" the woman asked.

"He hurt it running yesterday. By last night it was infected, this morning he could barely walk on it. He's been getting worse fast."

She nodded. He cringed as she inserted an IV into Tim's arm, then gave him a shot of something.

"You some kind of a doctor or something?" Jake asked.

She looked over her glasses at him and didn't answer. Jake backed out of the room and sat down on one of the cots.

He had to hope no one knew about this place or he and Tim would get pinched the minute folks heard about what happened.

He lay back on the bed, aiming to close his eyes for a moment, but fell asleep a minute later.

Wednesday, March 29, 1967

Tim opened his eyes slowly. He was tired, his body ached, and a dull pain throbbed at his ankle.

He looked around, confused. A second later a dark face hovered above his own.

It was a woman, a Negro woman, and she shined a light in his eyes and a thermometer was shoved in his mouth. He spit it out to ask what the hell was going on.

"Keep it in or it goes in the other end," she said.

Tim frowned. He tried to turn his head, and the thermometer was popped in his mouth again. She took it out a moment later.

"Sleep," she said. "You need your rest."

He frowned and shook his head. He had questions, but he couldn't form them enough to talk.

"Roundtree is holding his own. You have blood poisoning. Sleep."

He couldn't hear the rest of her words, they were lost in the haze in his brain.

He thought of alligators and cypress, weeping willow and water moccasins. He thought of the desert and home, dark hair spilled across his chest and grey eyes staring at him.

He slept.

Thursday, March 30, 1967

The next day he was able to eat and move around a little. He realized he'd been bathed at some point, his hair clean and his face shaved. The doctor told them Roundtree was at a hospital in the town, and he'd survive.

"What about Josie?" Tim asked.

The woman—Doctor Dennis—didn't know.

"The Lafayette police are crawling all over town and the prison. I didn't ask why, but it's likely the reason no one's come here looking for you."

Josie must have found a home for the papers.

People came and went from this little cabin, mostly Negro people seeing the doctor. She handed out antibiotics, cough syrup and wrapped sprained ankles. Some paid her in cash, others in eggs, meat and other goods.

"You're a doctor?" Tim asked her later that day.

She nodded.

"A real doctor?"

She rolled her eyes and nodded again. "Howard University medical school."

"Why practice here?"

"Where else?" She handed him his antibiotics. "It may be 1967, but down here it's still Jim Crow's south. Many of the hospitals won't allow coloured doctors to practice. I'm extra lucky, being a woman on top of that."

"Guess that makes me luckier," Tim said. "Otherwise you wouldn't have been here."

"You got that right," she said. "You'd be dead."

"Your bedside manner could use some work, you know."

"Your Josie sent a note," she said, handing him a paper.

He went to the window and waved Jake inside. It was hard to read, her printing was bad and her spelling worse, but she'd drawn a map and a time for the next day.

Jake came into the cabin and sat down on the cot next to his, looking at the note. He looked as tired as Tim felt. They didn't say anything to each other, since the third bed was occupied. Josie's note said nothing but to meet the next day, so they had no idea what was happening.

They packed up Friday morning, and the doctor wrapped Tim's ankle. It was sprained in addition to the cut and infection. He could walk on it, but not far. He was so weak he wouldn't be able to walk much at all anyway.

"Don't get it wet. Finish those antibiotics, and if it gets red and warm, go to a hospital," Doctor Dennis said. "Keep it wrapped. The sprain will heal in a few weeks."

He was shocked to see himself in the mirror. It had only been a few days he was so sick, but he was rail thin and looked like he'd been through the wringer. Of course, Jake didn't look much better, so he figured the prison had done most of the work on them.

"We don't have anything to pay you with, unless you'd like a carton of cigarettes."

She raised an eyebrow.

"Long story," he said.

"I suspect all of your stories are long," she told him. "You should quit smoking before it kills you."

Tim huffed out a laugh. "Dozen or more things'll get me before the cancer sticks will."

"I don't doubt that. Tripod fracture on the left face along with a naso-orbital-ethmoidal fracture as well, and if I'm right your nose has been broken more than once."

"Twice."

She looked at the chart she held. "Transverse injury along the stomach—I'm guessing a knife— "

"That was me," Jake said with pride. Doctor Dennis gave him a stern look and continued.

"Dislocation injury of the left shoulder, recently healed. Multiple healed lacerations of the back, and now you can add sprained wrist, sprained ankle and sepsis to your list of woes."

"You left out smoke inhalation, a few concussions over the years and a broken rib or three."

The doctor looked over at Jake.

"Hey, don't look at me, he's a disaster," Jake said.

"Stab wound to the arm," the doctor said, gesturing at Jake's arm.

"That was me," Tim said with pride.

"I ride rodeo, and I've dislocated elbows, torn a bicep, busted my knees, torn hamstrings, and this guy still comes out worse."

"More injuries on you two than the entire bayou," Doctor Dennis muttered.

"And we still don't have a way to pay you."

"Josie took care of it."

"Josie?"

The doctor nodded, but said nothing more about it. "Best be on your way."

Tim nodded. He still felt woozy on his feet.

He headed for the door, eager to get the hell out of the Pelican State. He turned back to the doctor.

"Thanks," he said.

She nodded, then went back to her patients.

Tim walked outside and was startled to see the cube truck sitting there. He looked at Jake.

"Found the keys in your pocket."

"Roundtree brought them," Tim said.

"I spotted it when we came in," Jake said. "Walked over and took it right out of the lot like nothing. We better ditch it when we get back to Nevada. You used a fake ID to pay for it, right?"

Tim nodded.

"Where did she say to meet?"

Jake looked at the note Tim held.

"Next parish. Ten minute drive maybe, according to this map."

They followed the map and pulled over at the side of the road, making sure the truck was hidden in the brush. He had no idea where the sheriff was and what had happened, and Jake, who'd been hiding out at the doctor's cabin clinic with him was just as clueless.

A big pickup truck approached from the south. Tim stepped from the side of the road.

The pickup skidded to a stop a few minutes later, and Josie Landry jumped out, her feet bare, her hair unkempt as always.

"You're okay!" she said, throwing her arms around Tim.

Tim noticed Jake raised an eyebrow.

"Oh, your arm!" she exclaimed, looking at the thick bandage on Tim's forearm and wrist.

"Sprained," he said. "Won't kill me."

"Your leg would have," she said seriously.

Tim nodded. "Got a load of antibiotics, that swamp doc you sent me to had me hooked up to an IV, all kinds of stuff. Still hurts like a bitch. How's Roundtree?"

"He's going to make it. They had to take him to Baton Rouge, and he had to have surgery. It was touch and go, but he'll be okay," she said. "His wife let me borrow his truck to come out here. That reminds me. Your things."

She hauled two big paper bags out of the truck bed. Tim peered inside. His boots and belt, along with his ID. Jake was already tossing off the dirty prison issue sneakers to pull on his Justin boots.

"Where's Jean-René?"

"Jail, in another parish. They haven't figured out what to do with him yet. Because of all the bogus convictions at the Strikersville prison, his conviction is being questioned. They might retry him, and if they do, he might have a better chance, especially with Hickom and Lee dead. Striker was there, but

I think he'll sink those two to avoid more charges. I may have to say something about what happened."

"Will you?"

She nodded. "If it helps Jean-René. He doesn't want me to, but I don't want him going away for doing right beating up Hickom."

Josie glanced down at his arm again, then over at Jake.

"They raided the prison, went through all these files in Striker's office. Oddly enough, they found no record of either one of you."

"Yeah, imagine that," Tim said innocently. Josie stared at him, searching for an answer, then laughed and leaned against the truck.

"I told them I never knew your names. Said you was from Texas."

"Good girl," Tim said, a wolfish grin on his face.

"Striker and MacGregor are in the cell next to Jean-René. I can't tell you how satisfying he finds that. They found MacGregor in the bayou, treed by a gator."

"Serves him right."

"Striker lost a lot of blood. He would've died if it wasn't for Jean-René keeping him alive. They found Lee's body in the bayou. At least part of it."

"And the papers?" Tim asked. "You gave them everything on Striker and MacGregor?"

Josie shook her head. "I gave them nothing. I put the papers in Roundtree's pocket when I got to the hospital. His wife found them when the nurses gave her his clothes. I suggested she go to the neighbouring parish to report it all, and she did."

"You didn't do it yourself?"

"The town wouldn't think it was nothing but grudge," she said. "Roundtree's wife isn't Cajun, she's not bayou. They think Roundtree was a hero, collecting information to expose them. I'm happy to let the town think it. He'll make sheriff after this, I guarantee."

"Where are you going to go?" Tim asked.

"Back to the cabin, of course. Back to Gummy. Hopefully Jean-René won't be in jail for much longer. I go back to my life. And you, cher?"

"We're getting in this fucking truck and driving straight to Nevada, no stops," Jake said, punctuating the air with a finger. "Goodbye Cajun country."

Josie grinned at him. "Too much for you, cher?"

"Yeah, and I ain't afraid to say it." Jake walked over and appraised her. "You did okay out there. 'Cept for that boneheaded move getting up and walking over to 'em like a wrapped up Christmas present."

She made a face. "You would do the same to save someone you love."

"Yeah, fat chance on that, I make better decisions than you," Jake said.

Tim's laugh was long and genuine.

"The doc said you settled up our bill."

Josie nodded. "I'll go in two days a week and cook and clean in the clinic. I'll bring in some catfish. C'est bon."

"Don't know how we're gonna settle up our bill with you."

She smiled at him. "You did, cher. Jean-René is safe, and Hickom and Lee are dead. MacGregor and Striker are gone. No one else had done it. If anything, I owe you."

"We better move," Jake said. "I'm not looking forward to an entire road trip listening to you grouse about your ankle and your hand and forgetting how I saved your life."

Tim turned back to Josie.

"I'm never gonna hear the end of this," he muttered. He raised his voice toward Jake. "And you didn't save my life. You helped me walk. You were a glorified crutch."

"That saved your ass."

Tim rolled his eyes.

Josie's voice was quiet when she spoke. "He's your friend. Whether you think so or not."

"He's gonna be the longest punishment I ever served driving back to Nevada," Tim said. He looked down at her. Her freckles stood out, and her eyes looked tired, but there was some relief in her face now.

"Take care of yourself, kid," Tim said.

"Thank you," she said.

She glanced over at Jake, then at Tim again. Jake rolled his eyes and wandered toward the back of the truck to give them some privacy.

Josie stepped toward Tim and put a hand on his chest.

"So you'll be okay?" she asked.

"I'm always okay."

She smiled at him, then leaned up and kissed him, making him want to stay in Louisiana for one more night.

"Come on, Kelly, let's move." Jake picked his nails with his switchblade.

"I gotta go," he said. He walked to the truck and opened the passenger door. "Take care."

"You too. Both of you." She looked from him to Jake. "Try to stay out of trouble?"

Jake laughed, and he couldn't help but join in.

"Can't promise you that."

Jake started the engine and pulled a u-turn off the dusty shoulder, sailing up the road toward the highway.

Tim looked in the side mirror, seeing Josie wave. He held a hand up, and watched her until she disappeared from view.

He looked forward at the long stretch of road before him and took in a deep breath. It was time to go home.

Monday, April 2, 1967

They pulled into Las Vegas late Monday afternoon. The drive was slow and arduous. Tim couldn't drive since his ankle was too weak to operate the clutch and his wrist too sore to shift gears. Jake complained the whole way about the fact he had to drive.

They'd spent a few nights at motels along the way, selling a carton or two of the cigarettes to afford it. Jake groused about losing his guns, the only thing missing from his bag of belongings, but the closer they got to Vegas, the lighter the mood in the truck.

Tim sighed in relief when the Hacienda came into view in the distance. They passed McCarran and the Dunes and Tim relaxed. He was home.

Jake stopped the truck at the warehouse and they unloaded Tim's half of the cigarettes just inside the old loading dock. Tim wasn't much help with the physical labour, and Jake complained about that, too.

He wouldn't put it past some of the boys to snag a few cartons of cigarettes, so he couldn't keep them in the loading bay for long. No one was there right then, but it was early on a Monday evening. The boys would probably show up later.

"You wanna get food?" Jake asked him.

Tim thought for a minute. "Drop me at home."

Jake dropped him a block from his house, and Tim wasn't sure he'd make it up the street at first.

Tim was glad to see his car was still in the driveway. He had debated where to leave it, but figured even his father wasn't stupid enough to sell it.

It was late in the day, the sun already a whisper on the horizon. His father's car wasn't there, and he was relieved.

He was surprised to find his mother in the kitchen instead of at work.

"You're not working?"

"Timothy!"

His mother dropped the pot, and green beans splattered around the kitchen. She sprinted through them and threw her arms around him.

"What's got into you?" he asked.

"What's got into me? Lord in Heaven! Timothy, where have you *been*? You said it was going to be a week or a week and a half trip."

He closed his eyes. He hadn't even realized. He'd been gone just over a month.

"We ran into some trouble."

His mother put her hands on her hips. "Police trouble?"

"No, ma," he said. It wasn't a lie. MacGregor wasn't a sheriff anymore. "Car trouble."

"And you couldn't have called your poor mother? I thought you were dead in a ditch! I called every hospital in Southern Alabama looking for you. Look at you! What happened?"

Diana materialized in the doorway.

"She figured you took off on us."

Diana launched himself at him and hugged him hard and quick, then stood back and shoved him.

"You are such a jerk!"

He looked down at the floor. Jesus, he should've called once they were out.

His mother stalked back across the kitchen, cleaning the beans off the floor.

"I'm sorry, I should've called." His mother collected the beans in the pot then went at the linoleum with a rag. "You really thought I took off? That I left you guys without a word, no goodbye?"

His mother stood up and set the Corningware dish on the counter.

"It crossed my mind."

"Ray said you probably took off for keeps," Diana said.

"I see you haven't gained any brain cells while I was gone. Ray's a moron."

"Don't start. Where were you?" Diana looked him over. "Jesus, what happened to you?"

He rubbed a hand down his face. His wrist had hurt too much for him to get a decent shave on the road, and he knew he looked rough.

"Had some car trouble."

"I heard you went with Jake Wheeler. Did he do this to you?" Diana asked.

"No. I had to keep an eye on him."

"For what?"

"Needed his help," Tim lied. "I found a supplier. Going into business selling cigarettes."

"Legally?" Diana asked, an eyebrow raised up artfully.

"'Course legally." He walked into the kitchen and picked up an orange and peeled it. "I've got a business going. Cigarette machines."

His mother stared at him. "This is really legal?"

"Sure is," he said. "I already have five machines, and already have one bar agreeing to take one. Now that I have a cigarette supplier the others will follow."

His mother pursed her lips, but she didn't look angry anymore.

She knew as well as he did who ran the cigarette machine racket in the city. Knowing he had one in already went a long way to being legit.

He discarded the orange peels in the garbage and noticed his mother's eagle-eye gaze.

"What?"

"You're limping. And Diana's right, you look a fright. What happened?"

He sighed. Nothing ever got by her when he wanted it to.

"I got hurt, had to stay in a hospital."

"Hurt? How?"

He didn't want her to see the marks. It was too obvious it was a restraint of some kind.

"Sprained my wrist and my ankle," he said, splitting the difference between the truth and a lie. He held up his wrapped wrist. "May have been out of it a day or two."

"What happened? A car wreck?"

"No, just issues moving the boxes around. Bunch fell, I didn't get out of the way in time."

Diana, her arms crossed, knew full well he was full of it based on her expression. He didn't think his mother believed it either.

"You still could've called. Where was this hospital?"

"Some podunk town in Louisiana," he said. "Small hospital, small town. Wouldn't let me call long distance."

His mother, lips pursed, looked him over. "Could've called collect."

"Like we can afford that," Diana huffed.

"Why aren't you at work anyway?" he asked.

"Traded shifts, I'll be going in early tomorrow and working a double."

The rent was due. She always overworked herself when the rent was due.

He didn't say anything, didn't bring up his father, who was probably at a bar drinking the rent away. Soon, with those machines, he'd be able to provide a little cash for her legitimately. As it was, he snuck it into the cookie jar when he could.

"I gotta go find Bill," he said.

"You should shave first, you look like a bum," Diana said.

He shoved her out of the kitchen as best he could with his bad arm.

His mother looked at him, and put her hands on his cheeks and kissed him.

"You need to rest. Have a shower, I'll make you soup."

He kissed his mother and shoved Diana out of the door way, getting a shove in return. It passed for affection with her.

He took a detour into the bathroom and found the electric shaver and made himself look presentable. His face was sunken and drawn—he looked like he'd had the worst flu of his life or something.

He turned on the shower but didn't get in, not wanting to risk his leg. He ducked his head in and washed his hair. He was tired from that exertion and swallowed two aspirin before he went into the kitchen. He finished the soup his mother had made, then left the house against her protests.

He got into his car, his head starting to ache. He'd move the cigarettes into his office at the warehouse, then organize things with Bill tomorrow. He started the car and struggled the first few blocks with the pain in his ankle and wrist. Luckily the drive wasn't long.

He pulled the car into the alley by the warehouse. The warehouse windows were dark, but that didn't mean much. With no electricity, they relied on lanterns at night and you couldn't always see if there was anyone there.

He saw a figure lurking around the corner and pulled the Browning out of the hidden compartment in the door. Tucking it into the back of his pants he approached the stairs to the warehouse.

Jack Wheeler materialized from the corner.

"What the hell are you doing here? Haven't we seen enough of each other lately?"

"Forgot these in the trailer." Wheeler shook a bottle of pills. His antibiotics.

"Thanks," Tim said, his voice more subdued since he knew the asshole wasn't there to mess things up. "While you're here, lend a hand. I need to get the cartons hidden in my office. They're in the loading bay, and those jokers won't be able to resist snagging a few cartons for themselves if I leave them there."

"Your *office*? This place is a piece of crap." Jake stared at the building. "You really gotta stop trying to make this shit sound important, you're no Johnny Moro."

"You're gonna be no longer for this world if you don't shut up."

Tim limped his way up the stairs to the steel door and unlocked it. Everyone was gone, and the place was deserted. He was relieved. The road weariness was getting to him, and he just wanted to flop down on a mattress and sleep.

He walked over to the loading bay where he'd left the cartons, and he and Jake began hauling them across the room, down the hall and into the office that had a lock. He was out of breath on the second trip and had to sit down for a minute.

He walked over to the table against the wall and lit two of the lanterns in the main room, giving them some light.

He looked at the back and frowned.

He walked over to the small ice box and rifled in a box next to it. Pulling out a battery powered flashlight, he switched it on.

"What's wrong?" Jake asked.

Tim said nothing and walked to the back of the building, shining the light around.

"They're gone."

"What's gone?" Jake asked.

"The machines. The goddamn cigarette machines. They're gone!"

He shined the flashlight everywhere. A noise at the door caught his attention, and he spun around, his hand on the butt of the Browning. The door opened with a creak, and Tim shined the beam at him.

"Whoa, whoa, it's me," came Bill's voice. "Who's that? Jimmy?"

"Not exactly."

"Tim? Where the hell have you been?!" Bill strode into the room with his own light, looking at Jake and then Tim. "What the hell happened to you two?"

Tim glanced over at Jake. His face and arms were as scratched up as his were, from all the running in the bayou. Jake had lost weight too, and his face looked drawn and tired. No wonder his mother didn't believe a word he'd said.

"Long story. It involves crooked sheriffs, a prison break and alligators, but we'll get to that later. Where the hell are the cigarette machines? Did you get them in somewhere? Get a truck for them?"

Bill shifted his weight, looking at Jake, then Tim, then the door.

"Bill," Tim said, his voice measured. "Where the hell are the machines?"

"Well, you were gone a long time. A month with no word. We assumed you got pinched for this deal, and that could net you some serious time. And the boys were getting restless, they needed money . . . so . . . "

"Jake, you wanna step outside?" Tim asked.

"Hell no, not right now." Jake sat down on a ratty old chair, a grin on his face.

"The machines, Bill."

"Well . . . we kind of . . . sold them."

Jake's laughter was loud and long.

"You sold them. You sold the fucking machines." Tim spun around, paced a few steps, then paced back. He counted to ten. He took deep breaths. He pinched the bridge of his nose. He wanted nothing more than to knock Bill's head off his shoulders, but he had a bum wrist.

Jake was laughing so hard he had tears streaming down his face.

"Well, we still got one, it's at Rett's. Nothin' in it, but it's there."

"Bill, you see all these cigarettes we got here?"

"Yeah."

"You're gonna find machines for them. And they're gonna be sitting in here tomorrow afternoon."

"Well, that's gonna be—" Bill stopped when he looked at Tim. "Tomorrow afternoon. Got it."

Bill swallowed audibly, then looked around the room.

"I gotta go find a pay phone."

"Call an undertaker while you're there, Billy boy!" Jake laughed. "Jesus Christ, this is the best day I've had in a long time."

Bill left the warehouse, and Tim sighed.

"If you don't stop laughing, I'm gonna bury my boot up your ass." Tim ripped open a carton of Pall Malls and opened a pack, lighting a cigarette. There wasn't enough nicotine in the world.

"I wish I had a camera. Your face, man," Jake laughed.

Tim turned around and grabbed Jake by the collar of his shirt, dragging him to the door. Ordinarily Jake would've fought back, but he was laughing so hard he could barely keep himself upright. Tim tossed him outside and closed the steel door behind him, the laughter fading.

He wandered down the hall, looking at the stacks of cigarettes in his office. He locked the door so he wouldn't have to see them.

He went into the room he slept in, kicked the sheets away and lay down. He picked up the small transistor radio, and flicked it on. Sinatra was singing "That's Life" and even he couldn't keep a straight face for that.

He smoked his cigarette down, cursing the loss of the machines, the stupidity of his gang, the entire state of Louisiana, and every gator on the planet.

He closed his eyes. Like Sinatra said, he was going to have to get back in the race.

How, he didn't know.

If you enjoyed this book, please leave a review on Amazon and/or Goodreads.

Acknowledgements

Thanks to Summer Wallace Minger for all the comments and editing, as well as being the sounding board for the ending. I think we can all agree that I should maybe give Tim a break now and then . . . but this is not that time.

All errors in geography, flora and fauna are mine, as the closest I've been to Louisiana is Google and Wikipedia, along with episodes of NCIS New Orleans.

I also gave Tim a pretty quick recovery from sepsis. Chalk it up to a good constitution and artistic license.

This story was loosely inspired by an NCIS episode called "Chained" where DiNozzo, undercover as a bad guy, is chained to a suspect in antiquities theft during a set-up prison break. As they drew heavily on *The Defiant Ones*, I drew on the antagonistic humour DiNozzo and Jeffrey shared.

About The Author

Jennifer Samson (she/her) is the author of the coming-of-age *Sin City* saga (currently at four full length novels and two side novellas) and co-author of the dark comedy/thriller *The Final Cut*, the first in the *Billie and Diana* series. She has been published in the literary journals *Thursday* and *The Lyre,* as well as the BoldPrint book *Friends.* Her work has been featured in the Brookline TAB, Toronto Star, Ottawa Citizen, and Edmonton Sun.

She enjoys fine-nibbed pens, Hilroy loose leaf paper, corner store candy, adorable cats, and beating her Goodreads Reading Challenge every year. Being Canadian, a love of hockey goes without saying.

She is a member of Gamma Xi Phi, a predominantly African American, anti-racist, non-hazing, all-gender professional fraternity for artists and creators where she currently serves as National Secretary. She is also a member of Alpha Phi Women's Fraternity.

She currently lives on the unceded traditional and ancestral territory of the Sḵwx̱wú7mesh (Squamish), səlilwətaɬ (Tsleil-Waututh) and xʷməθkʷəy̓əm (Musqueam) Coast Salish peoples.

You can find her on Goodreads, Bluesky and Pinterest. She's probably there instead of editing.

* * *

Sign up for my newsletter and receive free ebooks and information on new releases - https://tinyurl.com/arieswriting

Arieswriting - www.arieswriting.com
Goodreads - www.goodreads.com/jennifersamson

Jennifer Samson Booklist

The Sin City Series
(Crime/Family Saga)

Piece of Work
Sin City
Tilt*
The Dead Woman
Neon and Tinsel*
Bayou Bound

Coming Soon:

Under The Gun

*With MB Miller

The Billie and Diana Series
(Comedy/Thriller)*

The Final Cut

Coming Soon:

Curtains

*with M.B. Miller

Join my newsletter at https://tinyurl.com/arieswriting for free ebooks and news on my latest releases.

www.ingramcontent.com/pod-product-compliance
Lightning Source LLC
Chambersburg PA
CBHW071435260626
47170CB00008B/2722